DANGEROUS GAMES

Takeback 3 of 6

RILEY EDWARDS

D1596382

BE A REBEL
Riley Edwards Romance

Dangerous Games
TAKEBACK Book 3

Cover design: Lori Jackson Designs

Written by: Riley Edwards

Published by: Riley Edwards/Rebels Romance

Edited by: Rebecca Hodgkins

Proofreader: Julie Deaton, Rebecca Kendall

Dangerous Games

Ebook ISBN: 978-1-951567-20-0

Paperback ISBN: 978-1-951567-24-8

First edition: March 29, 2022

To my family - my team – my tribe.
This is for you.

1

"ONE MORE MONTH and I'll have the money."

Seeing as I had three hundred and forty-one dollars to my name, and I was three months behind on rent that was a whopper of a lie.

Another month would only mean I'd be four months behind with no hope of paying, but I couldn't lose my bakery.

"Sadie—"

I adjusted my phone cradled between my shoulder and my ear and I begged, "Please, Mr. Johnson. One more month and I promise I'll be caught up on my rent."

"Have you spoken to your parents?"

At the mere mention of my parents, my heart sank. I could not and would not burden them with my problems. Since they'd left Idaho for warmer weather, they were finally free of the day-to-day bullshit my younger brother, Josh, brought into their lives. And Josh's brand of bullshit wasn't your average, every day, run-of-the-mill bullshit. When my baby brother puts his mind to something, he doesn't dip his toe in, he goes *all* in, then rolls around in it until he's covered in the stench of whatever bad news he's gotten himself involved in.

Unfortunately for me, I still lived in Coeur d'Alene, thus I was still involved in the day-to-day shit that my brother was swimming in. Not only was I around to witness it, but he also made it a habit of showing up on my doorstep asking for help.

This help was normally in the form of money. Lots and lots of money.

"No!"

"Sadie, darlin', you know your parents would want to know."

Mr. Johnson was right, and he knew he was because he knew my parents. He also knew my brother. Furthermore, he knew why I was having money trouble because I had to come clean with him, the bank, and all my vendors about what Nate Dickhead Mallard had taken from me.

"Mr. Johnson, in the five years I've had my bakery not once have I asked my parents to help me and I'm not starting now. They're in Florida enjoying their life and you know precisely why I'm not going to bother them with this. I promise I'm figuring it out. I just need another month."

"That boy," Mr. Johnson mumbled. "Hate to say it, but he's a bad egg. Born that way. Nothing your parents could've done differently."

Man-oh-man, that was the truth. But I'd go one step further—Josh was a rotten egg, and if you weren't careful his stench would seep in and cling to you for eternity.

"Okay, Sadie," he relented. "One more month. But that's all I can give you."

One month.

I had one month to come up with the money to save my bakery.

Thirty days.

I closed my eyes against the onslaught of emotions. Emotions that did not fill me with elation Mr. Johnson was giving me more time before he evicted me. Dread hit hard and fast. And when I opened my eyes and looked around my beloved bakery, fear and sadness also crept in. I'd worked tirelessly to make Treats a success. I'd been smart with my money and had started small, only buying what was absolutely necessary and only scaled up when I was turning a profit. And only took out a loan to get better equipment when I knew I could make the payment. I'd done everything right.

Except I hadn't.

It had been me who'd foolishly been taken in by Nate Mallard. It had been me who'd been swept off my feet by a liar and thief. And finally, it had been me who'd trusted Nate.

Now I was going to lose everything.

Absolutely everything.

"Thank you, Mr. Johnson."

"Sadie." I didn't miss the pain in Mr. Johnson's tone. He didn't like this any more than I did. But he, too, was running a business and had a mortgage to pay. Family friend or no friend, he wasn't running a charity.

"I appreciate your generosity," I rushed out.

I heard the front door push open and looked up just in time to watch the back of a man walk out. Not just any man, Reese Turmel's fine backside in a pair of his signature barley-colored cargo pants. He must've owned fifty pairs of the same color. The only variation to his daily uniform was the shirt he wore. Today's was burgundy. Going or coming, I'd know the stretch of that fabric anywhere. It was debatable—and I'd spent *a lot* of time doing just that—which was the better view. The front won out only by the tiniest fraction and only because Reese was insanely hot. Magazine cover hot. Or as my friend Letty Welsh would say, book cover hot. But the back of him was sexy as hell. I put money on it he worked out at least three times a day to keep his ass as firm as it was and his back muscles as wide as they were.

Well, I'd put money on it if I had any.

"I wish you'd reconsider calling Frank and Mary," he pushed.

That was never in a million years going to happen. I would lose everything before I burdened my parents with my troubles.

"I have a few things in the works. If they don't come to fruition I'll consider it," I lied.

The part about having a few things 'in the works' was the truth, if you deemed me selling all my personal belongings in an effort to pay my rent 'in the works.'

"Fair enough. Have a good day, Sadie, and be well."

"You, too, Mr. Johnson."

I lowered my phone from my ear and disconnected the call. And in a moment of weakness, I scrolled down until I found my thieving ex's name and hit go.

As I expected, the call went straight to voice mail. Unsurprisingly, the box was full and I was unable to leave a message. Not that it mattered, I'd already left thirty. Hence why the box was full.

I dropped my phone on the cream quartz tabletop that, like everything else in the bakery, had been painstakingly chosen to fit my vision. Elegant but inviting. Pastel pinks, dark grays, and glossy black. Pretty but not overly girly. From the black and white chevron tiles that made a diamond pattern on the floor, to the stark white bakery display, to the storm-cloud gray walls, to the shiny black exposed metal beams on the ceiling, to the tables and light gray chairs, I'd spent hours and hours carefully choosing every color, every piece of furniture. And that was just the front of the house. My kitchen was the same. The mixers, the ovens, the metal spatulas, the cake pans, all the way down to the fillings and frostings.

All me.

All mine.

And for what? To have it all stolen from me.

My no-good, stealing ex and my piece-of-shit brother who'd bled me dry.

Never again would I trust another person. Not with my money, not with my business, not with my heart. Nothing. No one was ever going to get anything from me ever again.

"Sadie?" Jamie, my only full-time employee, called from behind the counter. "Phone."

I wanted to sit and wallow, but that wasn't what I did. I plastered a fake-assed smile on my face and went back to work.

I finished my call with a very excited bride-to-be, who'd happily rambled on about marrying the man of her dreams. Being as such, he'd of course given her an unlimited budget to plan the wedding of the century—because that was what the man of *her* dreams would do.

Gag.

I had much lower expectations—the man of *my* dreams simply wouldn't clean out my bank accounts. Speaking of such, it had taken a great deal of effort not to burst the woman's bubble as she waxed poetic about her perfect husband-to-be.

Gag.

If I hadn't needed the wedding cake, the bridal shower cupcakes, and the rehearsal dinner desserts order so freaking badly I would've told the naïve woman to run. No man was perfect. They pretended to be until you let your guard down, then when they knew they had you hooked —*bam*, they showed their true colors.

"Holy crap," Jaimie whispered.

I stopped arranging the cupcakes in the display case and looked over at Jaime counting the money from the tip jar. Technically it wasn't *the* tip jar, it was whoever was working the counter's tip jar, and today those tips would belong to Jamie.

"He's generous, but this is..." she trailed off and held up a hundred-dollar bill.

I didn't need her to clarify who "he" was.

Reese.

He always tossed a five into the tip jar, which was well above the standard twenty percent. Hell, it was over a hundred percent when he was buying a four-dollar coffee and a little less than when he added a muffin.

Then I remembered his fine ass waltzing out of the bakery earlier. My eyes sliced to the table I'd been sitting at talking to Mr. Johnson. Not close to the counter but not far.

Reese heard.

My eyes went back to Jaime and they narrowed on the bill. Before I could say anything, she was holding it in my direction.

"Here. This is too much."

It was good she thought so, or I would've had to take a hundred dollars out of the till to give Reese back his money.

No way in hell was I accepting charity from Reese—or anyone.

This was my problem. I'd stupidly gotten myself into this mess and I'd get my damn self out.

I plucked the money out of Jaime's hand, gave her a

tight smile, and walked around the display case showcasing today's specials. This week I'd gone with a pastel theme. Beautifully frosted cakes and cupcakes, lavender, baby pink, creamy yellow, mint with contrasting fancy sprinkles all in bold metallics. The other side of the case was almost empty after the morning rush but it had been stocked with cinnamon, blueberry, lemon-poppyseed, chocolate chip, and banana nut muffins. As well as freshly made donuts and croissants.

I hadn't meant to notice, but seeing as I was the owner, I tended to pay attention to what my regulars ordered. I thought it was something a little extra I gave my patrons; I knew most of them by name and greeted them as such. I also knew their coffee orders so that when they came up to order I could ask "your regular?" My customers liked the little extras I gave them, and I liked the smiles they gave in return and the repeat business. So, I knew Reese always got a lemon-poppyseed muffin when he came into Treats, further I knew in the morning when he came in, he ordered a caramel macchiato with three sugars. If it was the afternoon, he ordered a large caramel iced coffee with extra whip and three caramel chocolate chunk cookies. It wasn't the drink preference I hadn't meant to notice; it was his obsession with caramel and massive sweet tooth that didn't jibe with his wide shoulders, muscled biceps, and flat stomach. Of course, I'd never seen what was under his clothes, but I didn't miss the way his shirts fit and there was no beer belly in sight, meaning I wasn't too far off about his workout schedule.

Those were my thoughts as I marched my happy ass out of my bakery, down the sidewalk two doors, and entered Smutties bookstore. And there he was, all six feet and some change of masculine beauty walking out of the back room.

Naturally, Reese stopped where he was and made me continue walking to him. The man was not stupid, nor was I hiding how pissed I was. So, he didn't miss my anger directed at him, yet his smug ass made me go to him.

Figures.

I wasted no time making my way across my friend's kickass bookstore. When I got to him, I held out the hundred-dollar bill. My haste was mostly for self-preservation. Whenever I was in Reese's presence I tended to forget. And what I forgot were the important lessons my ex had taught me.

Men sucked.

No matter how pretty the packaging was, what was underneath was never, ever worth it. And the prettier that packaging, the more the man thought he could do and say whatever he wanted because his looks would buy forgiveness. And since Reese was far better-looking than any man I'd ever seen—so far better-looking he was in a universe all of his own—I knew with certainty he'd be no different than the rest.

In a nutshell, it was false advertising.

Good-looking equaled asshole. If I ever decided to date again, and that was a huge *if,* I was finding myself a less-than-average-looking man. Which meant that Reese and his flirting was out of the question.

"Here."

Reese didn't take his eyes off me when he asked, "Why are you giving me money?"

Games.

The guy loved to play games. The last time we got into a verbal scuffle I ended up dumping his beloved caramel iced coffee over his head. It wasn't one of my proudest moments and it led to me having to clean up a sticky mess, but Reese was the only person I knew who could drive me to violence. My ex had cleaned out my bank accounts, and as much as I wanted him to pay me back then find himself in jail, I didn't have the desire to throat punch him like I did with Reese.

And why did Reese get under my skin? Why did I feel like my heart shriveled to the size of a peanut every time I saw him? I knew the *why*, it was just that I was denying it. I'd sworn off men, I'd told myself I'd never, ever get involved in another relationship again. Yet every single time I saw Reese my chest got tight and anger swelled because I couldn't have him.

The universe had screwed me over, giving me Nate instead of Reese.

So what did I do? I flirted and teased and tortured myself. I got as close to him as I could then I pulled back. And this was how it had gone for months.

In another life, Reese would be mine. I'd pull out all the stops and work hard to get him to fall for me. But I didn't have another life—I had this one and it was shitty.

"I'm not. I'm giving you back *your* money."

My temper flared when he feigned ignorance and held up his hands.

"Why would you think that's my money?"

"Because I'm not stupid. No one in their right mind would put a hundred dollars in the tip jar, Reese."

His smile only pissed me off more.

And when he switched to his smooth, flirtatious tone, that yearning I had to strangle him rushed to the surface.

I needed to leave—pronto. I waved the bill. "Take it."

"That's not mine," he lied.

It was the easy lie rolling off his tongue that did it. White lies turned into fabrications which led to outright deception. My anger morphed into hurt and shame. Why did everyone think they could lie to me? Did I come across as an easy mark? Or did people mistake my kindness for me being a naïve twit who'd believe anything?

"Sadie, honey—"

"Please don't," I cut him off. "Whatever game you're playing I want no part of it. I wish you didn't know but you do and since you heard you know how bad it is. I don't have time for bullshit. So, please, Reese, take your money back."

"Yeah, Sadie. You're right, I heard. So don't be stubborn and take the tip."

Ouch.

Jeez, that was embarrassing, but at least he told the truth. But it was the truth of my situation that burned like acid in my stomach. I was on the verge of losing my dream. The last thing I needed was some jerk thinking I needed or wanted his pity.

"I don't need your charity."

I dropped the money, uncaring if he picked it up or not, turned, and made my way to the front door. I did this ignoring my friend Letty's concerned stare. I also did it thinking that if Reese told Letty what he'd overheard I was definitely punching him in the throat, right after I kicked him in the shin.

I was barely out the door when Reese came rushing after me.

"Sadie!"

His very loud, very gruff call had me turning my head to look at him over my shoulder.

"Leave me alone."

I turned back to watch where I was going and caught sight of my brother standing in front of Treats.

Seriously?

What was this, shit on Sadie day?

Josh's gaze went from me to over my shoulder. I didn't need to look again to know what my brother saw. A pissed-off jerk who didn't know when to mind his own business. So I understood why my brother's eyes widened, but what I didn't understand was the fear I saw. Sure, Reese was bigger than Josh, and he was ticked off, but I still didn't get why my brother looked scared.

The closer we got to Josh, the more that fear multiplied until Josh took two steps away from me.

So much for my brother protecting me.

Another thing to add to the list of reasons why my brother was a loser.

And if my day hadn't already been total shit, my brother in a black leather vest with a patch that announced he was a prospect would've plummeted my mood straight down to the deepest pits of hell. There were a few MC clubs in the area, but there was only one creepy motorcycle gang I knew my brother would gravitate toward—the criminal, outlaws. Those were his people. Not the clubs who did charity runs, not the clubs who got together to ride and share their love for motorcycles, but only on the weekends because they were respectable men who held down jobs. Nope, those clubs weren't Josh's style. So, I didn't need to see the Horsemen patch on the back to know which group of men my lowlife brother had chosen to prospect for.

Fuck my life.

Just when I thought it couldn't get any worse, it did.

"Why are you wear…" I stopped myself midsentence deciding I didn't want to know why my brother was wearing a tattered leather vest. "Never mind. Not my business. Why are you here?"

"I need to talk to you," Josh told me but his eyes were still on the man behind me.

And when I stopped, Reese stopped. His chest hit my back, his hand went to my hip, and if there'd been any space between us—which there wasn't—Reese yanking me back would've alleviated it.

"Fuck me," Reese sneered. "Didn't make the connection."

Connection?

I felt a nasty ball of humiliation form in my throat, and try as I might, I couldn't swallow it down to object. Not that there was much to protest; Josh was my brother, we were indeed connected by blood. But I was not him. I didn't participate in illegal activities. I didn't drink or smoke or gamble or do whatever it was that my brother did with his money that left him always broke.

But, wait, I was now broke, too.

Flat broke.

And just like my loser brother, it was no one's fault but my own.

2

JOSH PIERCE.

How in the hell had we missed that the newest prospect of the Horsemen was related to sweet Sadie? Actually, that was precisely why—Sadie was sweet. She was the quintessential girl next door. Couple that with her owning a trendy bakery and no one would guess her brother, younger by the looks of it, would be a scumbag.

"Who are you?" Josh feigned ignorance.

"You know who I am, asshole. Now answer Sadie, why are you here?"

Sadie's already-taut frame jerked right before her back snapped straighter and she turned to granite in my arms. Which pissed me off more than I had been when I overhead her begging for more time to pay her rent. And I was pissed. Not because no one on my team had put two and two together linking Josh to Sadie. Not because I was irritated that she'd refused the hundred dollars I'd left in the tip jar. And I wasn't pissed because her brother was a monumental prick.

No, I was pissed because I'd thought a lot about what it would be like to have Sadie in my arms. And not once had I pictured the first time I felt her pressed up against me, she'd be stiff as a board and facing off with a criminal. And it sucked, because now that I had her close, I could smell the cinnamon and sugar that clung to her clothes which made me want to drop my lips to her neck and see if she tasted as good as she smelled.

I didn't need the confirmation that the idiot standing in front of me was nothing like the woman in my arms; so when Josh pushed his shoulders back and puffed out his chest, he not only proved he was an asswipe but what he said next proved irrevocably he was also a total fucking moron.

"If you know who I am then you know you better show me some respect before you buy yourself a world of hurt." Josh finished his tough-guy threat with a jerk of his chin that made him look more foolish than threatening.

"Oh my God," Sadie whispered, then said louder, "did you really just say that?"

"Asshole knows better than to disrespect a Horsemen."

I tried, I really did, but I couldn't hold back my laughter. I laughed so hard I shook with it, which meant Sadie went along for the ride. The unfortunate consequence was that Sadie's very nice ass rubbed against my crotch. Again, something I'd given a lot of thought to, the way she'd feel moving against me. But not like this. Not when I couldn't fully appreciate her beauty and not when I couldn't express just how remarkable she felt.

"You laughing at me, bitch?"

Josh took a step toward us, and without thought, I pushed Sadie behind me. Her squeal of surprise told me I hadn't done so gently and that pissed me right the fuck off. Both the need to protect her from her asshole brother, who should've been the one showing concern for his sister, and the fact I'd scared her.

"This is your one warning, motherfucker. Whatever it is you think you're gonna do, don't. But if you're dumb enough to step to me, you damn well won't be doing it in front of your sister's bakery."

I felt Sadie's hand plant on the middle of my back and her other went to my shoulder and again disappointment washed over me. Not because I didn't want her hands on me; I damn well did, I just didn't want them on me in the middle of a drama with her brother.

"You calling me dumb, asshole?"

Josh took another step closer. Evidence was suggesting that not only was Josh dumb, he was also stupid as fuck.

"Sadie, go back down to Smutties. Tell Letty to lock the doors, I'll come—"

"No."

"Babe—"

"No way, Reese. I'm not leaving you."

Leaving me.

Not her brother.

Me.

Damn, that felt good. So good, it pissed me right the fuck off.

"Step up, asshole," Josh unwisely taunted.

"Oh, please," Sadie snickered from behind me. "Since when do you talk like that? Step up? Who do you think you are, Mr. Billy Badass? Jesus, Josh, Reese has three inches and fifty pounds of muscle on you, he'd kick your ass. Which, honestly, you're such a pain in mine, it might be fun to watch. But I know you. You wouldn't take your licks like a man; you'd call Mom and Dad and bamboozle them into paying your medical bills."

"Fuck you, Sadie."

"You're done," I announced. "Turn your ass around and leave."

"I'm far from done. I came here to talk to my sister and I'm not leaving until I talk to her."

"I think Sadie opening with 'why are you here' was a pretty good indication that not only was she not expecting a visit but wasn't happy you showed. If you want to talk to your sister, I suggest you call her, and if she doesn't pick up you can take that as a read, she doesn't want to talk to you."

"You good, brother?" I heard Davis Wright ask from behind me.

Perfect timing.

"Take Sadie to Smutties," I told Davis.

"No!" Sadie's denial was punctuated by her nails digging into my shoulder. "Josh, please leave. I don't need this in front of my bakery. Actually, I don't need this at all. I know why you're here and the answer is still no. And not just because you already owe me over three-thousand dollars. I told you I didn't have any more to give you and I wasn't lying. I don't have it. So please stop calling me and asking."

"I told you I'm working on something. I'll pay you back."

Three-thousand dollars? Sadie was having money troubles, behind on her rent, and this motherfucker owed her three-thousand-fucking-dollars.

"You got until the end of the week to pay your sister back," I growled.

"Sister?" Davis grunted. "Fuck me. This asshole's sweet Sadie's brother?"

I felt Sadie step closer. Her forehead hit my back and I knew she was hiding from the embarrassment. Though she didn't have one thing to be embarrassed about. Josh's life choices said not one bad thing about her.

"Do you know who you're fuckin' talking to?"

Christ, not this again.

"Yeah, asshole, I know I'm talking to a fucking prospect," Davis started. "Says so right there on your pussy vest. The question is, do you know who *you're* talking to? Don't know how Zeus runs his club. Don't care to know. Don't know how much he allows his prospects in on. But you'd have to be the stupidest fucker on the planet not to have heard who we are. You'd also have to be seriously dim not to see where your sister is right now. And just in case you're not smart enough to put it together I'll spell it out for you—she's standing behind Reese, meaning he's shielding her from you. In other words, your sister's now got protection. You should run back to that dump you call a clubhouse and spread that shit far and wide. And while you're doing that, let it sink in so you don't forget."

"Fuck—"

"I see you're not playing this smart," I cut him off before he dug himself a deeper hole. "Now this has gone on long enough. We're in front of Sadie's business. I've asked you to leave. You don't do that now, I'm calling the cops. It'll suck, you standing out here causing a scene when your sister's got cakes to sell, but I can't stop you unless I physically remove you. Which isn't an option while I got your sister curled into my back."

Josh's ugly scowl turned into an even uglier smile when he spat, "Pussy."

I looked to my right. Seeing Davis now right beside me, I smiled at my friend.

"*Right.*" I chuckled.

Josh's eyes darted between Davis and me, and just when I thought he was going to do the smart thing and walk away, he did the opposite.

"This isn't done, Sadie," he threatened.

Three things happened simultaneously. Sadie jolted at her brother's threat. Davis moved and in a gentle but forceful movement pulled Sadie away from me and wrapped his arm around her shoulder.

And I rushed Josh.

My hand went to his throat and I walked him back five steps before I dipped my head and my forehead hit his.

"I warned you, motherfucker. You didn't listen. Now you're gonna learn the hard way how badly you just fucked up."

I shoved Josh back, watched him stumble, and advanced again.

"You don't—"

"No, *you* don't know. I see you again, we got trouble, the kind that's gonna land you a stint in a hospital bed. I see you near Sadie, I hear about you harassing her, that hospital stay's gonna turn into you having a permanent limp. You think to threaten her again, bring any of those fucked-up, pieces-of-shit Horsemen around, you won't have to worry about the limp because I'll fuckin' end you."

"That's my sister," he lamely protested.

"You're right she is, which begs the question why you're jacking her around. You got a week to come up with the three thousand you owe. No joke, Josh. Seven days. She doesn't have cash in hand, me and my team will be at the clubhouse to collect."

"I can't—"

"You fuckin' will. Period. You find a way or serious as fuck, I'll be at the clubhouse."

"You do that." Josh smiled.

"I see you think Zeus will have your back. Good luck with that."

I heard a sharp whistle. I stepped away from Josh and glanced over my shoulder. Sadie looked angry as hell shoving away from Davis. My friend was doing his best to keep her contained while not putting his hands on her.

I didn't bother sparing Josh another look. I turned my back on him knowing he wouldn't make a move on me. The guy was dumb enough to talk shit but wasn't stupid enough to take it further.

I made it to Davis and Sadie, nabbed her hand, and started to walk her to the front door of her bakery.

"I'll be over to fill you in when I'm done talking to Sadie."

Davis gave me a chin lift, a smile, and he was on his way back to Smutties.

We entered Treats. Sadie followed me, but when we got to the counter, I stepped to the side to allow her to go first. She walked us behind the counter, pushed open a swinging door, then led me through the kitchen to her office.

The back space was bigger than I'd thought it would be. It was also spotless. Stainless steel racks full of baked goods lined the wall opposite the big industrial ovens. It smelled just like she did, cinnamon and sugar with hints of lemon and freshly baked bread. I was still inhaling the goodness when she pulled me into her office and slammed the door.

And when she turned to face me, those gorgeous eyes of hers were sparking fire. Her shoulders were back, her spine was ramrod straight, and her hands were balled into tiny fists.

"What the hell was that?" she spat.

"Sadie—"

She took a step closer, lifted her hand, jabbed a finger at my chest, and continued to hiss, "That was bullshit."

"Listen to me."

"No! You listen to *me*."

Sadie rocked forward, her hand flattened on my chest, but she gave up her futile attempt at shoving me when my hand came up and circled her wrist. Sadie's head tipped back to look up at me at the same time I was dipping my chin to look down at her. She glared at me up close, then her eyes started roaming over my face, pausing on my lips. Her gaze came back to mine and I had an altogether different Sadie standing in front of me. The fire was still sparking in her baby blues but now they were blazing with something that looked a lot like lust. Straight up, rip-your-clothes-off lust. The kind that superseded rational thought. The kind that overruled good judgment.

I knew I was right when she attacked.

Her mouth hit mine, her tongue spiked out, demanding entrance and I was all too happy to oblige. I opened for her, felt her lips part, and her tongue glided against mine. Upon my first taste, I knew I was fucked. I wanted more so I took it. My head tilted, she followed my lead, and I deepened the kiss. Sadie's hand on my chest moved up and I released her wrist. The moment I did, it traveled up and didn't stop until she was digging her fingertips into the back of my neck. Her other hand went under my shirt. At the feel of her nails scraping their way up my spine, I turned us, pushed her back against the door, and she moaned into my mouth.

It was the moan that snapped my control. No, it was

the sexy-as-fuck sound coupled with her nails and the taste of her that made me lose control. My hand went to the front of her jeans. I had the button undone, the zipper down, the tips of my fingers sliding into her panties when I lost Sadie's hands—but only so she could shove her jeans down over her ass. Then they moved again going to the front of my cargos. While she worked at freeing my cock, my hand slipped down, and it was my turn to groan when I found her wet. So fucking wet she was dripping. From a kiss. I groaned again when Sadie fisted my hard-on, and with a firm grip, she slid from root to tip. She was not gentle—not her grinding down on my fingers, not her tongue dueling with mine, not the way she was jerking my cock.

Christ.

I twisted my hand, added another finger, and Sadie went wild. Her hips bucked and she broke the kiss but only to cry out.

"More," she pleaded against my lips.

Fuck.

"You gotta tell me how much more you want."

Her hand stopped on an upward glide and her thumb grazed over the sensitive tip.

Fucking hell.

"I want this."

To explain what *this* was she tightened her fist around my cock.

My free hand reached around to my back pocket. I pulled out my wallet and fished out a condom. I dropped my wallet and searched her face for any sign of hesitation. I found none. Seeing nothing but excitement and hunger, I slid my fingers free. Sadie whimpered and I liked that sound. I liked it too fucking much. I liked knowing she was

getting off from just my fingers, but I had something better
to give her.

I spun her around, yanked her shirt off, and tossed it
aside. Next came her bra. Once I had it unhooked, she did
the rest and tore it down her arms. When she was done with
that, she shimmied her panties down until they caught on
her thighs and couldn't go any lower.

I stepped back and took my fill. Jeans down to her
knees, shoes still on, panties pulled tight against her legs,
and her sexy bare ass on display.

Jesus fuck, that was so hot my cock twitched as I rolled
the condom down my length.

Once I was done, I moved closer, pressed my chest to
her back, dropped my mouth to her ear, and growled,
"Hands on the door, Sadie."

I guided the tip through her wet and paused.

"Hands higher, above your head."

Her hands slid up the door until they were where I
asked. It was a struggle, seeing as her legs were trapped,
but inch by inch I worked to get inside of her. And with
every inch Sadie took, my hands on her hips shook. She
was tight as all fuck, especially since she couldn't spread
her legs, so tight I had to fight my need to slam home and
get busy fucking her. The only thing stopping me was I
didn't want to hurt her. And impaling her on my cock
while I was in that state would undoubtedly bring her
pain.

"More, Reese."

"Not yet."

"Please."

It was her whispered plea that had me bending at the
knees, and with one hard thrust, I drove my cock deep.

I barely heard Sadie's swift inhale over the roaring in

my ears. The feel of her pussy taking all of me—so snug, so warm, so fucking wet—was damn near my undoing.

"Holy...*Reese*," she moaned loudly.

I curled tighter against her back, glided my right hand over her ribs, then diagonal, cupped her left breast, and pulled out to the tip and slammed back in.

"You still want more, baby?"

"Yes."

Her answer wasn't moaned, it wasn't a whispered plea, it was hissed.

I used my thumb and forefinger to roll her nipple and asked again, "More?"

Sadie's head dropped forward, her ass tipped up, and she arched into my hand playing with her nipple.

"Everything."

I felt the muscles in my neck jump.

Everything.

I couldn't give Sadie or any other woman everything. But I could give her this. Hot, angry sex against the door. I could give her rip-your-clothes-off-lust and orgasms. I could give her my mouth, my cock, my fingers, any combination of the three, and I could do that all day and night until she was boneless and begging for me to stop. I could fuck her until she was sore.

But I couldn't give her everything. And since I couldn't, I fucked into her harder, only pulling out a few inches before driving my cock deep. Sadie came up onto her toes and I rolled my hips and held her where I wanted her.

"Mouth," I rumbled against her neck.

Sadie lifted her head and turned it toward mine. But before I took it, I asked, "Fucking you rough, baby, you sure you're good?"

She nodded and closed the distance, and just like the

first time, she kissed me. She did it with wild abandon. Nothing held back. Not the way she was groaning down my throat, not the way she was working her hips with mine, and she sure as fuck couldn't hide her hunger. I liked all of that more than was healthy. I liked it in a way I knew I was coming back for seconds and thirds. Only, next time she'd be naked on a flat surface where I could take my time.

It didn't take much longer for her orgasm to build. The first flutter around my cock had me ready to explode. And from there it built higher and higher until she broke the kiss to pant my name against my lips as her pussy convulsed.

Fucking hot.

Three more strokes, I drove in deep while slamming her down and spilled into the condom.

Good goddamn.

It took her longer to come down than it did me. But when she did, I had a different kind of wild on my hands. Sadie jerked forward, my still-hard cock slipped out of her, and she turned and plastered her back against the door like she was trying to melt into it. Faster than they came down, she yanked her panties up and settled them over her hips. Next, she tugged up her jeans. When she was done with that her hands came up in a futile attempt to cover her chest.

"Step back."

"Not until you look at me."

She didn't look at me. Her gaze went around the room, the floor, the ceiling—anywhere but me.

"Step back," she repeated.

"Told you, not until you look at me."

Slowly, she dragged her eyes up my chest. They lingered on my throat for a moment before her attitude firmly snapped back into place and her narrowed eyes met mine.

"You okay?"

"What?"

"Did I hurt you?" I asked softly.

"No, you didn't fucking hurt me, Reese."

Her gaze dropped to my still condom-covered cock and she groaned. This was not the same sexy, pleasure-filled sound she made while we were fucking. This one was full of regret. I didn't like that one fucking bit. And I hated it even more when her arms crossed over her chest to further hide herself from me.

"Don't do that, Sadie," I warned.

"Do what? Fuck you? Too late for that. Act like a dick-starved slut and jump you? Too late—"

"Stop." I took a step forward, my hands went to her neck, and I gently tipped her head back. "Don't do that either."

"You need to leave."

I bet she'd like that. But I wasn't leaving until I knew she was okay.

"Not until we talk."

"No more talking. No more touching. No more fucking. No more coming to my bakery. You're gonna leave and we're gonna pretend this never happened."

It was safe to say the situation I found myself in was a first. Actually, more than one first. I'd never had angry sex against a door, not even with my ex-wife. When she pissed me off or vice versa, the last thing I wanted to do was get anywhere near the bitch. And she felt the same, though her reasons were probably different than mine seeing as she'd been fucking someone else while my ring was still on her finger. And not before and not after my ex-wife had a woman ever kicked me out after sex. It was always the oppo-site, me trying to extradite myself from a situation I didn't want to be in.

"Sorry, Sadie, but that's gonna be impossible seeing as that was off-the-charts hot and every second is burned into my memory. Every sound you made, how wet you got, how hot and tight you are, how quickly you came with just my cock and me playing with your nipple. All of it. Every single second. So, fuck no, I'm not pretending that didn't happen. And just to say, it's gonna happen again."

I didn't miss the tremble, nor did I miss the way her eyes flared. She might've been pissed she let me fuck her against the door in her office, but she damn well enjoyed it.

"That's never gonna happen again."

"Baby, you're right in front of me."

"So?"

"I can still taste you on my tongue. I still got your excitement on my cock, and, baby, you were so fucking wet you were dripping down my legs. So, with all that, I don't get how you think you can lie to me. I see you, Sadie. I can still *feel* you. You can't fake what we just had. You got off on it just as much as I did. And not for some fucked-up reason, like you spouted off, because it was a long time coming and you know that, too. Though, warn-ing; next time, I'm tasting something else, and I suspect when I get my mouth between your legs it's gonna be just as sweet."

Sadie opened her mouth to say something but promptly clamped it shut. Which was smart because I would've called her out on her denial.

Nature being what it was, necessitated me to step back to handle the condom. But before I went in search of a trashcan, I tagged Sadie's shirt off the floor and handed it to her. She grunted her thanks and to my dismay, she wasted no time covering herself.

I glanced around her office, taking in the tidy space. Finding what I was looking for next to her desk, I moved that way. Much like the front of her bakery, Sadie's office was an extension of her personality. Soft pinks contrasted by bold white with glossy black accents. Soft and bold. Sweet, pretty, cute with a backbone of steel. That was something I seriously liked, something that had drawn me to her since the day I met her. A friendly smile that made you want to stick around just to see it again and again. Witty comebacks that denoted her intelligence and humor. Her dedication to her business was evident—from the employees she hired to the delicious treats she baked to the time and effort she'd put in to making Treats a place you wanted to visit. But it was her 'take no shit' attitude that had sealed it for me. There was something extremely appealing about a woman who not only knew her mind but spoke it.

The day I'd complimented her on her muffins, I was indeed talking about the lemon-poppyseed goodness I kept coming back, day after day, to buy. But Sadie took in my wink, my smile, the teasing tone in my voice and took my compliment to mean something she didn't take kindly to. I then found the iced coffee she was delivering to my table poured over my head. And damn if I hadn't found that appealing, too.

All of her grit and attitude, along with a smart and funny personality, wrapped up in a beautiful package with killer curves and I was hooked. Now, knowing she could let go, turn wild, and had no hang-ups about sex, I was seriously fucking hooked.

That was, no hang-ups until the deed was done, then she closed down and called herself a slut. I made a mental note to have a conversation about that at a later date. A time when she wasn't kicking me out of her office.

I tossed the condom, zipped and buttoned my cargos. I hadn't removed a single article of clothing and I'd only gotten Sadie half undressed before we went at it. Sadie would likely disagree but that only added to the hotness factor.

"I'm asking you nicely," she said softly. "Please forget about everything you heard today."

So, she was trying a new tactic. Sweet Sadie was back.

I turned to face her and I was taken aback by the sadness I saw. I could deal with her pissed, angry, sweet, and turned-on, panting my name while I fucked her. What I couldn't deal with was her looking like her world was crumbling around her. Which after finding out she had money troubles and a shithead for a brother, I'd reckoned she was getting buried under a pile of shit.

I would not add to that.

I wouldn't let her swing, either.

However, I would back down. For now.

"I'll be back in a week with the money your brother owes you."

"Reese—"

"Sadie," I interrupted her. "I'll be back in a week with the money Josh owes you. In the meantime, he tries to fuck with you I wanna know. But since I know you're not gonna make that call to tell me, I'll be watching."

"I don't want you watching!" she fumed.

I ignored her protest and made my way back to the door. When I got there, I didn't stop until I was crowding her space. My lips dropped to hers and with the tiniest provocation, she opened for me. That was to say, all it had taken was my chest pressed against hers and my tongue sweeping her bottom lip before her hands went to my waist and she eagerly participated in a deep, wet, insanely great kiss.

And just to prove my point, my hand went under her shirt and my thumb found her pebbled nipple. The kiss lasted until she moaned. Then I broke the kiss but didn't pull away when I muttered against her lips, "See you soon, Sadie."

I moved her away from the door and left.

3

"EVERYTHING'S FINE, MOM."

I was going to hell. Straight to hell with a fast pass in hand. You know, the permit that lets you cut the line to the front. Yep, that was me, Sadie the fast pass holder first in line to meet Satan.

I'd hit an all-time low lying to my momma.

"Sadie Marie, you don't sound fine."

"Hang on." I put the call on speaker then lied some more. "Sorry, I'm doing a little spring cleaning."

"It's fall," she reminded me.

Damn.

"I was too busy in the spring so I'm doing it now."

I gently folded my favorite plum-colored belted dress that did wonders for my figure. Tight but not hoochie-mama tight. V-neck that showed off some cleavage yet remained PG rather than X-rated.

"How's Dad?" I attempted to redirect the conversation away from my spiraling out of control life.

"I'm worried about you," my mom murmured, and my heart clutched.

Both because she sounded worried, and because I was placing yet another fabulous dress in a box to be mailed to its new owner.

"There's nothing for you to be worried about."

Lies. All lies.

It was debatable which of her children my mother should be more worried about. Her son who'd hooked up with a gang of dirty motorcycle-riding criminals or her daughter who was going to lose her business in less than a month. I figured my brother won the worry-mom stakes considering his bullshit could land him in jail. I'd just be jobless and homeless but I'd be both without a criminal record so there was that.

"Have you heard from Josh?"

Shit, *shit*, shit.

I knew that was coming.

"Um. It's been a few days."

Five days to be exact.

Five long, tiring days trying to avoid Reese after our little episode in my office. Who was I kidding—there was nothing *little* about Reese. And we didn't have an episode, I'd gleefully, happily, hungrily banged him against the door. Okay, so technically he banged me, and he did it to spectacular results.

Gah.

Just thinking about it made my cheeks burn and my lady parts tingle.

Best sex of my life.

Which was sad. When I was with Nate, I thought we'd had good sex. We'd been in a committed relationship that had been comfortable. Now six months removed from the year-long relationship I'd come to a few uncomfortable realizations. I never loved him. And for obvious reasons, it was clear he never loved me. But at the time, I'd liked him. He'd been good company, fun to be around, someone to help carry the load, but never had he made my heart race. Never did I get a feeling in my belly that made me jittery when I saw him. And I'd never, not once in the year we were together, jumped him the way I had Reese. I'd started dating Nate then stayed with him because I'd been lonely. I was out of sorts after my parents moved to Florida and Nate had been convenient.

Worst mistake of my life.

A knock on my front door pulled me from my thoughts. My gaze went across my living room to the door and for the first time in my life, I wished I had X-ray vision. If it was Josh and I didn't answer right away he'd start banging. And if I still didn't answer he'd resort to yelling my name.

"Hey, Mom, let me call you back."

"Are you expecting company?"

It was ridiculous that my mother actually sounded excited at the prospect of her thirty-six-year-old daughter having someone stop by her house.

Prospect.

Shit, fuck, and damn.

"Nope. Probably a Girl Scout. I'll—"

"Don't be silly, the Girl Scouts don't sell cookies this time of year."

Of course, my mother would know that. I, myself, had never been in the Scouts but I'd had an obsession with Thin Mints since my mother had given me one at three. I'd partly blamed her for my love affair with all things cookies.

There was another knock. This one louder.

Crap.

"Mom, I really have to go. I'll call you later."

"I'll just wait on the phone while you answer."

"Mom."

"You can never be too careful. The town's getting bigger, crime's going up. I mean, just a few months ago, that nice Kiki girl was murdered."

It was quite possible my mother was the only person other than Kiki's family who would describe Kiki Welsh as "nice." She was four grades behind me in school and I still heard about the trouble she caused. And by the time Kiki had graduated high school, she'd also graduated from being a mean girl to a straight-up bitch. But I'd never say that out loud and she did die saving a little boy's life. So obviously, she did have some nice in her, it just rarely came out.

"Mom—"

Another knock. This one loud and impatient.

"Just get the door, Sadie."

If there was ever a question where I got my stubbornness from, I'd have to look no further than my mother.

"Fine."

I left my phone on the kitchen table hoping she wouldn't hear when I throat-punched my brother for showing up at my house, uninvited and unannounced.

Something Josh did from time to time. Normally when he needed money or wanted me to feed him. Never was it to just stop by and have a chat. And since Reese had threatened him the other day, I was surprised it had taken my brother this long to find me and lay into me.

I went to the window and pulled back the curtain, wondering why I'd gotten one of those Ring cameras. Then I remembered I didn't have one because I was freaking broke. Then I stopped thinking about cameras and my dire financial situation and started gawking.

Reese's head turned and his gaze hit mine. He looked unhappy, as in un-*fucking*-happy. Deep scowl, eyes squinty, brows pulled together. He jabbed his finger in the direction of my front door and I shook my head. Those downturned lips got thin as he reached into his back pocket and pulled out his wallet.

Memories of the last time he'd pulled out his wallet assailed me.

Really great memories that I was ashamed to admit I'd replayed a thousand times in the last five days.

Reese stepped closer to my front door and bent at the waist, meaning I lost sight of his upper body and what he was doing.

"Who's there?" my mom called out.

"No one."

"No one?"

Before I could think up another lie my front door opened and Reese waltzed in.

Holy shit.

"Sadie, answer me."

Reese's gaze snapped to my dining room.

"It was no one, *Mom*. They were looking for my neighbor."

Thankfully, Reese didn't miss the emphasis and remained silent. Though he did walk farther into my house.

What the hell?

"I really wish you had a more active social life. You're young, you should be out enjoying all the varieties life has to offer."

Seriously?

Someone shoot me.

"I love you, Mom. I appreciate your concern, but I really have to go."

"Right. Spring cleaning in the fall instead of going out on a date. It's been six months since you broke up with

Nate. I will admit he was a very good-looking young man, nice and polite, too. But, Sadie, honey, it's time to move on."

I hated remembering my parents had met him once when they'd come to visit.

Reese's lips twitched and one of his eyebrows lifted, his amusement clear.

"Asshole," I mouthed.

The lip twitch turned into a smile and the *asshole* winked.

"I'm not hung up on Nate. I've just been busy with the bakery. I'll start dating again when things slow down."

Epic lie.

I wasn't ever dating again.

Which made looking at Reese so painful I wanted to close my eyes against the agony.

"We're very proud of you, honey. We know how hard you work. It's just there's more to life than work and we want you to be happy."

Dagger to my heart.

How proud would my parents be if they knew how stupid I'd been? How proud would they be if they knew I was behind on my rent—both personal and business? How proud would they be if they knew my business loan was nearing default?

"Thanks, Mom," I choked out. "I'll call you tomorrow."

"Okay, I love you, sweet girl."

"Love you, too, Momma."

I rushed to my phone to double-check that she'd disconnected before I turned back around. Unfortunately, Reese had moved with me, so he was so close I almost ran into his body. I teetered back knowing what happened when I touched him and not wanting a repeat.

It seemed there was a theme to my night—big fat honking lies.

I wanted a repeat. I wanted lots and lots of repeats with slight variations of what we'd done in my office. I wanted it so badly I'd successfully avoided Reese for five days. If I saw him come into the shop, I hightailed my ass to the back. If he'd slipped in without me noticing and was already ordering when I did, I busied myself with something behind the counter, making sure my back was to him.

"Your parents don't know you're in trouble?" he guessed.

I wasn't in trouble. I was fucked.

"Get out."

"Who's Nate?"

"Get. Out!"

"Why haven't you told your parents you're behind—"

I should've taken a breath or ten. I should've picked up the phone and called the police to report an intruder then stood there and waited until the cops showed up and cuffed him. I should've done twenty other things than what I did.

But I couldn't know until after I'd opened my mouth that Reese was the type of man who, once you gave him an inch, took that as encouragement to keep pushing.

"My parents don't know because they're in Florida. They're there partly because they were tired of Idaho winters and wanted warm weather year-round. Partly because my mom loves the beach and my dad loves my mom and wants her to have everything she loves. But mostly they moved to get away from my brother's dysfunction which isn't your average, everyday, run-of-the-mill bad behavior. Josh is unrelenting. He's an ass who likes to spread his misery whenever he can. My parents got fed up and moved. They're happy. Truly and completely happy. I'm not going to dump my bad life choices on their doorstep when they're finally free to live their lives without my brother showing up every other day for no other reason than to upset them. And Nate is none of your business."

"You're wrong."

I was wrong?

I jerked back, putting more distance between us. Reese didn't like this. I knew because he took a step closer, negating my efforts.

"Wrong about what?"

"Your parents are not in Florida living the good life worry-free. I don't have kids, but I do have good parents, and even though I'm an adult I know they still worry about me, and they do that regardless they know I got no troubles. So, your parents, knowing their son is the definition of trouble, are not worry-free. They're fretting about their son. And the fact they're doing it from Florida because they needed to escape their son means they're doing it daily."

He was correct. My parents worried daily about my brother.

"Another reason why I'm not going to tell them."

"Bad choice, Sadie. When life gives you shit, best thing to do is reach out to the people who love you."

"Thanks for the unwanted advice. You can leave now."

"What bad life choices have you made?"

"Ones that aren't your business."

"When are you going to clue in, I'm making it my business."

Red hued my vision.

"Is this fun for you? With everything I got going on, are you getting off on fucking with me? Huh, Reese, is this some sort of sick game? Kick the girl while she's down?"

If my vision colored, Reese's face turned to thunder.

"Told you then and I didn't lie. I got off huge fucking you."

"That's not what I'm talking about and you damn well know it."

"I'm ignoring the fucked-up shit that's coming out—"

"Fucked-up shit," I sputtered. "What's fucked-up is you showing up at my house."

"Who screwed you over?"

My insides boiled, my blood heated, fury struck. Yet I was speechless.

"Tell, me, Sadie. Who fucked you up? And please, don't play me as the fool and deny it. First, you spew some jacked shit about being a dick-starved slut, which we both fuckin' know is not why we tore into each other the other day. And just now you asking me if this shit is fun for me is equally, if not more, jacked-up. Someone's fucked you over. Did this Nate guy do this to you?"

"Why would you think—"

"Textbook," he cut me off. "Women have a bad habit of internalizing then projecting the shit some asshole force-fed them. A woman who's confident in who she is does not see herself as a slut, much less say that garbage out loud. A woman who has not been jacked around by a man does not automatically think that the next man who comes along is fucking with her when in reality what he's doing is trying to help a friend."

"Friend? You're not my *friend*."

"Sadie, I've been inside you."

Gah!

"Would you stop freaking talking about that! And just because we had sex doesn't mean we're friends. I'm sure you've had lots of sex with women who were not your friends."

Either that or he had a lot of friends, because he was seriously good at sex. And he was a fantastic kisser. And he got an A-plus for dirty talk.

"We're not talking about me. We're talking about you."

It was then something struck me.

"Did you come here thinking you were gonna get me in bed?"

"Totally jacked," he mumbled irately.

Reese's gaze went from me to the table where I'd been packing up clothes that needed to be shipped. His eyes narrowed on the dresses and shoes, then I watched as he caught sight of the invoices I'd printed. After that he looked around the rest of the room, turning to take in the living room as well. I knew what he saw, and unlike my mother who I could lie to and tell I was spring cleaning in fall, Reese would figure it out.

"You're selling your stuff."

Yep. There it was. Meaning his statement was just that, a statement, not a question. And since it was such, I didn't feel it warranted a response. Further from that, I was so embarrassed I'd been reduced to selling my personal belongings to pay my bills I couldn't say anything. All the words were trapped in my throat, and I was fighting back tears of frustration.

"Sadie?"

"Please don't," I whispered.

All the anger had drained out of me until all that was left was humiliation.

Reese stepped closer and when he was within range his arm came up, his hand went to the side of my neck, and his fingers slid under my hair before they curled in and squeezed.

"You're selling your stuff, sweetheart," he repeated gently.

I'd never heard Reese's voice so tender. It was a weird thing to think about, especially now, while I was mortified. He knew I wasn't just broke, I was sell-my-clothes broke.

But I couldn't help pondering which Reese was more dangerous to my sanity. Bossy, growly Reese. Sweet, gentle Reese. Or teasing, flirty Reese which was who he was when I'd first met him.

The man had three different personalities.

All dangerous in their own way.

But this soft side, it would do the most damage.

I knew he'd hurt me in a different way than Nate did. I would one day recover from what Nate did to me. But Reese...he could lay the hurt on me in a way that would shatter my heart.

Yet I still didn't run.

I stayed and held my ground.

I'd learn later it was both my best and worst decision.

4

THERE WERE a lot of unpleasantries about my job. Over the years, Takeback had been involved in hundreds of human trafficking rescues. I'd seen a lot of women, children, and men in despair. I'd seen hopelessness, anguish, sorrow, desperation. You name it, I'd witnessed it.

I'd seen fear and vulnerability.

And I was seeing it right then.

A different kind than I'd seen on the faces of the victims we'd helped. But there was no mistake, Sadie was exposing a fragility I hadn't expected to see.

Not weakness, though she'd likely call it that.

There was strength in her despondence.

Sadie's eyes darted around the room, her shoulders sagged, her back hunched forward along with her chin tipping down, and finally, she looked at her feet.

She was embarrassed I knew what she was doing, maybe even embarrassed she had to do it, but she was doing it. Sadie wasn't the type of woman who'd lay down and allow things to happen to her. She wasn't the type of woman who was going to lose without first putting up a fight.

She'd sell her clothes, shoes, and by the look of her home, other things besides.

What she wouldn't do was crawl into a corner and give up.

Something else I liked about her.

"How bad is it?" I asked.

"Bad," she whispered, still looking at the floor.

Fuck.

"Your brother's got two days to pay you back what he owes you. Will that help?"

"No."

Fuck me.

Sadie's jaw clenched, her neck tensed under my palm, and I braced. She was coming out of her stupor and coming to understand what she'd shared.

Her gaze came up and as soon as her eyes locked with mine the soft slid out and the hard crept in.

There it was, that backbone of steel mixed with no small amount of fortitude.

Good goddamn, I liked that.

Way too fucking much.

"Since you've brought it up," she snapped. "We need to talk about Josh."

Hell, yeah, we did.

Her brother was a piece of shit. I'd been sitting on what I'd found on him for days wondering if Sadie knew about Josh's record. And I'd been doing that because she'd been ghosting me. Five days of that bullshit was all I could take, hence me showing up on her front stoop.

"We got a lotta stuff to talk about," I reminded her. "But if you wanna start with your brother, you can tell me if he's tried to call you since the day in front of your bakery. I know he hasn't made contact otherwise."

"How would you know that?"

Was she serious?

"I told you I'd be watching."

"And I told you I didn't want that."

"So you get to watch me but you don't want me watching you?"

"I don't watch you!"

Her lie was punctuated with a sexy, low snarl. She also belatedly realized I had my hand on her neck and we were standing close. Something she rectified with a step back and a shrug, disengaging my hold.

"Right. So, I guess I imagined all those times I've caught you staring at me when I'm waiting in line, or when I'm sitting at a table with one of the guys enjoying my coffee."

"I don't stare at you," she sputtered.

That was a lie.

I'd caught her on many occasions staring at me when she thought I couldn't see. She did this mostly when my back was to her, and my back was to her so I could watch her stare at me using the front windows that ran the length of her shop. She also stared at me while I was waiting in line to order, but she only looked at me when she thought my attention was on my phone and when I'd look up, she'd quickly avert her eyes.

"You do. Wanna know how I know? Because from the moment I walk in I seek you out. Because I watch *you.* Because you find reasons to come out from behind the counter when I'm sitting at a table. Because you don't send an employee over to deliver my coffee, you personally bring it to me."

"Damn, Reese, you've got a mighty big ego."

"Nope. Just calling it straight."

"Hate to tell you but you got it wrong."

Sadie's arms crossed and her gaze went over my shoulder. There was also color blooming on her cheeks. She knew damn well she watched me, same as I couldn't take my eyes off her whenever she was near.

"If you say so."

"What's that supposed to mean?" she hissed.

"It means I'm giving in and I'm not gonna argue with you because I know I'm right."

She wisely let that go and asked, "Why are you here?"

"You really have to ask that?"

"I just did, so, *obviously*, yeah, I have to ask."

Damn, she was cute as all get-out when she was riled up and throwing sass.

"You've been dodging me."

Sadie pursed her lips, one side hitched up, and she squinted her eyes before she drawled, "So, you didn't miss it then?"

Oh, yeah, she was cute as fuck when she was being a smartass.

"Hard to miss you scampering away every time I came in to see you."

"I don't scamper."

"Then what would you call it?"

"Me, politely telling you—"

"Baby, to *tell* me something you gotta use your words like a big girl."

Sadie bent slightly at the waist, leaned in, and spat, "Don't be a dick."

"It's not *me* being a dick, Sadie."

"You're...you...you're calling me a dick?" she stammered.

"Yep."

I watched Sadie straighten and as she did this her arms uncrossed, fell to her sides, and her brows pulled together.

"Okay, Reese. You win. I'm the dick. And since I'm that, I don't understand why you'd waste your time coming over here. I feel like I've said this to you about a hundred times; I don't have time for what game you're playing. But since you're not catching the hint, I'll spell it out. The other day what happened on the sidewalk was bullshit. I don't want you involved—"

Before she could finish, I asked, "Do you know who Zeus is?"

"I've lived here my whole life, Reese. I know who Trevor Lawrence is and I refuse to call him by his stupid club name. I've known him since I was like six when he was just a scrawny little kid getting picked on during recess. And I knew him in middle school when he found his inner asshole. And I knew him in high school when he honed those skills and became someone anyone who was smart feared."

Trevor was no longer scrawny. Though he was still an asshole and he'd ratcheted up the asshole to criminal and was now the president of the Horsemen.

"Do you know Tug Anderson?"

Sadie's torso jerked and her features filled with sorrow. Sadness I knew was for Brooklyn, Rhode, Remington, and the Welshes. Tug and Kiki Welsh had kidnapped Remington. Remy had almost died that day. Tug and Kiki had died. Kiki by jumping in front of a bullet fired by Tug meant to kill Remy. Tug died with Rhode's bullet in his forehead.

"Yes. I knew Tug."

"Right. Did you know that while Tug was alive, he was pimping out women? Junkies he forced to work for him. But before he died, he branched out to clean women he could rent out for more money."

"What?"

I didn't miss the disgust on her face, nor did I miss the way she wheezed out her question. And it seriously fucking sucked talking about this sick shit with a woman who was sweet, sometimes shy, funny, smart, and beautiful. Sadie owned a bakery, for God's sake. She walked around smelling like a sugary dessert and tasted even better. So I found no pleasure in explaining to her why I was now very much involved, whether she wanted me to be or not.

"Since Tug died, leaving his stable ripe for the pickin', Zeus stepped up and took control. That means the Horsemen went from dealing drugs and whatever other fucked-up shit they do to keep themselves in booze and Harleys to selling ass."

"Holy shit."

"Holy shit's right, Sadie. Your brother's a part of that."

Her eyes widened a fraction and fear crept in, which negated her rebuff. "He's a jerk but he'd never hurt me."

"You might think that, and you might even be right, but the men he's running with wouldn't bat an eye at fucking you over. And that, Sadie, means I'm at your back. You can tell me you don't want me involved. You can say it over and over, you can scream it, you can do your best to push me away, but you're gonna fail. There's zero chance I'm walking away."

"Why does he do this shit?"

I figured her question was rhetorical, and if it wasn't I didn't have an answer for her, so I remained silent.

"His whole life he's been a pain in the ass. And not just a little one, a huge one. So big, my parents had to move to Florida to escape the shit he continued to dump on them.

And what happens when they leave? He turns to me and piles me under his shit, knowing that I'm not going to let my baby brother drown. But he doesn't care that *I'm* drowning. He doesn't offer me help. And he knows because I told him what happened. He knows I can't afford to give him more money, but he keeps coming around to ask, then gets pissed at me when I tell him I don't have it. What kind of brother does that? Why on earth would he think it's a good idea to join the Horsemen? Everyone knows to stay the hell away from them. If they're in a bar, you turn your happy ass around and leave. You do not go in and have a drink. You don't strike up a conversation with one of them. And you sure as hell don't prospect for them."

I had a response to that. "What happened?"

"Huh?"

"You said your brother knows what happened because you told him. So, what happened?"

In an instant, everything about Sadie changed. She went from being upset about her brother, ranting about him being a pain in the ass, to wary. Then very, very angry.

"None of your business."

Every word was enunciated and clearly underlined in bold. Her tone left no room for argument, yet I pushed.

"I see you're not getting it, Sadie, so I'll lay it out for you. I'm making it my business. I was doing that before I found out you've got a brother who's mixed up with a bunch of assholes. I was doing that before I found out your brother owed you money. I was doing that before that scene in front of your bakery. I was doing it before I fucked you in your office. I was doing it before I came over here and saw you were selling your goddamn clothes. I made the decision when I came in to get my afternoon fix and heard you on the phone asking someone to give you more time to pay your rent. But that decision was carved in stone after what we shared."

I watched her eyes narrow. She was pissed and getting more so by the second. Perversely, I found it a turn-on—not her anger, but the fire I saw flash across her features. Sadie wasn't going to back down; she'd go toe-to-toe with me and do it happily. She'd do it not to be argumentative but because she was the kind of woman who wouldn't back down, and that was a huge turn-on.

"I don't know what you're talking about. We didn't share—"

"Tell me who fucked you over?"

"No."

"You remember what I do?"

"What you do?"

"Yeah, Sadie, what I do. Takeback. You remember I find people, right?"

Realization dawned.

Sadie was friends with Brooklyn and Letty. Brooklyn was engaged to my teammate Rhode which was the reason my boss Wilson McCray had moved Takeback's operation from Arizona to Idaho. We couldn't afford to lose Rhode's expertise and Rhode understandably wanted to be in Idaho with his son and fiancée. Sadie's friendship with the women meant she knew what Takeback did, and even if she wasn't friends with them, we didn't hide who we were therefore Sadie would know because the whole town knew.

"You wouldn't dare," she spat.

"I'm not sure how I can make this any clearer for you, but I'll try," I started. "Not only will I dig through your life, but I'll also dig through your finances. I'll dig through your brother's. I'll comb through everyone you've had contact with in the last year. So, not only will I do it, I'll do it happily and thoroughly."

Sadie sucked in a breath, puffed out her chest, and took two steps, not stopping until she was in my space. I fought the urge to breathe her in, to lean in, run my tongue over her throat, and see if she tasted as good as I remembered. To haul her ass back to her bedroom and do all the things I'd been dreaming about doing to her. The only thing that stopped me was her accusation I was only there to get her into bed.

"*I'm* not sure how *I* can make myself any clearer, Reese, but *I'll* try," she mocked. "Stay the fuck out of my business. This is not a joke. This is not fun for me. My life is so screwed up right now, I can't see my way out of it. *I'm selling my clothes!*" she roared and threw her arms wide. Then quietly, in a whisper, she repeated, "I'm selling my clothes, Reese. Do you know how embarrassing that is? I've worked my ass off for years to build my business. I've worked seven days a week, twelve-hour days to build something I'm proud of. Something that is *mine*. And now I'm working just as hard to save it. So as embarrassing as it is, I'll sell everything I own if it means I save my business. What I will not do, is fight with you about it. My problems are not yours. I did this to myself, and I'll fight like hell to get myself out of it. I don't need you poking around in my life, invading my privacy. I don't need you showing up at my house, breaking in. I don't need you leaving hundred-dollar tips. I don't need jackshit from anyone."

When she finished, her chest was rising and falling like she'd run a marathon. One she hadn't trained for because she was seriously huffing and puffing.

"How'd you do it to yourself?" I asked quietly.

Much to my dislike and dismay, tears formed and within seconds spilled down her cheeks.

Fucking hell.

"You're not listening."

"Baby, I am. I'm listening to every word. But it doesn't jibe. I know how hard you work because in all the months I've lived here I haven't seen you take a day off. I can't say I'm at Treats every day, but damn near close. And the times I don't go in but I'm at the bookstore, I see your car parked behind the bakery, so I know you're there. What I don't see is you driving an expensive car. I don't see you kitted out in expensive clothes, jewelry, and shoes. I don't see you not showing up at work going on vacations. You keep saying you did this to yourself but that doesn't fit with the woman I know you to be. And I know exactly the kind of woman you are because you're selling your fucking clothes, Sadie, not sitting in a corner sniveling."

Sadie angrily swiped at the tears and shook her head.

"Seems to me like I'm sniveling now."

"There's a difference between tears of frustration and crying in a corner and you damn well know that. I get you're embarrassed. I understand what it feels like to be humiliated. I know how hard it is to swallow the bitter taste of indignity." I paused when Sadie's chin dipped, and her eyes slid to the side.

I lifted my hands and cupped her wet cheeks. It was risky but necessary. I needed her looking at me but at the same time, touching her brought on a different kind of need. The kind that went beyond the obvious sexual tension. The kind that made me want to pull her close and just hold her. The kind that I couldn't afford to allow myself to feel.

Been there. Done that. Never doing it again.

"Let me help you, Sadie."

"No!"

Her refusal was curt and soft, but she might as well have shouted it in my face.

"No strings. No one will know. Just a friend helping a friend."

Sadie's stubborn blue eyes held mine when she repeated, "No!"

"You'd rather lose everything you worked so hard for?"

"I'd rather shove toothpicks in my eyeballs than take a handout."

That wasn't strength; that was sheer stubborn stupidity.

"You being stubborn doesn't prove anything. No, actually, it does. It proves you'll let pride stand in your way. It proves you got an ego. It proves you got further to fall before you come to realize that accepting help doesn't mean the success you've achieved isn't still all yours. It also means you're confusing humiliation with humility. There's nothing fucking wrong with needing help and taking what's being offered. But there sure as fuck is something wrong with turning it down because you can't set your ego aside. With that being said, my offer stands. A no-strings, no-interest loan. I'm not gonna beg you to take my money, but I hope like fuck before you lose your business you come find me."

I dropped my hands and stepped back.

"Reese—"

"I'll be back in a few days with the money your brother owes you. And when I do, I don't wanna catch shit about it. That money is owed to you. It's not me or your brother giving it to you."

With that, I turned to leave. My gaze went around the room wondering what she'd already sold and cataloging the rest. I wanted nothing more than to stay and argue until she agreed to let me help her. Every instinct I had screamed to fight with her and for her. And that was a red flag. A big ass mental stop sign.

It had been years. So long ago, some men might've forgotten. But I remembered. The betrayal and cynicism were branded on my heart. The embarrassment I felt when I found out my wife was a cheating bitch still churned in my gut.

Feelings and emotions were off-limits.

I opened the front door and for the first time since I'd come home from deployment and caught my wife in bed with another man, I had to force myself to leave a woman's house. I had to remind myself I felt nothing.

Thankfully, I succeeded.

5

HOW WAS it possible to be in a room full of women yet feel totally and utterly alone?

My twice-monthly book club meeting had just ended. Five other readers plus Brooklyn, Letty, and Mrs. Simpson were milling about chatting.

All smiling.

All happy.

But not me.

I was feeling a lot of things, but not one of those feelings was happiness. Dread and shame were my constant companions. And if that wasn't bad enough, fear and anxiety pushed in throughout the day. Then there was Reese. Thoughts of him didn't have to push in because they were always at the forefront. The memories bombarded me. Everything he'd said, what we'd done, how I felt when I was in his company, how I felt when I *wasn't* in his company, and his offer.

No strings, no-interest loan.

I'd turned him down for all the reasons he'd stated. Pride, ego, stubbornness, and embarrassment.

But he'd forgotten one—fear.

I was scared to get too close to him. I was scared of making the same mistakes. I was scared I'd do something stupid like kiss him again. Which would lead me to feeling other things. And I knew that was the case because I'd felt them. Under the lust was a twinge of longing. A pang of irrational sorrow for a man that I could never give myself to. But that didn't stop me from wanting him.

Fingers snapped in front of my face, and I blinked until Letty's smile came into focus.

"Please tell me you were thinking about a certain tall, green-eyed man who missed his calling as a cover model and not the hot wolf-shifter-alpha who bites his mate. Not that I'd blame you, Lance is a sexy beast and I might ask my man to act—"

"Jeez, Letty." Brooklyn laughed. "TMI."

Letty shrugged and smiled at her best friend.

"Like you didn't dog-ear that scene for Dulles to read when you get home."

"Of course, I did. But I'm not going to advertise it."

Incidentally, Letty called Brooklyn's fiancé Rhode, Dulles. I didn't understand the nickname and sometimes Letty switched it up and called him Magus, which I still didn't get because if anyone should have a Viking nickname it was Letty's future husband River. The guy was huge. But his nickname was Pen Pal or sometimes Male BFF. I understood those nicknames because I knew of River before he'd shown up in Idaho. Letty and he had been friends for years. Though, during the years I'd been friends with Letty and had been involved in her book club I hadn't known they'd never met in person. Nor had they ever exchanged photos. Something that made my romantic heart swoon.

I mean, how sweet was it that River fell in love with

Letty without ever seeing her? His love for her was real and true.

"Have you been drinking?" Letty asked with a giggle.

I jolted and quickly glanced around looking for who Letty was speaking to. But it was just the three of us.

"Are you talking to me?"

"Yes, girl. You're zoning out."

I wasn't zoning out. I was freaking out.

It had been two days since I'd seen Reese. And in those two days, he had not come into my bakery once. So my freak-out was multi-faceted, starting with my brother's deadline to pay me back. Next up was how Reese planned on getting Josh to pay up since he was always broke. After that was the fact I hadn't seen Reese and I couldn't remember the last time I'd gone two full days without catching a glimpse of him. The other night, I had flat-out lied when I denied watching him. I totally did, and yes, this included checking out his ass. It was a perverse obsession. I'd turned into a masochist torturing myself daily then promising myself I'd stop giving in to my need to see him.

But I never stopped. I studiously kept an eye out. But for two days, nothing. And that caused my freak-out to intensify. I should've been happy I'd pushed him too far. I'd been a royal bitch to him and now he'd leave me alone like I'd demanded.

I wasn't happy.

I was angry and I knew that was irrational as well.

"Long day," I told Letty. "You know how it is."

"Damn right I do. Two sisters kicking ass in the business world."

Letty's beaming smile made my stomach clench.

I was failing.

She was kicking ass.

But my demise was mine and I wasn't the kind of woman or friend who dims someone else's light to plunge them into my darkness.

The smile I returned felt fake. Yet, I plastered it on my face and buried the sick feeling that was threatening to pull me under.

"You're always kicking ass, my friend."

That was not fake. It was the truth. Letty had dreamed of owning a bookstore and damn if she hadn't done it, then she made it thrive.

"On that note," I continued. "I need to get home. Unlike you, I open at seven for the morning coffee rush."

I passed out hugs and waved my goodbye to Mrs. Simpson. The older woman reminded me of Liz Taylor—a throwback to Hollywood's glitz and glamor. She used to be Letty's neighbor before she and River bought a house and moved in together. Letty being a good person recognized Mrs. Simpson's loneliness and offered her a job. Mrs. Simpson worked when it suited her. I adored spending time with her. She was a riot, but she was also astute. Nothing slipped past her. So I'd been avoiding being in her presence when there weren't a gaggle of people around. Like now, with other book club members in attendance, Mrs. Simpson would never ask me what was wrong. She was far too classy for that.

But one day, she'd catch me alone and ask and I would lie to her like I was lying to everyone else. Something I already felt guilty over and I hadn't even done it yet.

Lying sucked.

Each one piled on top of the one before until you had a castle of deceit.

The hell of it was, I knew one day I'd be locked in that

castle all alone wearing my crown of deception, cloaked in misery of my own making.

It wasn't pride that would be my downfall.

It was fear.

Self-reflection was a bitch.

Introspection gave me the clarity of my actions, but I lacked the strength to pump the brakes to prevent the fiery crash that was coming.

Those were my thoughts on the short drive home. That was until I saw Reese's silver Range Rover parked at the curb and my heart started to beat wildly in my chest. I pulled into my driveway, turned off the ignition, and barely folded out before Reese was cruising up my walk. He didn't greet me by the car. He didn't even acknowledge me on his way to my front door.

I wasn't sure what that meant, but I knew it wasn't good.

Damn.

I'd done it. I'd successfully pushed him away.

"Reese—"

"Inside," he clipped.

His gaze went from me to the street. His eyes narrowed and I glanced over my shoulder to see what caught his attention. A white compact car that should've been put out of its misery about twenty years ago slowly drove by.

"Sadie!"

His tone dripped with impatience, but more than that, it held an edge of unease. It was the unease that made me rush past him to unlock the door. As soon as I had my key free of the lock, Reese reached around me and with his chest pressed to my back, he turned the handle, and shuffled us in.

"What's wrong?"

Reese didn't answer. He locked the door, tagged my hand, and pulled me farther into my house. All of this was so abrupt, and with an abrasive vibe rolling off of him it scared the shit out of me. Not because I thought Reese would hurt me, but because I had a feeling Reese had seen Josh and that meeting hadn't gone well. I was going to repeat my question, but the words died when Reese rocked to a halt like he'd slammed into an invisible brick wall and his head swiveled around my living and dining rooms.

I didn't have to look. I knew what he saw. Yesterday, I'd sold my dining room table and chairs on Marketplace and my kickass coffee table, along with the matching side tables sold on Swap and Shop. The buyer picked those up today on my lunch break.

"Jesus fuck," he growled.

I remained quiet as Reese yanked my hand and moved into my kitchen. When we were next to the island he dropped my hand, reached into his back pocket, pulled out a thick envelope, and tossed it on the butcher block top.

"Three grand," he announced.

Holy shit.

Josh paid.

That was impossible.

My gaze went from the envelope to Reese, and I took in his scowl. Everything about him was cold. The kind of cold that froze your insides and made it hard for your heart to pump.

"What happened?"

"Your brother's a motherfucking idiot."

Perhaps the sisterly thing would've been to get pissed at Reese for talking shit about my brother. But since Josh had demonstrated *repeatedly* over the years that he was an idiot and recently he upped the idiocy to new heights that could indeed be described as seriously screwed up, I decided not to pretend there was a sibling bond and get to the heart of the issue.

"What did he do?"

"To me? Not a damn thing. Saw him, and before I could ask, he handed me the cash and smartly walked away."

That sounded good. So I wasn't seeing what had Reese so angry.

"Okay," I cautiously started. "So why do you look mad?"

"Mad?"

"Well, you look murderous but since we're talking about my brother, and even though I don't like him much, I'd prefer my parents not to have to bury their child. So, I settled on mad in the hopes you'd forget that you wanted to commit a felony and instead explain to me what happened."

My eyes dropped to Reese's lips in time to watch them twitch.

Damn.

It had only been two days, but it felt like a lifetime since I'd seen him smile.

"I didn't think it was possible to get more pissed at your brother." Reese's mouth stopped moving but his eyes continued to roam my face. They were doing this searchingly. I didn't know what he was looking for, but I supposed he found it when he parked his gaze and said, "But seeing you're back to your normal cute, it pisses me right the fuck off I gotta squash that to explain to you just how big of an asshole your brother is."

My normal cute?

Obviously, I knew Reese found me somewhat attractive, or attractive enough to have sex with. So I knew he didn't find me to be repulsive. But since I'd never been called cute before I didn't know what to make of it.

"That doesn't sound good," I murmured.

"None of it's good," Reese confirmed. "Had occasion to sit down with Zeus. This meeting was arranged before I knew Grinder was—"

"Wait, who's Grinder?"

I'd never heard that club name, which wasn't surprising since I didn't hang out anywhere the Horsemen did. Treats wasn't exactly biker unfriendly but none of the Horsemen had ever stepped their dirty motorcycle boots inside my girly bakery before. *Praise Jesus!*

Reese's eyes flared and I didn't take that as a good sign.

"Josh's club name," he informed me.

"Grinder?" I felt my lips curl. "That's a stupid name. How'd he get stuck with that?"

"Babe," Reese mumbled and shook his head.

Everyone knew club names were earned. Unless you were Zeus. Rumor had it Trevor had coined his own nickname as the god of all gods when he'd started the Horsemen. But everyone else as far as I knew earned theirs. It was the biker way. What could my brother have done to get stuck with Grinder?

"Does he grind the gears—"

"Babe, leave it."

Now I really had to know.

"Tell me."

Reese shook his head again, but this time added, "Trust me, Sadie, you don't want to know."

Now I really, *really* had to know.

"Trust me, I want to know."

Reese leaned his hip against the counter. His eyes held mine and there it was—the feeling in my stomach I always got when I saw him fluttered. That was, it fluttered when I wasn't pissed at him for barging into my problems. But with

Reese standing in my kitchen after not seeing him for a few days—even if he was only here to drop off the money he'd gone out of his way to get from my brother—I realized how much I missed seeing him. And if he came in with Davis or Jack or one of the other guys he worked with and sat at one of my awesome bistro tables, inevitably I'd hear his laugh or see his smile, and I missed that, too.

"There are things a sister doesn't want to know," he returned. "And *trust me*, this is one of those things."

The only thing I could think of that a sister would never, under any circumstances want to know about her baby brother was his sexual exploits.

Ack.

Gross.

"So it's about..." I trailed off unable to vocalize the word, deciding that Reese was right, I didn't want to know. "Never mind. Don't tell me."

"Good call."

Reese's quick comeback, not to mention the relief I saw in his eyes, had me thinking I was right. Grinder was a metaphor for some sort of sexual act, I absolutely had no desire to know about.

Gag.

"Okay, back to your story," I prompted.

"Right. Met with Zeus and a few of his lieutenants. He wanted to make it clear the Horsemen had no knowledge of what Greg and Dora Thomas were doing and they were not involved in Letty's kidnapping."

Greg and Dora Thomas were horrible people. The local newspaper had printed an article about them that didn't scratch the surface of their depravity. Greg had abducted Letty for reasons I wasn't privy to, and the papers didn't say. But he died in a car accident while fleeing with Letty. It was a miracle Letty had lived. Dora Thomas was now in prison serving twenty years. I couldn't think of a better place for the vile woman to live out the rest of her days.

"I could see how having to breathe the same air as the Horsemen would be unpleasant and piss you off but what does that have to do with Josh?" I asked when Reese didn't go on.

"After your brother gave me the money, Zeus felt like talking. Not about Letty's kidnapping or Greg Thomas owing the Horsemen a fuckton of money. Instead, he decided to run his filthy mouth about you. Seems Josh shared with his brothers you got money problems. Further, he shared you got these problems because of that guy, Nate. Zeus happily informed me they got you covered. What the jackass wasn't happy about was me sharing with him in terms he couldn't misinterpret was that you are off fucking limits. Something I told your brother when we had our thing in front of your shop. Something he fucking ignored. Now, he's got his felonious band of brothers looking for Nate and he put you on their radar."

My heart was pounding wildly and I could barely catch my breath. I was pissed Josh had mentioned Nate's name. I was even more pissed Reese knew Nate was involved with my money troubles. Now he was going to ask uncomfortable questions about my ex that I didn't want to answer. If he hadn't *already* looked into my finances like he'd threatened. But all of that took a back seat to Zeus talking about me. I didn't ever want to be the topic of conversation for any of the Horsemen, but Zeus was the worst of the bunch.

"Why would he do that?" I wheezed.

"Can't answer that, Sadie, except to say your brother's a grade-A idiot. Now we got more to talk about."

My pulse kicked up a notch. My hands shook. My lungs

started to burn. And lastly, that flutter I felt in my belly had turned sour.

There weren't a lot of people I feared. The Horsemen as a whole scared me. Trevor by himself I was petrified of, and my damn brother knew that and knew why. The guy was creepy as hell and a pervert and my brother knew that, too.

"I don't want Trevor to know anything about me," I blurted out.

Everything about Reese changed. He'd gone from disgusted and mad to alert and lethal. This happened in the blink of an eye. So quickly, I didn't have the chance to process this before he pushed away from the island and closed the minimal space between us. So quickly, I wasn't ready when both his hands lifted and went to the sides of my neck. His thumbs at my jaw put pressure there until my head tipped back and he peered into my eyes. Watchful, wary, cautious.

And when he spoke, his tone was just as cautious as his stare. "There a reason why you look so freaked? He ever hurt you?"

Yes, there was a reason I was freaked. Trevor was...there hadn't been a word invented yet for what he was.

"He's bad news."

"That he is, baby. But we've talked about him before and none of those times have you looked like you were scared."

"Well, none of those times were you telling me that Trevor was talking about me. I've done everything I could do over the years to not be anywhere near the Horsemen, but especially Trevor. First, because they're all crazy. I know that's not a nice thing to say but they are. They don't care about anything or anyone who doesn't wear their patch. They start fights, they sell drugs, they beat people up who owe them money, they smash windows out of cars for fun, they harass women and if a man tries to step in, they'll jump him. None of that says normal, well-adjusted behavior. They scare me. But Trevor's in a league of his own. He preys on women. So, I wasn't all that surprised when you told me he's now pimping them out."

"What do you mean he preys on women?"

The sour in my belly started to churn as the bad memories started to invade.

"He doesn't like hearing no, so he ignores it," I told him.

I felt Reese stiffen. His fingers pressing into the back of my neck spasmed, which made his soft, gentle tone come across as harsh and grating.

"Did he ignore you when you told him no?"

"Not me," I rushed out. "A friend from high school. Trevor messed her up and Josh knew because she came home with me after it happened. Josh saw Lori. He saw her ripped shirt. He saw the bruising. He saw her huddled on the couch with my mom. He heard her crying. And he knew it took my mom an hour to convince her to call her parents. Josh knows it was Trevor. He knows I'm scared of him because he's creepy as fuck, has no moral compass, and has no issues hurting women. So, knowing all of that, why would my brother mention my name to that asshole?"

"*Fuck!*"

I startled at his vicious curse, which made Reese's face harden in a way that scared me.

"I would never hurt you."

The hardness slipped from his features; however, his tone was just as vicious. Or maybe it was simply adamant, but in my current state of fear-induced panic, I couldn't differentiate between the two. Fear of Trevor. Fear for my brother. Fear that what had happened to Lori would happen to me. And as soon as that thought hit my brain, guilt crashed in.

"Sadie, did you hear me?"

"I don't want him to hurt me."

"No one's gonna hurt you."

"But Trevor will. You don't know him, Reese. You don't know what he did to Lori. If he did that to me..." I paused to swallow the bile creeping up my throat. "I hate myself for even thinking that. God, what kind of person does that make me? She's my friend, or she was before she moved away. And she moved because she was so afraid it would happen again, she couldn't stay here. I know what he did to her and I'm a horrible person for thinking—"

"Sadie, stop!" He punctuated his demand by stroking my jaw with his thumbs. "It doesn't make you a horrible person to not want a man to violate you. It doesn't make you a bad friend. No one, man or woman, should have to go through what your friend did."

He was right—absolutely. But it didn't take away my guilt.

"Listen to me," he continued. "No one is going to hurt you. I promise you, baby, Zeus isn't going to get anywhere near you."

It was nice and all that Reese would make that promise, but Trevor did what he wanted to do. Period.

"You don't believe me," he rightly surmised.

"Trevor does what Trevor does. He always has. He was smaller than the other kids his age, but he was mean. He grew bigger and taller, and that meanness grew right along with his size. By the time he hit high school, everyone was scared of him, even the teachers. He's never cared about consequences. And now he's the president of an MC and he cares even less."

Reese kept his eyes locked on mine, but he dipped closer. I'd worked myself into a panic, but I wasn't so far gone I couldn't appreciate the brown striations that streaked through the green of his irises. The contrast made the green look emerald. Couple that with his dark, spiky lashes framing his eyes perfectly, the color, the shape, the intensity was a sight to behold. He was beautiful in every way. From his chiseled jaw to his perfect bone structure, to his well-defined muscles, to his mop of dark brown hair that high-lighted his golden complexion.

If I'd only met him a few years ago, before my life turned to shit. Before I'd met Nate. Before he'd stolen my life savings and cleaned out my accounts. Before the drama. Before I decided never to trust again.

"Sadie? Did you hear me?"

Hear him?

"Huh?"

"I promise."

I believed he meant that. I also believed he thought he'd be able to keep that promise. But I knew better and since I didn't want to argue, I agreed.

"Okay."

"I know you don't trust me, but..."

I felt it happen inch by inch. Starting at my toes and working up from there, every muscle seized. I knew Reese felt it because he stopped speaking and the severity of his stare deepened.

"Nate," he murmured.

Oh, no.

Nope.

I didn't want to go there.

"Don't."

"He's the one who fucked you over."

"Don't."

"He's the one that put that wariness I see in your eyes. He's the one that turned your thoughts. All the good you got inside of you, he used it, then jacked you around."

He was right about that; Nate did use me. But it was humiliation I felt, not wariness.

"I don't want to talk about him."

"I get that. You didn't want to talk about it the other day either and I gave you that play. But earlier I found out he's the reason you got money problems. So, now, we gotta talk about him. Not only because he screwed you over worse than I thought but also because your brother has set the Horsemen on him, and I need to know what I'm dealing with."

Things just kept getting worse and worse.

I didn't want to talk about Nate, but I wanted the Horsemen trying to track him down even less.

Suddenly I felt defeated, utterly exhausted. I was so over the emotional rollercoaster I was on I wanted to jump off. I wanted to throw my hands up and quit. I wanted to scream and pitch a fit, rage against the world, and while I was at it stomp my feet. But I couldn't give up. I had to fight until there was nothing left to fight for.

"You know I'm tired of having no control over my life," I told him softly. "It sucks that you're right and I have no control over that either. I have no good options. Either I tell you and hope you can stop Trevor, or Trevor does something he feels he should be paid back for. And I'd rather owe you than him."

Reese's eyes narrowed and his brows pinched together.

"Owe me?"

"Yes, owe—"

"Did I ask you for anything?"

"Well, no. But you went out of your way to get the money Josh borrowed from me that he had no intention of paying back. You should take a cut of the three grand; you know, like a finder's fee. And now…"

I stopped speaking. Perhaps I never should've started if the low guttural rumble was any indication. Then that sound got louder and more defined and I clamped my mouth closed completely.

"I'm gonna pretend you didn't just say that."

I thought that was a splendid idea, so I nodded.

"Can we go sit on your couch or is someone coming by in the next five minutes to pick it up?"

"Are you making fun of me?"

"No, baby, I'm being dead serious. It didn't escape my notice some furniture's missing, so unless you were robbed, I'm assuming you sold it. So, is the couch sold or can we sit on it?"

"No, *Reese*, it's not sold, but hopefully by tomorrow…"

Oh, boy. The rumble was back and this time it sounded even more annoyed.

"Have you eaten dinner?" He abruptly changed the subject.

I hadn't but I wasn't going to tell him I planned on eating a Cup Noodles if I got hungry. So I lied.

"Yes."

And being the broke-ass woman I was, I didn't have anything to offer him, not even a drink other than water, so we stood staring at each other silently.

"Don't lie to me."

There was so much concern in his tone it softened the blow of his demand.

"I haven't eaten. But I'm not hungry."

And that was the truth. Trevor. Nate. My brother. The Horsemen. They'd stolen my appetite. Not to mention, the impending conversation about how my ex screwed me over. None of those topics were conducive to me stomaching dinner.

Then there was Reese.

The man could inspire a thousand fantasies. He could fuel dreams and fulfill desires. But he'd never be mine. He wouldn't be the one who got away. He wouldn't be a regret. He would be the one who should've been.

My *if only*.

If only I'd met him before.

6

I HAVE NO GOOD OPTIONS.

I couldn't stop thinking about what Sadie had said. I was actively and with great effort ignoring the stab I felt in my chest that she didn't consider me a good option. But more, I was ignoring why I felt that stab. Why when she was close, I felt the need to touch her. Why I couldn't stop thinking about her. And lastly, why it had taken ungodly restraint not to go to her in the last two days.

"I thought you wanted to go sit?"

Sadie's question drew my attention back to her.

I'm tired of having no control.

Fuck.

I was treading on thin ice trying to navigate through a field of landmines. One misstep and I'd be swimming in the frigid water, but worse, I'd set Sadie off. She'd sold more stuff in the last two days and I couldn't help wondering what else she'd sold that I couldn't see. Did the woman still have a bed to sleep on? Did she have food in the fridge to eat? And this was where the road got dicey, and I didn't know how to proceed. My first instinct was to demand we go to dinner so I could get a proper meal into her. My second was to disregard her protests and order five pizzas so she'd have leftovers. Neither of those options would win me any favors. She'd be pissed I was forcing something on her she didn't want, taking away more of her control. Even if what she was controlling was the food she ate.

Totally fucked.

And did I care if she was pissed as long as her belly was full?

Nope.

I didn't care. My need to take care of her won out. But I picked the option with less chance of an argument.

"I'm fuckin' starved. Is there anything you don't like on pizza?"

"Why would it matter what I like on my pizza?"

She sounded outraged, but even if she didn't, her hand going to her hip and her eyes getting squinty would've been a dead giveaway I'd failed in my endeavor.

"Because I'm not gonna eat in front of you; it's rude."

"So leave."

That wasn't going to happen. I hadn't seen her in two days, not even a glimpse of her. I'd avoided going to Letty's bookstore precisely so I wouldn't pop into Treats for a fix.

"We got stuff to talk about," I reminded her.

"The story about how Nate screwed me over won't take that long. By the time your food arrives, I'll be done. As a matter of fact, we don't even need to sit. He stole all my money. The end."

I might've blinked a few times. I definitely felt my blood boil, and I most certainly should've curbed my reaction.

"He stole your fucking money!" I roared.

I watched Sadie flinch away from me for the second time, which only fueled my anger.

"I don't wanna tell you again, Sadie, I would never hurt you. No matter how mad I get, you're safe with me. Always."

"You don't look mad. You're back to looking homicidal."

I reckoned I did. Though premeditated murder would've been a more accurate description of what I was feeling.

"And yet you're safe."

"You didn't look into me?" she asked.

I hadn't. For some reason I wanted the story to come from her. I wanted her to trust me enough to tell me. That was a bad call made worse by Grinder sharing details with Zeus I didn't have.

"I wanted you to tell me."

Sadie blew out a stuttered breath, prompting me to drop my hands before I did something stupid like close the distance between us and kiss her. There was more I needed to know but we weren't going to have the conversation standing. I wanted Sadie comfortable, or as comfortable as she could be sharing something she didn't want to share. There was a sliver of my conscience that wanted to give her the privacy she wanted. A small part of me that felt like an asshole for demanding something of her she didn't want to give. I would've given in and left the topic of her ex off the table if the Horsemen weren't involved. But Zeus knowing about Sadie's troubles was a game-changer. There was no telling what that asshole would do and with the new knowledge of what he'd done to Sadie's friend—and I didn't believe that was a one-time occurrence, though once was fucking bad enough—I needed the whole story.

It was with that in mind, I tagged Sadie's hand and tugged her toward the couch while at the same time pulling my phone out to order dinner.

"Sit. I'll order—"

"Should I bark for you, too? Or do you prefer yes, master?"

It was perverse the way her attitude turned me on.

"Yes, master works for me. But just to say, you wanna go down that road and play, be prepared to go all in."

Her mouth dropped open. Maybe in shock. Maybe she was plotting to castrate me. Maybe the thought of me tying her up and fucking her silly turned her on as much as it did me.

"Red!"

Interesting.

"Red?" I asked. "Is there a reason you know what a safe word is?"

"I read a lot."

I knew she did. When I'd first met her, she'd go into Smutties and leave with an armful of books, something I hadn't seen her do in quite a while. I also knew what kinds of books Letty sold. It was called Smutties for a reason. The store was filled with romance books. Or as Brooklyn described them—steamy, sexy, smut romance.

I called them genius.

Any man not reading these books was missing out—big time. And the part they were missing out on was the front row look into the way a woman's mind worked. And if you read enough of these books, by enough authors, you gained important knowledge about the kind of intimacy women craved. And newsflash: most of the time it wasn't sexual but emotional. Which would be helpful for a man who wanted to win a woman but was having a hard time keeping one. It was interesting to read from a woman's point of view how she viewed the opposite sex. However, the more I read the more I noticed a theme. Book after book, across genres, written by a variety of authors, seemed to put heavy emphasis on foreplay. So much so it made me wonder if there were men out there who either didn't know how or didn't put in the effort. This was mind-boggling to me. And there was one sex act in particular that got a lot of page time. Which to me was a clear indication men all over the world were falling down on the job and not eating pussy. At least not correctly.

Shameful.

"Right."

"What? I do."

"I know, I've seen you in Smutties buying books. So I knew what kind of books you read. I just didn't take you for kink. Small town I could see, or cowboys, maybe even PNR, or—"

"How do you know what PNR is?"

"Who doesn't know what paranormal romance is?" I teased.

Once again, her mouth gaped open.

This time, I knew it was from shock.

I took advantage of her bewilderment and gently suggested, "Take a load off and I'll call in a pizza. After that, I'll tell you what I know about romance."

"You read romance?" she inquired.

However, she did this while taking a seat, so I threw her a bone.

"I'm partial to romantic suspense. Small town is okay. PNR's not my style. But I just started a new rom-com and I have to say, it's better than I thought."

Sadie's eyes went as wide as saucers.

It was cute.

It also made me want to kiss the fuck out of her.

What I wouldn't tell her was, my teammate Davis Wright suggested the book.

I pulled my phone out and called in three large pizzas while Sadie's eyes went from wide and bewildered to narrow and knowing.

She knew my game but didn't call me on it when I sat next to her on the couch.

"Good thing you're selling this couch, baby, it sucks," I told her, trying to find a section of the cushion that didn't collapse under my weight.

Unfortunately, while I was doing this I missed her smile, but I didn't miss her burst of laughter.

Christ, I missed that sound.

She used to laugh all the time. Same with smiling. Both came quick and frequently. But both were a rare occurrence now.

"I know. I bought it because I liked the way it looked. But three months into owning it I hated it."

"Why didn't you get rid of it and buy something new?"

"Because it was three months old and that would've been wasteful."

"It wouldn't have been if you sold it."

"Then what? The new owner keeps it for three months and decides they don't like it and throws it away? Our landfills are overflowing. I didn't want to contribute a six-month-old couch to the problem just because I thought it was uncomfortable."

"A Greenpeacer," I mumbled.

"An environmentalist," she corrected. "And you live on this planet, too, Reese, I hope you recycle."

I did recycle, but if I owned a shit couch that was uncomfortable and lumpy, I would've tossed that shit out immediately and bought something new.

Since the couch in question was currently listed for sale, the conversation was moot. And since the pizza was ordered I wanted the topic of Nate to be done by the time it arrived so she could relax and enjoy dinner.

"How'd you meet Nate?"

Sadie's face registered surprise, her head jerked, and she hesitated before she asked, "Why?"

"I just wanna know how you met him."

I understood her hesitation when she told me, "He targeted me, if that's what you're really asking."

That was exactly what I was asking.

"How do you know?"

"Well, my first clue was the PI I hired told me Nate's driver's license was fake. The second clue was Nathan Mallard came into existence a month before I met him. The next big, huge glaring clue was that Nathan Mallard ceased to exist a week after he cleaned me out."

What the hell, she'd hired a PI?

"Did the police make an arrest?"

"Nope. I made a report but the police can't find him. I paid for a PI for as long as I could but he wasn't getting anywhere and it was costing me a fortune."

Sadie had paid for a PI when two doors down from her bakery a team of investigators hung out on a regular basis.

What the fuck?

"Why didn't you ask one of us to run him?"

Sadie's shoulders slowly lifted, and her eyes slid away.

I knew why; she was embarrassed.

"You know the saying, everyone's one paycheck away from bankruptcy?" she asked instead of answering me.

"Yeah."

"Well, that was not me. I had five months of padding in the business account at all times. That was five months of rent, payroll, insurance, and loan payments. My bakery does well, so even after Nate cleaned out the account, I would've been able to pay my monthly bills. But the two months before he left, he stopped paying the rent, the insurance, and my business loan. It was a struggle to get those current. But I did it."

Five months of operating funds in the bank was a lot of money to steal.

"How much did he take?"

"A little over eighty-five K."

Fucking hell.

"If you got caught up, how are you behind now?"

"One of my ovens went out." Sadie huffed a laugh that held no humor and continued, "Of course, it was a year out of warranty, and I stupidly declined the extended warranty thinking if it ever broke, I'd pay out of pocket instead of paying monthly for something I might never use. Well, it turns out, out of pocket was over ten thousand dollars. I looked for a used one in good working condition instead of fixing mine but, good working condition on a sixty-thousand-dollar oven is more than ten thousand. So, I had no choice but to fix it. And that cut deep. That's a month's rent and half my payroll. Since I had to pay my employees and the bank threatened to call my business loan if I missed another payment, I couldn't pay my rent. And it spiraled from there."

Bad fucking luck.

And she'd wasted money on a PI.

And now she was selling her belongings.

"What's the name of the PI you used?"

"Why? He didn't find anything."

"I need any information he did find."

That was half the reason. The bigger reason was I

wanted to make sure the PI hadn't taken Sadie for a ride the same way Nate had.

"Wait, you're not gonna waste your time trying to find Nate, are you?"

Waste my time? The fucktard stole eighty-five K from her, and she thought me looking for the tool was a waste of time?

"Can't imagine why you'd think me finding the asshole who stole your money would be a waste of my time, except if you're back to thinking what you'd owe me if I did. So, I'm gonna put that shit to bed right now. Nothing. Hear me, Sadie, I want nothing from you in return for getting your money back. And while we're on this topic, it's important you get this, so I'll be thorough. The loan I offered you is still on the table. Tracking down Nate, taking your back with your brother and the Horsemen has fuckall to do with me fucking you. The two things are aside and separate from each other. I'm gonna repeat that, baby. I was clear in your office, I enjoyed what we shared, I want more, and I'm hoping we can come to a mutually pleasurable arrangement. But if we don't, I'm taking your back. If we do, I'm taking your back. So, the only question is, will I be doing that while at the same time spending time in your bed? But one has nothing to do with the other."

"A mutually pleasurable arrangement?"

"Straight up, yes, an arrangement. I'm not asking you for anything more than I can give. A really fucking good time. I don't want to be tied down and I'm not looking to tie you up." I paused to reconsider my last statement. "Second thought, I'm thinking tying you up would fall under the mutually pleasurable arrangement. But I think you feel me. I don't do relationships."

"*I* don't *want* a relationship," Sadie told me hotly.

"Good. Then it seems we're on the same page."

Before she could confirm or deny my assertion her doorbell rang.

Neither of us made a move to answer it.

And the longer I held her gaze, the deeper I was pulled in.

Then I started wondering for whose benefit I gave my no relationship speech. Me or her?

7

IT WAS strange how while we ate pizza, the conversation had turned to nonconsequential topics. Reese moving to Idaho and how he was adjusting. He didn't miss the heat of Arizona but wasn't looking forward to the bone-chilling cold of an Idaho winter.

And it was strange because I had never spent any time alone with him when we weren't bickering, and when we weren't doing that, he was easy to talk to. So easy, I'd picked up a slice of pizza without thinking about it. And it wasn't until my third slice that I noticed Reese was smiling.

He'd made it crystal clear he was interested in a no-relationship-sex arrangement. It had been on the tip of my tongue to agree to that but tell him he could shove his loan up his ass when the doorbell rang. But the longer we sat chatting about nothing, the ease of it, the flutter I felt having him in my house, the more I was thinking twice about the idea.

Sex was sex.

I could differentiate the two. Sex didn't equal love. But

it could and often did heighten emotions. It was easy to mix up friendship with something more when sex was involved.

So sex with Reese wouldn't just be sex. Not because we were such great friends and those lines would blur, but because I felt that flutter in my belly. When he was close, I couldn't take my eyes off him. And when he wasn't around, I looked for him.

Then of course there was the actual sex, which was a huge problem. If angry wall sex had been out of this world, mind-bending good, best I ever had, I was afraid of what it would be like if we'd had a bed and more than fifteen minutes. I'd likely expire from the goodness. Then I'd want more and more and more. And when he decided he was done with our arrangement and took it away, I'd be lost. Not lost without the sex, lost without him.

"How was your book club tonight?" he asked, picking up another slice of pizza.

He wasn't lying about how hungry he was. We'd polished off an entire large pizza and he'd dug into the second.

"It was good. Like always, Letty and Brooklyn are fun to be around, and now that Mrs. Simpson has started coming, she adds her own brand of uppity humor. She pretends that she's scandalized by the books when we all know she secretly loves reading them."

Reese grinned a knowing smile.

"Mrs. S is something else."

I agreed, she was the grandmother that everyone wished they had. Even at her age, she had all her faculties about her. She was smart as a whip and funny. It truly did hurt my heart having to avoid her, but I couldn't chance her asking me what was going on. I didn't want to lie to her. She'd likely take extreme offense. And I didn't want to find out if she held a grudge.

"Tell me about this rom-com you're reading," I prompted.

Reese's grin turned into a toothy smile.

God, he was beautiful.

"I was wondering when you were gonna bring that up," he started. "It's a sports romance. The hero's a virgin and—"

"*Jock Blocked*." I laughed. "Pippa Grant is awesome!"

Reese quickly lifted his hand, palm in my direction—the universal sign to be quiet—and shook his head.

"Stop! I'm only on chapter two. No spoilers."

No spoilers.

That was funny.

I pinched my lips, pressed my thumb and forefinger together, and pretended to zip my lips.

"Okay." I laughed. "No spoilers. But you're loving it, right? I mean, who doesn't love a flaming meatball?"

His smile widened and I was momentarily left breathless. This was not good. I shouldn't be sitting on my couch conversing with Reese about anything. But I really shouldn't be doing it when he was looking at me like he found me amusing. That smile of his got exponentially sexier. And really, I didn't come up with a flaming meatball, Pippa Grant did. So, there was nothing amusing about me. However, Reese was staring at me with his eyes dancing and his smile wide, and perfect, and dazzling like it was me who'd penned one of the funniest books I'd ever read. But, again, I didn't, Pippa did, and I needed Reese to stop smiling at me before I melted on the spot or worse, jumped him again.

"I admit, Mackenzie is my kinda woman."

Mackenzie?

Oh, right, Mackenzie Montana, the heroine. And she would be his kind of woman. Who didn't like a beautiful, smart, funny woman?

That wasn't me.

There had been a time I'd considered myself smart. But the whole Nate debacle proved that assessment incorrect. I wasn't beautiful, I was passably pretty. And I'd never been funny. I was too focused on my business to have fun. And before that, I was too busy learning everything I could about business management to have a good time.

God, I was a stick in the mud.

I was not a mascot-stealing, beautiful, smart, funny woman.

And that was the kind of woman that Reese would likely end up with. He wouldn't offer her a no-relationship-sex arrangement. He'd go all in to win her.

I was the kind of woman who got the scraps.

Sloppy seconds.

The crumbs.

The leftovers.

"Sadie?"

"I agree," I rushed out. "Mackenzie's pretty great."

"Where'd you go?"

"Huh?"

"You're looking at me, but you're somewhere else. Where'd you go?"

Damn.

Much like Mrs. Simpson, he was too observant.

"Sorry, my mind wandered for a moment."

"Got that part, Sadie. I'm asking where you went."

Abort, *abort,* abort.

"What other books—"

Reese denied my attempt to change the topic with a shake of his head and a verbal interjection, "Nope."

"Nope, what?"

"No more bypassing shit you don't want to talk about."

I found it annoying as hell that he knew I didn't want to discuss where my thoughts had gone, yet he was still pressing. It was rude and invasive and bossy.

I crossed my arms over my chest and leaned back as far as I could into the corner of my couch optimizing the distance between us.

"Let me ask you something. Why do you want to know *where I went?*"

"Because wherever it was, it wasn't pleasant. You went from smiling to frowning. You went from relaxed and laughing to stiff and uptight."

"That's me, Reese. I'm uptight."

"Bullshit."

He didn't know me well enough to call bullshit. And if he did know me, he'd agree. Which made the flutter in my belly turn into agitation. I didn't want Reese to know how uninteresting I was.

"I'm uptight," I reiterated then added, "And boring. My idea of a good time is hanging out in my sweatpants reading a book or lazing on the couch watching TV. I'd rather eat in than go out. I hate getting dressed up and I rarely put on more makeup than mascara and lip gloss. I don't like bars and nightclubs because there are too many people and I hate being jostled and touched. I don't like attention and I do my best to avoid being the center of it. I prefer the company of the people I'm close to, meaningless interactions with strangers do nothing for me. I hate dating because

I find the getting to know you stage is awkward. Which is probably why when Nate came along and started working for me, he made it easy and I fell for his lies. But that was the problem; he made it easy, too easy. I was lonely and he said all the right things. He didn't care I didn't want to go out on fancy dates. He didn't complain when I wanted to cook dinner at home. He didn't criticize me for my lack of social life. He never said a word. He didn't bitch. We didn't argue. We didn't bicker. There was zero spark. All of that should've told me something. If not a warning he was trying too hard, at least a warning that he was not the type of man I could fall in love with."

I was still pushed back into the corner of the couch, but Reese was now leaning forward. His elbows to his knees but his head cocked to the side staring at me.

Right at me.

Like he was no longer looking at me but staring through me.

Now I wanted to know where *he* was at because it was no longer in my living room with me. He looked miles away. Thousands of miles and his trip didn't look like it was a fun one.

Unfortunately, I didn't get a chance to ask.

He abruptly stood, his gaze still clouded with disdain. And there it was; I was too uptight and too boring to even hang out with. I should've been relieved, however, I felt no relief.

"It's getting late," he announced.

I said nothing when he picked up the pizza boxes and plates. I didn't get up when he walked them into my kitchen. I heard the fridge opening then closing, the faucet turned on then off, and finally, the plates being loaded into the dishwasher. I remained where I was when he reappeared.

Something had changed. Something big and scary.

My eyes traveled over the length of him, and I did this memorizing everything I could. I doubted I'd ever see him in my house again. He'd never stop by unannounced to argue with me about avoiding him. I'd never pull up to my house to find him in his Rover at my curb waiting for me. I figured his sex-only offer was now off the table, too, which made me want to accept it even though I would end up sad when it was over. And all of that made me wonder if he'd avoid my bakery, too. And the way my heart clutched at the thought was a reminder I was already in too deep with Reese.

A man who was not meant for me.

A reminder that I had to focus on getting my life back on track and forget about ever finding love.

"Just so you know," he bit out. "None of that says uptight or boring. It says real and honest. It says you're a woman who's comfortable with who she is. It says you're happy with the woman you are, and you don't need the attention of others to make you feel better about yourself. It says you're content and not a grasping, desperate bitch needing to find validation by tricking yourself out, fishing for men to notice you."

Reese barely took a breath before he spat, "Fuck Nate. The reason you didn't know what he was doing is because fuckers like him, con men, they perfect their craft. It's unlikely you were his first and men like him, they're smart, they watch and learn. They pay attention to cues and exploit anything they can. If they don't, they don't make money. The only thing you got right about him was, you know you're the type of woman who deserves that spark that was missing. You deserve a man who makes you light up, makes you catch fire when he's close, makes you think of only him. And you damn well deserve a man who feels that in return. Don't ever settle for less, baby. Any man who can't see all the beauty that is you is a fucking idiot and not worth your time."

With that, he left.

He'd said all that then just left me sitting on the couch confused.

Something told me the grasping, desperate bitch comment had nothing to do with how he perceived me and everything to do with a woman from his past.

I understand what it feels like to be humiliated. He'd said that to me.

I got up from the couch wondering if some woman had fucked him over. I grabbed my phone out of my purse, made my way to my extra bedroom, and looked around the room. I was not seeing the sturdy, well-made furniture I'd purchased from an estate sale years ago and refinished. My mind was too cluttered with all things Reese. The way he'd smiled at me. The way his eyes had danced with humor. The sound of his laugh. The way he'd scowled. And finally, the way the air in the room had changed when he told me not to settle for less.

He was telling me without coming straight out and saying it—he was not the man who would return feelings. Making him the "fucking idiot" or maybe I was the idiot for thinking about it. Which made me wonder why I wanted to know if I was right, and he'd been screwed over. Then I wondered why I cared so much.

I glanced around some more, needing to take pictures of the furniture so I could list it for sale.

I lifted my phone, but I didn't take the pictures.

I found Reese's number and debated whether to text or call him. Figuring he wouldn't answer a text while driving, I opted to call.

Then I held my breath while it rang thinking I was all kinds of stupid.

8

I HADN'T EVEN MADE it to the interstate when my phone rang. I didn't need to look at the display on my dash to know it was Sadie. I was actually surprised it had taken her as long as it did before she called me.

She might not have uttered a word before I left, but she didn't need to. It was written on her face—raw confusion. And I understood why she'd stared at me, puzzled at my turn.

Sadie had no way of knowing there was a war brewing. The battle had started months ago. I'd done my best to keep our interactions superficial and fun. Each week it became harder and harder. She kept herself distant but didn't. It was weird how she could be closed off but still draw you in. She was a frustration in that I knew better but couldn't stop myself from wanting to know more about her.

And now that I did, I was no less frustrated and a whole lot more intrigued.

Which meant it was time to make a decision.

My gut clenched and my hand itched to answer the call.

Then my ex-wife's voice played in my head.

Like my ex, Sadie was beautiful. She'd also said all the right things. Just like Ellie. Though it turned out Ellie had fed me bullshit. Outright lied, telling me what I wanted to hear. But once she had my ring on her finger, she went in search of more. Ellie was not happy living quietly, she wasn't happy with her husband being the only man giving her attention. And when she'd cheated, she'd blamed me.

I hit ignore and the ringing stopped.

Even though guilt gnawed at my insides it was for the best. I'd known better than to think I could carry on some sort of fucked-up arrangement with Sadie. She was unlike any other woman I'd ever met. Yet, I'd still offered and when I did, I saw the hurt flash in her eyes.

I was a motherfucking bastard.

And thinking back on things, I should've stopped her when she kissed me. And I never should've fucked her. Never should've put my hands on her. I knew before I had her I was playing a dangerous game. But once she caught fire, I'd been engulfed by her blaze, so lost in her heat I couldn't let her go.

But I had to.

The phone rang again.

I hit ignore and drove.

I was merging onto the highway when the third call came through. With everything going down in her life—her brother, the Horsemen, the very real threat of Zeus I never should've ignored the first two calls.

Now with a third, I had to answer.

"Is everything okay?"

"No," she clipped. "Why'd you send me to voice mail?"

That was not what I thought she was going to say.

"Are you okay, Sadie?"

"Who fucked you over?" she asked.

And the tables were turned.

I gritted my teeth and was at a loss how to play this.

My ex-wife wasn't a secret. But it was personal. And since I'd made the decision less than five minutes ago to let this obsession I had with Sadie go, talking about my ex wasn't conducive to disengaging. It was the opposite, yet if I didn't answer she'd continue to push.

"My ex-wife."

"Your ex-wife? You were married?"

"Yes."

I couldn't hide my disgust, though when talking about Ellie I never did.

"How'd she fuck you over?"

My jaw clenched tighter.

Sadie allowed a few beats of silence before she said, "Let me get this right, you get to demand answers from me. Things that make me uncomfortable to talk about, and like a dog with a bone you don't stop until I tell you. But you get to keep all your secrets."

Yes.

"She cheated on me."

More silence, then a screeched, "What? She...cheated... on *you*?"

I didn't miss the emphasis or the disbelief in her tone. Maybe if my head wasn't so fucked-up, her outrage on my behalf would've felt good. But the truth was, I *was* fucked-up. It had been years and I still couldn't get over the betrayal. It was not catching her in bed with another man. It wasn't that she'd shared her body, something she promised was only mine, with someone else. It was the lies I couldn't get over. It was the sweet way she'd whispered she loved me while I was on deployment but really, she was running around behind my back.

So many lies.

"Repeatedly," I ground out. "It started a week after I left on deployment and continued until I caught her. Once I left her, I heard from a variety of people around base what she'd been doing. The guy I caught her with wasn't the first. Don't know how many there were. Didn't care then, care even less now."

"You said you knew what it was like to be humiliated," she said softly. "Is that why? Your wife cheated and you felt humiliated?"

Jesus.

I thought back over my life and tried to think of a time when I'd been on the receiving end of an interrogation. And I couldn't think of a time. Luckily for me, my size alone made men think twice about confronting me. My teammates would question me, but there was a mutual respect that meant they picked up on my cues and dropped a subject before it slid anywhere near uncomfortable. And after I ended my marriage, I'd never given a woman the opportunity to ask me anything remotely personal.

Then there was Sadie. She defied all boundaries. And if I wasn't careful, she'd break down the walls I'd built to protect myself. Or knowing her, she wouldn't bother trying to break anything—she was smart enough to climb right over and do it with a pretty smile on her face.

And I was stupid enough to let her do it.

Meaning, I'd learned nothing from my disaster of a marriage.

"Yeah, Sadie," I snapped. "That's exactly how I felt."

"Why?"

Why?

What the fuck?

"What do you mean, why? My wife was fucking other men."

"So? That says something about her, not you. You weren't the one messing around behind her back. You weren't the one lying. I don't understand why *you* feel humiliated for something *she* did."

I blinked. That was pretty much all I could do before Sadie went on and she did so loudly and ferociously.

"I really don't get it. Why is it that the person who has been cheated on always feels the shame and embarrassment? And the cheater just gets off scot-free? The cheater is the only one who should be ashamed and embarrassed. She was your wife. She made promises she broke. Not you. So why would you be humiliated?"

My heart was frantically pounding in my chest. The thump of it frenzied and wild. For once it wasn't out of anger. I couldn't exactly put my finger on what I was feeling or why I was feeling it. I just knew it felt good.

Her fierce defense of me also calmed me. So my tone was no longer biting when I said, "She was my wife. And being that, meant I loved her. I made my own promises to her and one of them was to make her happy. I obviously didn't—"

"Why is that obvious?" There was a pause, but she didn't let me answer. "Never mind, I forgot you're one of those men who thinks it's your responsibility to shoulder life. Newsflash, Reese, it's not your responsibility. Any woman who's a real woman doesn't rely on a man to make her happy, she's responsible for her happiness. And if she's unhappy it's up to her to do something about it."

It was a damn good thing my exit was fast approaching. I was finding it hard to concentrate on driving while Sadie was making too much fucking sense.

Sense that I didn't want to see or confront. I was perfectly content spinning my wheels staying pissed at myself for not being a better husband.

"Just to say, she did find a way to make herself happy."

"That's not what I meant!" she exploded. "Are you being obtuse on purpose? Besides, in my experience women don't cheat because they're unhappy with their partner. They're unhappy with themselves and searching for something to make themselves feel better."

Fuck.

In her experience.

That felt like a blade sinking into my throat, taking my breath as it plunged deep. So much so, when it was safe, I pulled over to the side of the road.

"Personal experience? You've cheated on your man?" The question tasted like shit as it rolled out of my mouth.

"God, no," she bristled. "There's a reason my friend circle is so small. First, I'm a homebody and there's not a lot of people who understand that when I turn them down when they ask me to go out to bars or clubs with them, it's nothing personal. I just don't like going. But when they invite me over to their house for dinner and drinks I gladly accept. The other reason is I have no tolerance for liars. Like zero. Lying is a dealbreaker for me. And cheating is a form of lying. But that doesn't mean I haven't had friends who have cheated, and in those cases, it is because they were unhappy with themselves thinking something new or forbidden or dangerous will fill the void. It never does, so they jump from man to man doing the same shit over and over. And I just don't have time for that kind of insanity in my life."

The relief I felt was palpable. It was a physical solace that made my shoulders sag, and my head drop forward.

Of course, Sadie wouldn't cheat.

Another nail in her coffin.

Another reason on top of all the others that meant I had to find the strength to stay away from her.

"Is she the reason for your arrangement?"

Fuck.

"Sadie, listen—"

"Or is it just me?" she whispered.

Fucking hell.

"It's not you. At the risk of sounding like a pussy, it's me. It's how I live my life. Upfront and honest. I don't want to start something with a woman and have her thinking there's a chance of more when I'm not capable of giving that. The only way I know how to do that is by being straight from the beginning."

Jesus, could I sound like any more of a douchebag?

"So, I can take it as a read it's because of her."

"Yeah, it's because of her."

"Was this recent?"

"It was a long time ago," I muttered.

And for the first time, I felt embarrassed to admit that. I'd been nursing the hurt for far too long, being a pussy, not letting it go and moving on.

"I have an arrangement for you," she told me, and my muscles constricted.

"Sadie—"

"No sex. No loans. Friends only."

Friends only.

I'd been friend-zoned.

When in my life had that ever happened to me?

"My ego just took a hit, baby," I teased.

"Your ego will recover."

It wouldn't but I moved on to a more important topic.

"I want you to take the loan."

"And people in hell want water but you don't see Satan running out and getting it for them."

It sucked she was being funny when I was being deadly serious.

"Are you comparing me to the devil?"

"No. I'm offering you the only thing I have to give. My friendship. I'd like you to take me up on my arrangement. You can never have too many friends and if you give me a chance, I promise I'm a good friend to have. But I don't want money between us. You're already doing something for me, something big, something I can't do myself."

Goddamn, she was being stubborn about this.

"Your bakery's in jeopardy and I have the money. What kind of friend would I be if I sat by and watched you lose something you love?"

There was a stretch of silence and in those moments I thought she was taking what I said to heart.

I couldn't have been more wrong.

"You'd be a good friend. The kind that respected me and my wishes. This is important to me, and I need you to understand this. I thought about what you said, about my pride getting in the way of me accepting help. You might be right about that. But, Reese, I've worked hard, so hard you wouldn't believe. So while you might be right, it's my sword to fall on if that's what I choose. I know it sounds stubborn and stupid to you but if I fail, then I fail. There's a lesson to learn in that, I swear I'll learn it. But just as my success is mine, I need this failure to be mine as well."

I bit my tongue until I tasted blood. Why in the fuck would someone purposely fail?

Stubborn.

"Sa—"

"Have you ever had something that was yours?" she cut me off a-fucking-gain. "Just yours. That you worked for, and win or lose, it was yours. Something that meant the world to you."

"Yeah, baby, I have. And if it truly meant the world to you, you would do anything, and I mean anything to save it. I feel like I'm repeating this but, Sadie, you take anything, and everything being offered, and you thank the universe for the blessing."

"Maybe you're right," she mumbled.

There was no maybe about it.

I was flat-out right.

"You gonna take the loan?"

"I need to think about it."

My hands tightened around the steering wheel and I fought for patience.

Sadie didn't have time. She had three weeks to catch up on her rent or she'd be out on her ass.

"Is there a reason we're talking about this now over the phone when I left your house ten minutes ago and could've had this conversation face-to-face?"

"Honestly?"

"Is that a question?"

"I guess not." Sadie giggled, and I felt that sound slam into my chest. "It's easier talking to you over the phone. Or I should say, it's easier for me to be rational when I'm not looking at you."

What the hell?

"Why's that?"

She completely ignored my question and asked her own, "You didn't say, do you accept my arrangement? Friends only."

Sadie offering me her friendship was a gift. It was also

one that I knew would cut me. But it was the only thing I could give her beyond great sex and multiple orgasms. I wasn't blowing sunshine when I told her she deserved a man who could give her everything. No woman should ever settle but Sadie's brand of sweet warranted a certain kind of man. One who would shield her from all the ugly shit life could throw her way and let her be free to shine.

"Does me accepting your arrangement mean you'll tell me why it's easier for you to talk me when you're not looking at me?"

"Yes."

Fuck.

I was going to do it.

I was going to torture myself and be her friend.

Friends who did not fuck.

A bad feeling seeped in.

A feeling of loss stole over me.

And regret took root.

"Then I accept. But to clarify—do friends give compliments that could be construed as mildly veiled flirting?"

"I don't know, Reese, do you have anything better than complimenting my muffins? Because I have to tell you that was so lame, I felt compelled to dump a five-dollar coffee over your head. So, I can't promise you it won't happen again unless you step up your game."

I could step up my game until I had us so tangled together neither of us would know how to break free. But that was not what friends did.

"Careful what you ask for, baby. Now spill. I'm sitting on the side of the road and I'd like to get home sometime in the next decade."

"Why are you on the side of the road?"

"Sadie!"

"Fine. It's easier to talk to you when I'm not looking at you because I'm not distracted."

"Why would you be—"

"Don't play dumb."

"Woman, you have a bad habit of interrupting me," I grunted.

Deciding the heavy part of our conversation was over and it was safe for me to drive without courting veering off into a ditch, I pulled back onto the road and headed home.

"You've got a bad habit of asking questions you know the answer to."

What the hell was she talking about?

"Lost you, Sadie."

"You're good-looking." She sighed like it was hard for her to admit she found me attractive.

"You're not hard to look at either."

That was a gross understatement. Sadie was gorgeous. From her silky brown hair to her baby blue eyes, to her full breasts, to the curve of her hips, thick thighs, great ass, and tight, wet heat. Top to toe perfection.

I had serious doubts this friends-only shit was going to work. Days ago, I was being very honest when I told her I wanted to fuck her again. That had not changed. If anything, my desire had grown.

"Glad the sight of me doesn't burn your retinas," she returned haughtily.

Yep, this arrangement was very likely to explode in our faces. Especially when she was being cute and snooty. Two things that made me want to sink inside of her.

"Never done this before," I told her. "So, I'm unfamiliar with the parameters of our arrangement."

I turned on my blinker, checked my mirrors, and

switched lanes. This was done in silence as I waited for Sadie to say something.

The quiet had stretched long enough that I glanced at the dash display to make sure the call hadn't disconnected. Service was spotty the closer I got to my house.

"I might lose you soon," I told her.

There was nothing but silence.

"Sadie?"

"Shh," she whispered.

"What do you mean—"

"Shh."

That time it wasn't whispered, it was hissed. And it was done in a way that chilled my skin.

"Tell me what's going on!"

"I think I hear something."

My foot came off the accelerator and slammed on the brake.

"Where are you?"

Thank God for empty back roads in North Idaho. I executed a three-point turn and was backtracking at a high rate of speed before Sadie answered and when she did, I heard the wobble in her voice.

"I'm in the garage," she told me quietly. "I think someone's in my house."

"Leave. Go out your side door and run. I'm on my way to you. Do it now."

"What if I'm—"

It was my turn to interrupt her.

"Now, Sadie! Leave and run. I'm ten minutes out."

I pressed down on the accelerator, making ten minutes more like seven, thinking about her neighborhood and where she could hide. Sadie lived a block east of Coeur d'Alene High School. There was also a big church across the street from the high school that might or might not be having services, but if not, the parking lot would be dark and vacant. Same with the school.

"Does the senior living center on the corner have an office?" I asked as I merged back onto highway 95.

"Yes."

Her answer was partly muffled, partly breathy. I took that as a good sign she was on the move.

"Go to the senior center," I told her. "Get there as fast as you can but don't disconnect the call."

"Kay."

Yeah, she was definitely running.

I tapped the add call icon on my dash display and quickly found Wilson's contact. It rang once, then I merged the calls.

"Yo," Wilson answered.

"Who's that?" Sadie huffed.

"Hang on, baby. Wilson, I need you to get to Sadie's house. She's off Dalton and Fourth by CDA High School." I rattled off her address then I told him, "Possible break-in. Sadie's on the move to the senior center. I'm heading there to pick her up. Call me when her house is secure."

"Copy."

Wilson disconnected. Sadie's heavy breathing filled the interior of my Rover. The sound of her huffing and puffing enraged me further. Which was working in my favor, pushing the fear aside, leaving me angry.

Why the hell did I leave?

"I'm passing the Target," I informed her. "Where are you?"

"Cutting through someone's backyard. Almost there."

Smart.

"Good. Don't stop running until you get there."

I changed lanes, passed two tractor-trailers, and slammed back on the gas.

"What if I'm overreacting?" she wheezed.

"What if you're not and someone's in your house?"

"Fair point."

There was rustling then from far away I heard a muffled, "Shit!"

"Sadie?"

Nothing.

I looked at the display and my heart arrested.

Disconnected.

Fucking hell.

"*Fuck!*" I roared into my empty SUV and drove.

9

SHIT, *shit*, shit.

I pinched my lips together as hard as I could to stop myself from crying out. But the pain in my palms, elbows, and knees made it impossible to keep the groans from escaping. I patted the ground around me trying to find my phone but after the third attempt, I gave up and rolled to my hip, groaned some more, and finally got back to my feet.

I wouldn't say I was a total klutz, but neither was I the most athletic person on the planet. And I was definitely out of shape, but even being out of shape my spill was caused by a very large stack of logs. Which meant I didn't just take a fall, I tumbled over the logs, and landed on my elbows, shoulder, and knees. If there was a deer camera somewhere I was positive the recording would end up on the internet and millions could have a good laugh at my idiocy.

This time when I ran, I did it with a limp. It was a crazy thing to think but I was pretty sure at this point I was certifiably crazy anyway. I had fled my house after all. And I wasn't even positive someone had broken in, but I truly hoped someone had. And that was my crazy thought. Who wanted their house robbed? Me. I wanted my house broken into and ransacked. Something to make the pain worth it. My poor thighs hadn't seen this much exercise in years. And I was pretty sure my knees and elbows were skinned. And that hadn't happened to me since I was a kid.

I avoided all things that were physically exhausting.

Except for sex with Reese.

Stop.

Abort mission.

Friends don't think about having sex with their friends.

Thankfully the senior center came into view. My legs were giving out and my heart was pounding so hard it was nearing heart attack range. I rounded the fence at the same time as Reese's Rover skidded into the parking lot. Then the luxury ride demonstrated its superior braking system and did what the commercial advertised—fifty to zero in under two-point-five seconds.

Reese was out of the vehicle and running full sprint in my direction.

"Jesus, fuck," he growled and scooped me up into his arms.

I wheezed out a pain-filled breath.

"Jesus, fuck," he repeated.

Reese took off running back to his SUV, carrying me like I weighed nothing. Obviously, he wasn't out of shape. I would've appreciated this more if my shoulder wasn't throbbing with every pounding stride he took.

He wrenched open the passenger door, deposited me into the seat, and I watched him do a full-body scan.

"What the fuck happened?"

"I fell."

"*Jesus, fuck!*"

"You shouldn't say the Lord's name in vain," I scolded.

Reese's scathing eyes snapped to mine then they slowly closed. When they opened again the contempt was gone but there was a lingering look of fear. I blinked twice, just to make sure I wasn't seeing things. And nope, it was still there.

Then he confirmed what I knew in both words and deed.

First, he said, "You scared the shit out of me." Then he leaned in close and pressed his lips against my forehead.

I should've been wondering if friends kissed each other's foreheads. But I didn't have the willpower. His lips felt too good. So did his proximity and his concern. Before I could figure out which part I liked the best he pulled away.

"Buckle up, Sadie."

He didn't wait for me to follow directions before he stepped back and closed the door.

There were a lot of things I should've been freaked out about, and now that I was safe and not running through strangers' backyards some of my crazy subsided and I prayed my house hadn't been burglarized. I couldn't afford it, I needed to sell what I had left. I'd been putting off selling my TV so if that was missing it'd be a bummer. Then there was my phone, which was probably broken but I still needed to find it just in case because that was something I seriously couldn't afford to replace and I didn't have insurance on it.

Story of my freaking life.

Insurance.

If I'd only bought the stupid freaking warranty, I might not be so screwed.

I was never hanging up on those telemarketers offering extended warranties again.

Reese angled into the SUV just as his phone rang.

I glanced at the oversized, in-dash display that was bigger than my iPad. Wilson's name appeared and Reese touched the screen to answer the call.

"Are you there?"

"Yeah." Wilson's voice came over the speakers.

Jeez, the sound quality was so good, if I closed my eyes I'd swear I was in an IMAX movie theater. Which reminded me, I'd fallen over a stack of logs and was probably getting Reese's seat dirty.

I shifted and looked down at my funky, navy blue Hey Dude loafers and sure enough, they were caked in mud. The bottoms of my jeans and my knees were filthy.

Great. Awesome. Perfect.

"Front door was cracked open when I got here," Wilson continued, and my heart sank. "Did Sadie leave it open when she left?"

"No. I went out the door in the garage." Then I thought of something and looked over at Reese. "Did you lock the front door when you left?"

"Fuck," he clipped.

I guess that was a no.

"Davis is walking the street, checking the cars," Wilson carried on. "Give us five minutes."

"Copy."

Reese reached up, tapped the end icon, and turned to look at me.

"Damn, Sadie. Fuck, baby. I didn't think to lock the door."

Even if his tone wasn't so tortured, there was just enough illumination inside the car for me to make out his features and he looked devastated.

"It's not your fault. I don't always keep the door locked when I'm home."

One of his brows lifted, only one, and I thought it was cool he could do that. I couldn't. And I'd tried many times, standing in front of a mirror looking ridiculous as I attempted to get my facial muscles to do something they refused to do.

"That's not safe," he informed me.

"You're right. But it doesn't mean I sometimes forget until I'm locking up for the night."

There was a beat of silence and during this I took Reese in. Normally, he was downright good-looking. But him sitting next to me full of concern and anger that was not directed toward me was seriously sexy. Well, the concern was *for* me but for once he was angry *at* me. Though perversely, his anger at me for not wanting to take money from him was hot, too.

"You don't have an alarm," he weirdly stated.

"Reese, this is North Idaho, not the city. Of course, I don't have an alarm. As a matter of fact, I don't know anyone who has an alarm."

"Yes, you do," he countered. "Brooklyn and Letty have alarms."

I couldn't stop myself from rolling my eyes to the headliner, only instead of fabric, I found myself peering at a moonroof. Like everything else in the Rover, it was oversized.

"I'm afraid to know, but I think you paid more for this car than most people's down payment on their first house." My gaze swung back to him, and I finished. "And the only reason Brooklyn and Letty have alarms is because of Rhode and River. I know for a fact, neither had them before."

"They have them now," he unnecessarily reiterated.

"Do you have an alarm?" I inquired.

"I'm a man with an arsenal of weapons at my disposal."

I felt my eyes narrow on behalf of the sisterhood.

"Sexist much?"

"Let me rephrase." He smartly backtracked. "I have an arsenal of weapons I'm not afraid to use."

"That's not much better, Reese. How do you know I don't have a gun? And what's to say if someone broke into my home I wouldn't shoot them to protect myself?"

"Do you own a gun?"

Damn.

"That's not the point."

"Yeah, Sadie, it is. You live alone, with no protection. And your outside lighting sucks. You got no streetlights in your neighborhood. You need motion lights front and back."

"Motion lights?"

"Yes. Something to cut through the dark if someone approaches."

"What else do I need, lasers? That way I can fry every moose who wanders through my yard after I blind it with high-powered beams of light?"

"Don't be cute."

"I'm being serious. I love seeing moose in my yard." Reese tilted his head and stared at me like I had a screw loose. Since he had nothing to say I carried on. "And speaking of guns. I hope you keep yours locked in a safe. CDA is mostly safe but break-ins occur and gun ownership is a huge responsibility that includes keeping them out of the hands of criminals."

Reese blinked rapidly. Once he was done with that, he smiled and asked, "Are you lecturing me about gun safety?"

"No. I'm not *lecturing* you about anything. As a citizen, I'm merely asking if your guns are locked up."

"Yeah, Sadie, my guns are locked up and the one that is not is always within my reach. Now that we've established your love for seeing moose in your yard outweighs your desire to be safe in your home and I am indeed a responsible gun owner, maybe can we get back to you needing an alarm?"

No, we could not. Alarms were expensive. And even if I wasn't broke and in danger of losing my business, I still wouldn't waste money on an alarm. Not the installation of one and not the monthly fee to have it monitored. But luckily, I didn't have to explain this to Reese because Wilson was calling back.

"What's going on?" Reese asked.

"All clear to come back. We'll wait for you."

The line went dead.

"Do any of you say goodbye?"

Reese started his Rover and was moving through the parking lot before he answered, "Waste of time."

"Saying goodbye is a waste of time?" I sought clarification.

"Yep. We say what we need to say and that's it. There's no need to say goodbye when the other person knows the conversation is over."

"How did Wilson know you didn't have questions before he hung up on you? And what's with you not saying hello, either? You just start talking."

"That falls into the waste of time category as well."

He was kind of right but still, I told him, "It's rude."

Apparently, Reese felt any further conversation on the topic was also a waste of time because he didn't say anything so I carried on.

"Just to say, when we talk on the phone and we're getting ready to get off and you don't say goodbye and hang up on me, it'll piss me off."

"Noted," he mumbled.

Reese stopped at a stop sign and made a turn onto my street. He was correct, there were no streetlamps, however, most of my neighbors had their porch lights on as well as some sort of landscape lighting. I always thought it looked pretty; the darkness of the street even with the dim porch lights meant you could still see some stars. They weren't drowned out by city lights.

"And you could answer my calls with a hello, too. It wouldn't kill you to waste the millisecond it would take to be polite."

"Do you always babble this much when you're nervous?"

I wasn't nervous.

"I'm not babbling," I lied.

"Babe. You are. Everything's gonna be okay."

Reese pulled in front of my house and parked at the curb. My car was parked in my driveway since I was using my garage to store the furniture that had been sold. I might not want to blind the moose population, but I did take my safety seriously. I didn't allow strangers into my house when someone came over to pick up something I'd sold. I also wore a fake wedding ring *and* I made sure to slide in a comment about "my husband" at least twice during the pickup.

Anyway, my car was there, so that was good. And the front of my house looked...unburglarized. Was that a word? And could a house look burglarized from the outside?

Oh, God, I *was* babbling. To myself no less.

Yep, fleeing my house, running in the dark through my neighborhood had officially sent me to Crazy Town.

"Okay, I'm a little nervous," I admitted. "But mostly I'm really freaking mad I tripped and lost my phone."

"I'll find your phone."

My gaze remained on my house, but I was no longer seeing the pretty trimmed hedges that ran the length of my porch. My mind was no longer filled with thoughts of woe. All I could think about was a simple statement that sounded like a promise and how I believed Reese would keep his word.

He'd find my phone.

Something simple.

But I believed him.

10

BY THE TIME Sadie had trudged halfway up her walkway, I'd decided she wasn't staying at her house alone or at all. With each wooden step she took bringing her closer to her porch, she got stiffer and stiffer.

But it got worse when Wilson opened her front door. My boss made an imposing figure standing in the doorway with his arms crossed over his chest, a scowl on his face, and his angry stare aimed my way.

"You forget to tell me something?" he barked.

Sadie jerked to a halt, her body locked, and her gaze swung to me.

"Can we get inside before we have this conversation?"

Wilson didn't answer. He turned and disappeared into Sadie's house. Which was an answer, albeit a nonverbal one, which spoke to his level of displeasure.

"What's he talking about?" Sadie asked.

"Inside."

Sadie slowly looked at the empty doorway then back to me. Concern and fear etched on her pretty face. Or, more fear as it were. And that was when I was done. I could take no more. My decision to go easy, let Sadie come to the understanding she needed help, and then wait for her to accept my offer flew out the window when she looked at me with those big blue eyes.

There would be no waiting.

There would be no easy.

Not about the money.

The rest—the friends-only pact, the attraction, the giant step back I needed to take to keep distance between us wasn't going to work.

It was what it was.

And what it was, was dangerous as fuck, but I was going there, too.

"Why does Wilson look so mad?"

"Inside, baby."

It was fucked in a way I knew it wasn't cool, but when Sadie nodded and without further questions followed my directions, I felt the knot in my chest loosen. The woman was headstrong and too fucking obstinate for her own good. So, Sadie doing what I asked gave me hope I could wedge my way in and make her see reason without causing World War Three. Though if she wanted to battle, I was all-in to toe-to-toe and I'd damn well win.

This shit was about to be done in a way that would mean Sadie would be stress-free and breathing easy by tomorrow afternoon.

As soon as Sadie stepped over the threshold, her gaze went straight to Wilson.

"I'm assuming whoever was in your house didn't have enough time to haul your furniture out," Wilson started. "Please, for the love of God tell me you're remodeling."

Sadie's head whipped to the side, her eyes came to mine, and her confusion was clear.

"I didn't share," I told her.

"No, you didn't," Wilson confirmed. "Is there a reason why, when that shit-for-brains Zeus was talking about Sadie's problems, you shut him down but didn't fill me in?"

"Not my place." My answer was directed at my boss, but my eyes never left Sadie. Therefore, I didn't miss the way her lips parted or her swift inhale.

"It might not be." Wilson agreed amicably but I didn't miss the edge in his voice. "But you're wrapped up in this, and because of that, it makes it my business."

Unfortunately, Wilson wasn't wrong. We'd had issues with the Horsemen since we came to town and recently those issues had been escalating in a way that meant we were treading a fine line. None of us liked what Zeus was doing. We all wanted it stopped, we had the means to stop it, but in doing so we'd fuck a long-term undercover operation the Drug Enforcement Agency was conducting. But even the inside man for the DEA was getting antsy now that Zeus had taken on a stable of prostitutes. And seeing as Wilson was my boss and I was very much involved with Sadie and her issues, I should've told him. However, sharing Sadie's problems felt like a betrayal so I'd kept my trap shut.

"I don't disagree, but it's still Sadie's to share *or* not."

Wilson's gaze cut around the room. It didn't take a man with highly tuned instincts to put two and two together and come up with the correct answer. However, Wilson's intuition was so finely honed he not only took one look around Sadie's house and had come to an accurate conclusion about just how fucked her money situation was even if it had only been hinted at by Zeus, but he was also coming to a clear understanding Sadie meant something to me. Something more than the pretty woman I liked to look at and shoot the shit with when I grabbed my coffee.

What that 'something more' meant was a slippery path that could have me careening off a cliff if I wasn't careful.

Davis appeared at the mouth of the hallway, jaw tight, eyes narrowed, and Sadie scooted closer. The movement was small, just a shuffle of her feet, closing the gap between us. But it felt monumental. It felt like Sadie was seeking my comfort and protection from two very pissed-off men, even if they weren't pissed at her.

My teammate was far from stupid, and just like Wilson, it hadn't taken Davis long to understand what was going on.

"Place is damn near empty," he ground out.

"Um...I..." Sadie stumbled then trailed off.

Davis continued spitting out words and he did it angrily. "No forced entry. No sign of anyone tampering with the windows. No one sitting outside in their car staking out the house. Can't know if something's missing because there's a lot missing but I saw the furniture in the garage that matches the dresser and headboard in the guest room. But I don't know if you're moving that in or out. Or if you're rearranging since you have nothing but a mattress in your bedroom and clothes piled up in your closet."

Logically, I knew why Davis had been in her bedroom. Even if Wilson had cleared the house Davis would've gone back through to be safe. But it pissed me right the fuck off he'd been in Sadie's bedroom.

"Davis," I warned.

"Trying to be cool about this, brother," he returned. "But you forget, we all care about what's going on with her. And it would seem you held back after our meet with the Horsemen just how fucking bad the situation with her brother is. Need that intel now."

The situation wasn't about her brother. But the choice had to be Sadie's. She'd made it clear she felt she had no control over her life, and I wasn't taking this from her. I could run my investigation into Nate and the PI on my own. I didn't need my team at my back to find a pissant conman. Which meant I could help Sadie while still giving her the privacy she needed. Though the Horsemen situation was sticky, and Wilson needed to be briefed and I'd enlist my team to help me keep Zeus and his idiot gang away from Sadie.

"Shit," Sadie muttered and tore out of her living room.

All eyes followed her as she made it into her kitchen and stopped at the counter. Her chin dipped and she shook her head while chanting, "Shit. Shit. Shit. It's gone."

Fuck.

The three grand from Josh.

"I left the money on the counter," she continued and turned to face me. "We had dinner, then after you left, I started moving the furniture into the garage. I didn't think to put it away."

"The money from Grinder?" Davis inquired.

I couldn't stop my lip from curling at the sick fuck's nickname. Something else the undercover DEA agent was getting antsy about, Josh Pierce. The way he'd earned his club name, Sadie would never know. As a prospect, Grinder didn't have insider knowledge of the Horsemen's dealings. He wasn't in on club meetings, and he had no vote. But he did have responsibilities and those included taking and picking up the girls Zeus pimped out. Which meant he took as many freebies as he could. He did this roughly and bragged about it to whoever would listen.

Sick fucking asshole.

Sadie nodded but she did this while her shoulders slumped and with her eyes downcast.

If I already hadn't made my decision to end this for her,

the defeat I saw would've done it. In no fucking universe should Sadie Pierce be hanging her head, looking beaten down.

"Sadie."

Her eyes flicked up and when they did it took every bit of my control not to flinch at the sadness I saw.

"It's too much." Her hands came up, spread wide to her sides, and she glanced around the sparsely furnished space. "Everything. All of this is too much."

"Sadie, look at me."

She didn't look at me, she kept looking around.

"Earlier I was thinking I was ready to throw in the towel and give up. I'm so tired of being tired. I'm totally over being stressed out day in and day out. But I can't give up so I keep pushing."

"Sadie, please look at me."

"I lied to you," she blurted out and dropped her arms. "This isn't about wanting to win or lose on my own. It's not about owning my achievements or failures. I'm being stubborn because I don't know how not to be. I don't know how to give up. I don't know how to ask for help because I've never done it before. I'm the one who isn't the disappointment. I'm the one who doesn't ask my parents to bail me out. But I can sell everything I own, and it still won't be enough."

Sadie still wasn't giving me her attention. Instead, she was glaring at her couch like she was seriously pissed at it for not being worth the eighty-five large Nate had stolen from her. Since the couch was not going to turn into bars of gold no matter how long and hard she stared at it, I made another decision, one that was going to blow any chance I might've had of keeping the wolves at bay. I moved across the room, only stopping when I was standing in front of Sadie.

"Baby, I need you to *look* at me." Her gaze slowly rose to meet mine and when it did I leaned in until I knew all her attention was on me because I was the only thing filling her vision. "Now I need you to hear me. I'm covering your rent. And I'm also giving you extra to get you caught up on the rest." Sadie's lips parted to speak, and I shook my head. "Now is not the time to be hardheaded. Now is the time for you to listen and hear this clear, Sadie, I'm not taking no for an answer. This is ending for you. Right now. I'm not letting you lose your dream. You can fight me on this, but you can take it as a motherfucking vow I'm gonna win."

"You don't understand," she whispered.

"I damn well do. I understand that watching you struggle is a form of torture. I understand that coming in here earlier and seeing more stuff gone pissed me off in a way I know I'm not gonna let it go of. And I understand I'm putting the money in your account whether you want it or not."

The tears I saw brimming in her eyes strengthened my resolve, but they also reminded me I needed to go gently.

"Please, Sadie, let me do this for you."

"I don't know how to ask for help."

Her admission was whispered so softly if I hadn't been in her space I wouldn't have heard. But since I was close, I heard. I also felt the words hit my chest and start to burn.

I'm the one who doesn't ask my parents to bail me out.

This wasn't about Sadie being stubborn, it was about her brother. It was about him being a fuck-up, causing her parents grief, and now that she legitimately needed help, she was too afraid to ask them out of fear of disappointing them. And she wouldn't ask anyone else for help because she'd likely watched her brother use up his friends and burn bridges in the process. Sadie had learned through Josh not to be what she'd consider a burden.

Yet another reason he was a stupid motherfucker.

"Then it's a good thing you're not asking."

"Reese..."

She trailed off and when it became evident she wasn't going to say more, I went on.

"You are not your brother. Not even close. You don't borrow money from your friends and gamble it away. You don't ask your parents for money to blow it on booze. It is *not* you leeching off people who care about you so you can party all night then sleep your hangover off, unable to hold a job. That's him. You work your ass off seven days a week, twelve-plus hours a day running a business. It's you who goes into work every day, bakes great muffins and cakes, is good to her employees, knows her customers by name, and serves them with a smile. It's you who does this while so much shit is piling on top of you it would make a weaker person crumble. And when the threat of losing your business bears down, what do you do? You sell your shit. You do not curl into a ball and cry about it. You're not standing by, you're fighting. And, Sadie, any good fighter knows they use every tool given to them to win the battle. Accepting help doesn't mean failure. It means you're strong enough to win by any means necessary."

Sadie exhaled a slow ragged breath, and she gave a stilted nod.

Thank fuck.

The wetness that had been contained in her lower lids finally spilled over. My hands went to her face, my thumbs brushed the tears away before they could roll down her cheeks, and her glimmering blue eyes held me captive. But as spellbound as I was, I didn't miss Sadie's lips move to mouth "thank you." I didn't miss the emotion that had come over her. I didn't miss the depth of the meaning behind her gratitude and further from that, I didn't miss the relief.

Seeing all of that made every minute of frustration I'd felt over the last week worth it.

"My honor, baby."

Her eyes flashed in a way I liked a fuck of a lot. But before I could enjoy the warmth it had created, someone cleared their throat, reminding me we weren't alone and I'd probably said more than I should've in front of my friends.

"Hate to break up your huddle," Wilson started. "But we need to talk before I leave."

And he indeed sounded like he was unhappy to interrupt though he didn't mask the thread of impatience so it could be heard loud and clear. Something that didn't slip past Sadie's notice.

She blinked away the remaining tears and pulled herself together like the warrior she was. Her hands came up, rested on my forearms, and with a squeeze and a tight nod, she wordlessly told me she was ready to face Wilson.

Yeah, fuck yeah, the woman was a warrior.

I let go of her face but instead of allowing her hands to drop, I twisted at the last minute and tagged her hand and held on.

It wasn't until I turned around to face Wilson and saw his look of surprise that it hit me, I was holding Sadie's hand. I was in the midst of trying to remember the last time I held a woman's hand, thinking it was Ellie before I'd left on deployment. Just as the memories of my ex-wife started to sour in my gut Sadie's thumb rubbed the back of my hand. That slight brush effectively erased the images my mind was conjuring up, pulling me back into the room. No, that small movement pulled me back to *her* and I wrapped my fingers tighter.

"My problems aren't with Trevor or the Horsemen," Sadie announced. "My ex cleaned me out."

Wilson did a slow blink.

"Your ex cleaned you out?"

"Yep," Sadie popped the P, the nonchalant sound a direct contradiction to the tremble in her hand. "He took all the money in my accounts, but for months before that, he wasn't paying the bills and charged all my credit cards up. Stupid me didn't know this because I wasn't paying attention to the bills since he'd been paying them for months with no issue before he stopped paying them. And since I live as debt-free as I can, personal credit cards are only used in emergencies. So I didn't know they were maxed out until Nate took all my money and I tried to use one to pay a vendor's invoice."

It would seem Sadie had left out a few things from our earlier conversation since I had no idea about the credit cards.

"Did he have access to your personal accounts as well as your business?" Davis asked.

There was a beat of silence, which prompted me to give her hand a squeeze.

"Yes. And I know it was stupid. So freaking stupid, but I was slammed at the bakery and he was over one night and saw my electric bill was late. Not because I couldn't afford to pay it but because I was so busy at work putting in fifteen-hour days to get all the orders filled. So he offered to take over paying my personal bills as well. At the time when he offered, he sounded sincere, like he was trying to make my life easier. That's how it started, him convincing me he was looking out for me, telling me he wanted me to concentrate on baking cakes instead of sitting behind a desk for hours paying bills."

Fucking prick.

"So he was not only your boyfriend but he worked for you?" Wilson inquired. "No judgment, just trying to get the full scope."

"Yeah," she whispered her answer. "Every summer I hire seasonal help. With the tourists in town, the bakery can get crazy. Nate told me he was finishing his degree and was looking for work that would only take him through the summer." Sadie stopped to draw in a breath and on an exhale she said, "I should've known."

Not this shit again.

"Sadie—"

"No, Reese, I should've. This might be sexist but in all my years running my bakery a man had never applied. Not one application from a guy. But even putting that aside, he was smooth. Too smooth, like it was practiced. Even him asking me out was... I don't know, corny, or polished. I can't explain it."

"Try," I urged.

Sadie took a moment. and while she did her gaze went to Davis, then to Wilson. What it didn't do was slide back to me. On some level, I understood her embarrassment even though I knew she had nothing to be ashamed about. Something I'd thought I made clear.

"I knew he was into me, and I admit the way he was with me, always sweet and going out of his way to make me laugh or smile, made it easy for me to fall for him. One night after closing, it was just the two of us, and he came back to my office to tell me he was done and going home. But he didn't leave, he handed me an envelope. When I asked him what it was, he told me to open it. I did and it was his resignation. It wasn't a regular resignation though. It listed all the reasons why he had to quit, which included all the reasons he'd fallen in love with me. He concluded by saying he knew I'd never date an employee and he'd rather have his shot with me than keep his job. Obviously, I fell for that and he continued to work for me after we started dating. After a few months, he offered to help me in the office. I was overwhelmed and he said his degree was in accounting so I let him take over the bookkeeping. Some months later he said it would be easier if he could sign the checks instead of having to stop me from baking to sign them. I agreed and added him on my accounts as a signer."

Goddamn creep.

"Do you still have the letter?" Davis questioned.

"Yeah, in the safe at work. But I already showed it to the PI I hired, and he told me it was useless because it was typed and Nate didn't even sign his name."

"PI?"

"I'll fill you in on him later," I told Wilson, then asked Sadie, "Did he dust the letter or the envelope for prints?"

"You can do that?"

So that was a no. It was also an answer. The PI she'd hired sucked, which meant I'd be having a talk with him about the work he had done, if any, and see about getting Sadie's money back.

"Yeah, baby, you can do that. And we might not be able to do it now if the envelope and paper have been handled too many times, but we're still gonna give it a try. What about photographs or security footage?"

"I don't have any pictures. Another red flag. Nate said he hated his picture being taken and he hated social media and thought it was the downfall of humankind, but he was always taking pictures of me saying he loved to look at them before he went to sleep. And the security feeds at the bakery only stay in the cloud for seven days. But not surprisingly," Sadie lifted her hands and in air quotes and said, "someone," then dropped her hands and continued, "switched the settings so the cameras weren't recording at all."

Dead end.

"Did this PI you hired hook you up with a sketch artist?"

"He offered, but he said they were expensive. And by that time I was out of money."

Oh, yeah, fuck yeah, having a conversation with TJ Gayle just got scratched to the top of my mental to-do list.

"You got the name of this PI?"

Wilson's question was directed at me. He, too, wanted a word.

"Yep."

"Good, we'll set that up."

"Set what up?"

Wilson ignored Sadie and went on. "We need to talk about what happened here tonight. There were five patched Horsemen, including Zeus, that saw Grinder hand you that money. They also knew that money was for Sadie." Wilson stopped, pinned Sadie with a stare, and told her. "Not smart being a single woman living alone and not doing what you can to protect your home address. Took me two minutes to find you and I did it using Google. Starting tomorrow you're off public directories."

Sadie looked like she wanted to argue but at the last moment, she wisely kept her mouth closed and simply nodded

"I'm thinking we start with those five and move on from

there. I'll make a call and see if I can get the whereabouts of each of them, but that might take a few days."

Wilson was talking about reaching out to the under-cover DEA agent. Which was risky as fuck for the agent; it also communicated that Wilson understood exactly where I was at with Sadie and I'd want that risk taken if it meant keeping her safe. Fuck the money, I'd replace it tomorrow, but we needed a clear understanding of who in the Horsemen we were dealing with.

"In the meantime, I didn't like how our meeting ended with Zeus and I like it less now. He's changed in the last few months. Getting cockier. I already called Brasco and Kent and told them about my concerns. They're looking into things on their end, but they have to tread easy."

Jet Brasco was a detective at the Coeur d'Alene Police Department and our local contact. River Kent was Letty's man and new addition to the CDAPD. He'd moved to Idaho from Georgia and came with a list of references and recommenda-tions that were such the CDAPD were beside themselves to have him on board. And Jet being a good cop and a smart man, had worked his tenure to his favor with the brass and when Brasco's partner had retired, Kent had slid into that role.

They knew about the DEA agent, they also were smart, good cops and knew how close they could walk the line without crossing it and fucking the DEA's case. So I trusted that if they were looking into Zeus's sudden change of atti-tude they'd do that and not have the DEA breathing down our backs.

Belatedly I realized Sadie's grip on my hand had tight-ened to the point her nails were digging in, causing pain.

It was likely a Horsemen had been in her house—maybe even Zeus himself—and she'd expressed her absolute fear of him. I was betting it was her brother who'd broken in to retrieve the money he didn't want to pay back in the first place. It was a bonehead, fucked-up play that he had to know would bring my ire down on him.

But maybe that was what he wanted, and the more I thought on it, the more it became clear.

"It was Grinder," I announced.

"My brother?"

"He went out of his way to make the handover in front of the others. He also knows Sadie's scared of Zeus, he knows why, and he still told them about her money troubles and why she has them. He's pissed as all fuck at me for calling him out in front of Sadie's bakery. But he's more pissed I laid it out in a way he couldn't miss. Cutting off his access to his sister who he's been using as his own personal bank. He knew about her situation, but he was coming around to ask for more. He also knew coming over here to get that money back, whether it came here to sweet talk his sister into giving back or strongarming her, he'd know it would piss me off and I'd make a play. Whatever I decided to do would cause an issue. He's banking on Zeus getting pissed I fucked up one of his recruits. Meaning Zeus would have no choice but to save face and come after me, which would push Takeback to make a stand. That means war, which is exactly what Grinder wants. His punk ass cannot take me on, he needs the Horsemen, so he did what he did and made it so my hands are tied."

"I think you're giving my brother too much credit," Sadie said softly from beside me. "He's not that smart."

"No, you're right, what he is, however, is pissed Reese bested him." Wilson took over. "Not only did Reese get in his face but he made good on his threat and showed up to collect your money. Money your brother didn't want to give so he's looking for a way to fuck Reese. And he'd need the Horsemen to do it. Zeus's been playing it smart, keeping his shit tight, but recently he's made moves and like I said he's getting cocky thinking he's untouchable. And unfortunately, until I know what's changed, no one's making any moves."

That last part was for me. A direct order to stand down without Wilson saying the words. Still, his order was clear. It also irritated the fuck out of me.

"You staying here tonight?" Davis rejoined.

"Not unless you're willing to pull duty. Sadie doesn't have an alarm."

"I could do that."

"What's this?"

I glanced down, caught Sadie's eyes, and laid it out, "You're not staying here alone so I'm staying. But to be safe Davis is gonna be parked out front of your house visible. Someone thinks to fuck with you and they see Davis, they'll think twice. After seeing Davis out front, they still feel like fucking with you, I'm here. Either that or you're at my place. The choice is yours."

I watched emotions sail across Sadie's face, not a single one of them good. Some of them worse than others. When she finally settled on one, she asked, "Do you really think that's necessary?"

"What I think is I don't give a fuck if it is or not but it's what's gonna happen."

"Josh is my brother..." Sadie trailed off.

Her mind likely put two and two together coming up with Letty thinking the same about her sibling. Only it was Letty's sister who'd been involved in bad shit that led to a child being kidnapped, and ultimately to her murder.

"I see you're coming to the right conclusion, baby. But

just to be sure, I'll confirm that shit that went down with Letty's sister will not be happening with you and your brother. What is gonna happen is, we're gonna play this smart and part of that is me sleeping over and Davis staying out front. And tomorrow I'm going to work with you to check out your alarm there and make some changes. I want those feeds going to my office. After that, I'm coming back here and installing a system."

"There's no need to put in an alarm here," she argued.

"Sadie—"

"I'm moving out, so it will be a waste."

What the hell?

"Where are you moving?"

A look I didn't like took root in her eyes. A look that told me I needed to brace because I wasn't going to like her answer or her reasoning behind the move. I decided now was not the time to learn the where or why. It was time to end the discussion and get Wilson on his way, and Davis's ass planted in his car outside.

But first I needed to find Sadie her phone.

"Davis, will you hang in the house with Sadie a few minutes? I need to go find her phone."

"I'll go with. Or better yet, I'll look for it in the morning."

"Or, Davis will stay with you and I'll go find it like I told you I would."

Thankfully she read me right and gave in without further argument.

After she told me the general vicinity where she dropped her phone, I followed Wilson out to his SUV.

"I know you got plans tomorrow," he started. "But you need to make time to sit down with the team and fill us in."

What he meant was, I needed to have my ass at the

office so he could make sure his order not to move on Grinder had been communicated, and to give me shit for keeping what I knew about Sadie's issues to myself.

"I'll be there. But just so you know, I heard you about not contacting that fuckwad."

"I know you did, Reese, and I know you wouldn't push this into something that would fuck the DEA or us. I also get why you held back telling me about how bad Sadie's in the hole. Tomorrow's about briefing the team but also about me making sure your head's where it needs to be."

"I'm not tracking."

"Known you awhile. You've never made what your ex-wife did to you a secret." I felt my body tense at the mention of Ellie, and I didn't bother hiding my displeasure she was the topic of conversation. "I see that touched a nerve. I also saw how you were with Sadie. It's not lost on me there's something there. You know we got your back; however, we need to have it. But I gotta know if this is you moving to protect a woman you're fucking or a woman who means something to you. Either way, you'll have us. But Sadie's friends with the guys, they'll want that friendship intact when you're done with her so have a mind to that."

Red hot anger coursed through me until I felt my insides start to boil.

"You know you have my respect, so I hope you know I mean no disrespect when I tell you we're gonna have problems if anyone ever refers to Sadie as the woman I'm fucking. And as far as my bitch of an ex-wife is concerned, she fucked me over and did that in a way that made me never want to go there with another woman. But Sadie's not *another woman*, she's Sadie. It took me a while to understand what that meant but hearing her running, out of breath through the woods shook something loose inside me.

And if that hadn't done it, hearing her scream, then the line going dead certainly woke my shit up. A thousand thoughts raced through my head, none of them I care to think about now, but only one emotion planted itself in my chest—fear. At that moment, driving like an idiot trying to get to her, the realization hit pretty fucking hard she was something more. Gratitude for your concern, but right now I'd appreciate it more if we all concentrated on keeping Sadie clear of danger."

Wilson took his time studying me before he nodded.

"Glad to hear you're where you need to be with Sadie. And this is the last time I'll bring up your ex, but, Reese, the bitch never deserved the headspace you gave her. Glad you've decided to move on."

There was nothing to say to that, so I remained quiet when my boss gave me a lift of his chin and climbed into his SUV.

Then I went in search of Sadie's phone. Twenty minutes later I found it and was mostly over my irritation. By the time I was walking up Sadie's driveway, all ruminations of my ex-wife were gone and all that was on my mind was, I was happy Sadie was moving; it would save me the effort of installing outside lights.

Moose be damned.

11

IT WAS the dead of night. I was in my bed alone, Reese was on the couch, and I was debating doing what I was getting ready to do. It was stupid. I was a grown woman who'd lived on her own for a long time. But someone had been inside my house. And even if the general consensus was that person was my brother it was still a guess. I was freaked out, had woken up from a bad dream, and had been tossing and turning for an hour.

So even if it was stupid, I needed to see Reese. Then maybe after I visually confirmed he was on the couch I could get back to sleep and get a few more hours of shut-eye before I had to get up and get ready to go to the bakery.

I threw the covers back, swung my legs over the side of the bed, and padded to the door. I only hesitated a moment before slowly turning the knob and opening it. Equally quiet, I tiptoed down the hall and continued to creep into the living room until the couch came into view.

No Reese.

I blinked, praying I was still half-asleep, but when I refocused, he still wasn't there. The blanket was there crumpled on the couch. The pillow I'd given him was there. But Reese was not.

Irrational fear slithered up my throat.

Did he change his mind and leave?

Was Davis still out front?

The more I thought about being alone in my house the more I overreacted. There was nothing to be afraid of, yet I was scared and the kind of scared I was—the illogical, irrational fear that was born from my imagination—was quickly spiraling into outright terror.

I tore my eyes from the couch and glanced around the dark room, a space I'd walked through thousands of times. A place I'd always felt safe now felt perilous. Like I was one of those women in a Halloween-themed movie who went to investigate a sound while you sat in the theater yelling at her to hide in her closet. And when she got axed to death you felt no remorse because the woman was a boob who should've run.

Should I run?

Hide in my closet?

What was happening here?

Out of the corner of my eye I caught a shadow move, my tummy bottomed out, and I stupidly froze.

And I only unfroze when I heard, "Sadie?"

It was unfortunate that hearing my name did not relax me. I jumped at the sound like a frightened squirrel and twisted my body in an unnatural way that sent pain shafting up my spine.

"Where were you?" I snapped with way more attitude than was warranted.

Reese continued to walk through my kitchen, his big body on display—chest bare, tight boxer briefs that molded to his crotch and thighs—in a way that, if I hadn't already known what he was packin' I'd have a relatively good idea. Powerful, thick legs that right then were moving him closer to me.

"Bathroom."

Bathroom.

Right.

I was too busy trying to get my heart rate out of stroke range to reply.

Reese wasn't having the same issue, so he went on, "Everything okay? Why are you out of bed?"

No, everything was not okay. I was a total lunatic.

"Everything's fine."

Yep, I was still being snappy.

Reese stopped close, necessitating me tilting my head back or risk getting an up-close and very personal look at his very defined, smooth chest.

"You don't look okay."

"How kind of you to point out."

That wasn't snappy, it sounded angry.

Reese ignored my attitude and asked, "What woke you?"

I injected as much sarcasm into my tone as I could when I told him, "Oh, I don't know, a bad dream about the Horsemen breaking into my house and dragging me off to their lair to torture and kill me."

"Baby—"

"It's your fault." And before I could think better of it my hands lifted and I slapped them on his chest. "I was fine until all that talk about alarms and security. I've never felt unsafe in my home. *Never.* Now I'm having bad dreams and creeping around my house like a stupid girl in need of a protector."

"And you came out looking for me."

That was not a question, it was an arrogant statement that incidentally was correct. I had gone in search of Reese. I couldn't go back to sleep without knowing he was there on my couch, protecting me from imaginary bad guys.

"That's your fault, too."

Reese's hands went to my hips, then they slid around. One traveled up my back, the other around until it rested on the opposite hip, and I was caged in his embrace. This also brought our bodies closer together. His, as stated shirtless, mine in my thin pajamas that did nothing to shield me from the heat emanating from him. A warmth I wanted to soak in.

Danger.

Abort mission.

"Let's get you back to bed."

It was my bad luck his words caused an ill-timed shiver to move over me.

Friends only.

Reese was being friendly, not suggesting he take me to bed to do all those things he'd said he wanted to do to me.

I bet I'd have nothing but sweet dreams after a few Reese-induced orgasms.

What the hell is wrong with me?

"You can't take me to bed," I told him.

Slowly his mouth quirked into a smug grin.

God, that was hot.

"I was talking about sleep, Sadie, but if you got a better idea, I'm all ears."

My hands on his chest involuntarily flexed and wet gathered between my legs.

How lame was that?

All it took was a smile and my body melted for him.

"Friends only," I reminded him.

Or was I reminding myself?

"Yeah, Sadie, friends."

He'd left out the *only* part but I didn't have the chance to bring it to his attention before he let me go and tagged my hand. Next thing I knew he was pulling me toward the hall. Then down it, back into my room, and he didn't stop until we were standing at the side of my bed.

"Climb in."

I climbed in.

Reese turned and went back to the door. My heart clutched in a way I wish I could deny. It was not out of fear of being alone. It wasn't because I was scared. It was straight-up foolishness. My life was out of control, in a downward spin and I was fast approaching rock bottom. Sex would only further complicate my life but doing something as reckless as falling for Reese would destroy me.

Nate had fucked me over and I was living with the consequences. I knew with great certainty Reese would never steal, cheat, or lie. He was too straightforward and honest for that. But he would take something from me, even with all his honesty and careful warnings not to get attached, I would. Hell, even with all that was bearing down on me I'd still felt it from the start. From the very first time I'd clapped eyes on him, I felt the power of his draw. With a man like Reese, it was impossible to stop yourself from drowning in him. He put you in the thrall of wicked fantasies. He held you captive even as he held you at a distance.

He was the type of man who a woman would long for.

And right then, watching him leave my room I longed for him to stay. There was where the danger lay. I wanted him next to me—not to fuck me but to comfort me.

Reese closed the door and was on his way back to the

bed when a new fear mingled with elation rocked through me.

He was staying.

With me.

Oh, no.

His knee went to the mattress, I felt the bed move, then I felt his arm slide under my shoulders, and finally, I felt him shift me until my cheek had no place to go but his chest.

I felt all these things rather than saw them because I closed my eyes.

Pleasure and fear ricocheted.

I laid there stiffly, not knowing what to do or where to place my hand so I left it awkwardly smooshed between us.

Reese, not having the same problem, reached over, found my hand, and yanked it free. He placed it on his chest and I held my breath. He covered my hand with his much bigger one and I continued to hold my breath.

"Relax, Sadie."

Is he nuts?

On an exhale I blurted, "This isn't a good idea."

"Relax and get some sleep."

Now I knew he was nuts. There was no chance I was going to fall asleep pressed to Reese's side with my cheek resting on one hard pec and my hand on the other. His nipple was under my palm for God's sake. And if there had been any light in my room and I looked real hard I'd be able to see his other one—albeit crossed-eyed—but it was mere inches from my lips. With all of that happening, he thought I'd be able to sleep.

That wasn't nuts—that was pure insanity.

"Reese—"

"Baby, you got two choices. Option one, close your eyes,

relax, and get some shut-eye. Option two, I get creative, find different ways to relax you, and when you're good and exhausted you'll have no choice but to knock off. In case you're wondering, my vote is option two."

I felt a quiver between my legs that was so intense I might've experienced my very first mini orgasm.

"See! That right there is why this isn't a good idea."

"Sadie, I'm a man," he weirdly stated.

"Um, yes, Reese, I know you're a man. But I don't see what that has to do with anything."

"I'm a *man*. And being that, means I got control over my body. I was teasing you, baby. Nothing is going to happen that you don't want to happen. You could be butt-ass naked next to me and that'd still hold true. Now relax. You're safe. Totally safe, and that's from something happening that you're not sure about to someone breaking in here. Just sleep."

Reese had the wrong idea. I wasn't worried about him trying something. I was worried my control would slip and I'd do something that would push us further down the murky path.

"Do you want to be my friend?"

I felt Reese tense under my cheek. His strange reaction made me wish I could pull the words back in, but I knew I'd never get back to sleep until I understood the boundaries of our friendship.

There was a long stretch of silence. So long I was seriously freaked out that his answer was going to be no.

"Well? Do you want to be my friend, or not?" I pushed.

"Why are you asking?"

"Why don't you want to answer?"

"Because I get the sense however I answer is gonna bite

me in the ass later so I'm trying to find the angle you're playing."

I shifted so I could tilt my head and look at his face. Reese's chin was already tipped down, meaning that when I tilted up it brought my mouth close to his. This was a huge mistake. I knew how good those lips felt. I knew with a glide of his tongue he could highjack my thoughts.

Neither of us moved.

And the longer our breaths mingled, the longer we laid there perfectly still doing nothing more than staring at each other, the deeper I came to the realization that whatever game we'd been playing had morphed into something else. There was no flirtation, no teasing, no playful glint in his eyes.

Oh, yeah, something had changed. Unless I was reading him wrong, but I didn't think it was possible to misconstrue the fierce possession rolling off him. He was making it clear what he wanted, and it was not a friends-only arrangement. It wasn't even a sex-only pact between friends.

Between the fiery glimmer in his eyes and the wet that had drenched my panties—add to that the way my nipples had puckered and were aching—I was so lost in him, it didn't register he'd taken his hand off mine until he used it to brush my hair off my face. The feel of that so gentle it shocked me.

"What's happening?" I whispered.

I lost his eyes when they roamed my face and it wasn't until they came back to mine did he whisper back just as softly.

"Everything."

His breath breezed over my lips. The moment was so intense I fought the urge to hide from it. Intimate in a way the was indescribable and that intimacy turned into something more when he went on.

"I tried to stay away. Even before I knew you had trouble, I was battling with what to do with what was going on between us. Trying to keep it light, keep you at arms' length so if it went where I wanted it to go you wouldn't get hurt. I even tried to feed you that line of bullshit. But I was doing that to protect myself from you."

I jerked back from the force of his insult. He thought he needed to protect himself from me? Like I was a cheater like his ex?

"From me?"

"I've spent a lot of years working hard not to feel anything. Succeeded, too. Can't say I haven't liked and respected the women I've had, but beyond that, nothing. Not until I saw you behind the counter beaming your pretty smile my way. Fought against a variety of feelings I long thought were dead. Then I got to know you, and little by little you came out of your shell, giving as good as you got. Cracking witty comebacks, giving me more of you. Then that fight became a struggle. Memories were coming up of another woman who I'd taken one look at and lost myself in were in the forefront of my mind."

"I'm not her, Reese."

"I know, Sadie. You're far, far more lethal. That bitch destroyed me. But you, with your beauty, the raw energy I felt—and I felt it the very moment I saw you. The way you stirred something deep in me that I didn't even know was there. You'd fuck me up worse. You, I wouldn't recover from. So I moved to protect myself from all that."

There was so much to say yet I couldn't find the words. Everything he'd said was true, except in the opposite. *He* was the one who *I'd* never recover from. He was the one who would hurt me when he left. I was the one who needed to be smart and stay away from him.

"You're wrong."

"I'm wrong?"

I nodded and in doing so, the upward glide of my head brought our lips closer.

"Yes, you're wrong," I repeated, mostly to give myself time to find the words I needed to explain. "Us in this bed isn't a good idea because I want you here with me even though I know I'm courtin' a broken heart. It is not me who will hurt you. It is you who will hurt me, and I'll let you, Reese. Unlike you, I don't have control over my body when I'm next to you. I have so many problems right now it's not even funny. I should be so worried about them and how I'm gonna save my business that you never should've hit my radar. But you did, in a big way. And that should be a red flag."

"I am not that motherfucking douchebag," Reese ground out.

"I know you're not. And to use your words, the asshole destroyed me. Not emotionally. I didn't love him. And you wanna know how I know I never loved him?" I asked but I was too far in my head to let Reese confirm or deny if he wanted the knowledge. "When he walked into a room, I felt bland happiness to see him. When I see you, there's the feeling in my belly that makes me jittery and nervous. When I see you—whether it's you coming into my bakery or into Letty's store, the first thing I wonder is how long you'll stay. Again, to using your words, you are far more lethal than Nate. Not to mention the sex. The sex is a big problem."

"Why's the sex a problem?"

"Not a problem, a *big* problem."

Reese turned to stone and his gaze was suddenly infused with concern.

"Did I hurt you?"

The words came out tortured. So tortured my heart squeezed and I rushed to put his mind at ease.

"No, you didn't hurt me. You didn't do anything I didn't beg for. And that's the big problem. I'm not a prude, I've had good sex." Reese's growl gave me a shiver. Apparently, he didn't want to hear I'd been with other men, but he had no problem talking about the women he'd had. "What I mean is, it's never been like *that*. I've never attacked, I've never begged, and I've certainly never done anything like that while in the middle of an argument."

"Emotions were high, and we got chemistry. I'm still not understanding why that's a big problem."

I thought I was speaking English and it was on the tip of my tongue to ask him if he understood the language when his hand cupping my cheek—something he did a lot which I liked way too much—moved over my temple and his fingers slid into my hair.

"I don't want to be your friend." My heart clutched so hard I puffed out a breath. "I want to be more than friends. I wanna fuck you in your bed and in mine, and as off-the-charts hot as it was, I don't want to angry-fuck you in your office because all we got finally boiled over. I want us tearing at each other because we both recognize that we got a certain kinda passion between us that's explosive. I want to prove to you that you can trust I'm not gonna fuck you over and I want you to teach me to trust you. I want that enough to put myself out there and stop fighting it. But wanting it doesn't mean shit if you're not willing to drop that hand you've got up and let me in."

At some point, my heart stopped being squeezed, but a

new pain had crept in. Reese's honesty caused more fear than pleasure. However, there was no use lying about how good it felt to hear Reese tell me he wanted more. So good, it was the best feeling I'd ever felt. But with it came insurmountable panic—overwhelming and frightening and at the same time joyous and exhilarating. I wanted him to prove to me I could trust him and I want to teach him how to trust me so badly I was almost willing to scale the mountain standing before me.

But the reality remained. I was in the midst of a major life crisis, and I was scared to start climbing another hurdle.

"You said you were incapable of giving more," I reminded him.

"I was wrong. With *you,* I can give more."

"There's..." I started and stopped then tried again. "I don't know how..."

Shit, that wasn't right either.

The words all moshed together in my mind and the harder I tried to unscramble them the worse it got.

"I get it," he murmured.

"You do? Because I don't."

"You got a lot going on," he noted in an understatement. "Timing of this sucks. I get that. But, Sadie, I'm not gonna let that stop me. I have very few regrets in my life, and I'm not making this one of them. I get it would be easiest on you if I backed off, gave you time to sort your shit out, but in doing that we lose time. So, I'm not doing that. What I will do is stand at your side while you work out your problems. What I'm not going to do is let you go at this alone. I'm not standing by watching you struggle through it. We've decided you're taking the loan. That should get you caught up. You need more money, I'll give you that, too. The Horsemen won't be an issue for you because my team's gonna see to that. And when I track down Nate, he'll be paying you back what he stole from you and that will solve that. So, actually, the problems you had this morning you no longer have. Meaning, there's nothing stopping us."

The loan.

Fuck. How had I forgotten about agreeing to take the loan?

"Me borrowing money from you while we're…being more than friends could get messy."

"It could."

"Right. So then you agree it's not a good—"

"Nope. I agree it could get messy, not that it's going to. But I absolutely, one hundred percent do not agree that us moving forward is a bad idea."

"Reese."

I said no more because he lifted his head, bringing our lips a hair's breadth apart.

"How bad do you wanna kiss me, Sadie?" he asked against my lips.

Right against them. So close I felt them brush against mine as he formed his words.

"That's not the point."

Since my lips had brushed against his the same as his had mine, I was no longer clear about what the point was.

"Kiss me, Sadie. Then tell me this is a bad idea."

"That's not fair."

"Life's not fair."

"You're a good kisser."

"It's good you think that."

Through these exchanges, our lips were intermittently touching. Each word that was spoken had its own unique brush. Each "you" and "you're" added pressure. Each word that included an S was a barely-there swipe. It was erotic and sensual, and each syllable spoken caused throbbing between my thighs that was now constant.

"Kiss me, Sadie."

I didn't kiss him, not really, but I did slide my tongue over the swell of his bottom lip.

God, he tasted good. Just from that, a glide of my tongue, and I was already dizzy. But the lightheaded buzz changed when Reese's tongue slowly chased mine, giving me a hint of what I gave him.

I squeezed my thighs together which did absolutely nothing to quell the ache, and my fingertips pressed into his chest in an effort to stop myself from exploring all the hard planes that were on display. Right there for the taking. He wouldn't stop me; Reese would let my hand wander and roam.

"I don't want to get lost in you."

"I don't want you lost, Sadie. I want you right where you are."

"And where am I, Reese?"

"At my side."

I was quite literally at his side, pressed up against it, with my lips hovering close to his, having what felt like an important conversation. No, not important, a game-changing conversation after a night where he'd stayed to watch over me. This after I'd been a total bitch to him. I'd refused to see reason, but he hadn't walked away. I'd fought with him about him loaning me money, but he hadn't given up. I'd pushed him away, but he hadn't turned his back on me.

And for a man who told me he wanted nothing but sex he sure had done an about-face.

"Reese, you don't want—"

"Kiss me."

"What changed?"

"Kiss me and you'll know."

I didn't think kissing him would give me the answers I was after. As a matter of fact, I knew kissing him would leave me with more questions.

"Why don't you kiss me?"

"Because I promised you that you were safe. I promised you nothing would happen in this bed that *you* didn't want. I never break a promise. Not fucking ever. So that means, you have to kiss me."

I felt a flicker of hope.

"Promise me this doesn't get messy. Just that. I don't want anything else. I just need you to promise that no matter how this ends it doesn't get ugly."

Reese pressed his mouth against mine and muttered there, "Promise."

That was all I needed to hear.

My tongue retraced his lip, he opened over me, and I kissed him.

Not frenzied like our kiss in my office.

Not frantic and angry.

This was slower, sweet, gentle.

There was gliding and tasting. Our tongues touched and tangled.

It was unlike any kiss I'd ever had. Reese didn't deepen it; he didn't tilt his head to take my mouth nor did I. Our lips were barely touching, only our tongues were exploring, and for some reason that made the kiss so off-the-charts hot.

Reese pulled away, slanted back down, and kissed the corner of my lips. Then he moved to my jaw and dragged his lips along the curve of my jawline until he reached my ear.

"Do you get it now?" he whispered.

I had no idea what he was talking about. The only thing I was getting was that I did not possess the same self-control he did. I was ready to roll on top of him and pounce.

When he didn't go on, I shook my head.

"With the touch of my tongue."

My hazy mind still wasn't following.

"What?"

"That's all it takes."

"You're a good kisser," I reminded him and tipped my head to the side hoping he'd get the hint I wanted more of his mouth on me.

"That wasn't a kiss, Sadie, and you know it. That's the energy we got between us. I haven't touched you. I haven't even really kissed you. Yet your hand is trembling on my chest and your legs are rubbing together."

"Arro—"

"You had a bad dream and came looking for me," he cut me off. "That's what did it for me. Knowing that you woke up, were scared, and needed comfort and you came looking for me. I don't need to touch you to feel you. That's not new; tonight I just decided to stop fighting it. And whether you're ready to admit it or not, you already dropped that hand when you came out into the living room. You know there's something between us. You feel it, same as I do. No arrangements, no walls, no distance. We let this play out however it's gonna play out and we do that open and honest."

Open and honest.

I liked that.

And I did go looking for him even though I didn't think it was a good idea. I couldn't stop myself from going to him.

Plus, he'd promised not to let this end ugly.

What was I waiting for?

"Open and honest," I agreed.

His head came up, and without moving mine, my eyes went to him in time to watch him smile.

He had such a great smile.

"Good."

Reese put pressure on the back of my head and shifted until his head was back on the pillow.

"Let's catch some sleep now, yeah?"

Sleep?

He wants to go to sleep?

After he'd turned me on and did it to make a point—a point I'd conceded. And now he was suggesting we sleep.

What the heck was that about?

I was a little salty, so when I rested my head back on his chest, I didn't hide my frustration.

I felt Reese's big body start shaking and my frustration grew.

"It's not funny."

"It kinda is."

Jerk.

"Only because you're not the one lying here hot and bothered and uncomfortable."

Reese's hand covered mine and it was as if he was trying to kill me. He glided my hand over his stomach and kept going until my palm was resting on the hard ridge of his dick.

"Sleep, Sadie."

I didn't go to sleep.

I laid there for a long time with my hand cupped over his erection, my cheek on his warm chest, and my mind racing, going over everything Reese had said.

I must've done it for too long for Reese's liking.

"Relax," he whispered.

I felt his fingers sifting through my hair. His head turned and his lips went to the top of my head. He left them there and I closed my eyes.

Good or bad, I agreed to be open and honest.

Right or wrong, I was happy for the chance.

As the old adage went—only time would tell.

12

I WAS LEANING against Sadie's counter sipping coffee, checking my phone while she was in her bathroom getting ready for work.

Davis had texted he was leaving to go home right about the time Sadie's alarm had sounded at the butt-ass crack of dawn.

Now I was checking emails on my phone, and I was doing this vacillating between wondering if my still-stiff dick would ever soften and how it was possible after last night and all that was said I felt so calm. Not only calm but totally at ease.

I had no second thoughts. No anxiety. No concern I'd made a mistake opening up the way I had.

I'd fallen asleep with Sadie in my arms, and I'd woken up the same and all I felt was contentment. On a morning, this being the first I'd woken up in a bed with a woman since Ellie, after a night where I did nothing but hold a woman in my arms, something I hadn't done since before I left on my first deployment. On a morning when my head was sure to be filled with the garbage my ex-wife left me, I felt none of it.

There was no distrust, no worry, no sick feeling in my gut that Sadie would only show me what she wanted me to see, and once the thrill of the chase was over and she knew she had me she'd be out needing the attention of other men.

With all of that absent, I was pissed as fuck at myself for wasting time. Thankfully, it hadn't been a lot of it, but I'd wasted months. And that sucked for me, but it also sucked for Sadie. If I'd been paying more attention to what was going on in her life instead of acting like a pansy-ass fool I would've seen it sooner. Which meant I would've been able to put a stop to it sooner and she wouldn't have had to sell her clothes or her furniture. Though the couch wouldn't be a loss. But if her master bedroom furniture was half as nice as what she had in her guest room it was a shame she sold it.

"You don't have to wait for me."

I glanced up from my phone and my poor cock went from semi-hard to straight-up hardened steel.

It had been approximately twenty years since I'd executed a covert combat jack. And it was unfortunate at forty-one I was going to have to excuse myself to go rub one out.

"Sadie," I growled.

"What?"

I left my gaze glued to her bare legs and watched as the hem of her t-shirt brushed her thighs as she made her way to the kitchen.

"What do you mean what? You've been in there an hour and you're not dressed."

"I haven't been in there an hour. More like fifteen minutes. And like I said, you don't need to wait for me."

"Baby, you're not dressed," I repeated the important part.

Or at least the part my dick had homed in on.

"What are you talking about?" she asked, reaching up into the cabinet for a mug.

The shirt rode up. I caught a glimpse of her ass cheek and my dick twitched.

Fucking hell.

"I have on clothes, Reese, what's your problem?"

My problem was I'd had nothing but my hand for seven days and visions of her bent over taking my cock. And it was a toss-up which was worse—those visions being memories that were vividly seared into my brain so all I had to do was think about her and I could recall in minute detail how phenomenal she felt wrapped around my cock—or the memory of her sleeping in my arms.

"Fuck," I grumbled and attempted to distract myself by taking a sip of coffee.

"Why are you acting like I walked out here naked with a horsetail buttplug in?"

I choked the hot coffee down and was in the midst of a coughing fit wondering if it was possible to get third-degree burns in my throat when she winked.

It took a minute for me to get the hacking under control but when I did, I asked, "You think you're funny?"

"That was pretty funny, yes. And for the record, I do not own a horsetail buttplug. I read about pony play in a book."

That was the second time she'd admitted to reading BDSM.

Interesting.

"What about a regular plug, do you own one of those?"

Her nose scrunched and she shook her head.

"No."

"You ever tried one?"

Another shake of her head but the nose scrunch was absent.

"Maybe we can talk about buttplugs when it's not five-fifteen in the morning and I've had more than one sip of coffee."

"Right. I'm gonna hit the head while you finish getting ready."

Sadie lifted her mug to her lips but not before I saw her smirk.

"You got something to say?"

She didn't answer verbally but her big bright smile said it all.

"Wanna join me?" I asked.

Her eyes flicked to the microwave to check the time. When they came back to me her smile was still firmly in place, but a fair amount of flirtation had slid in when she said, "Wish I could but I got coffees to make. Besides, it doesn't look like you need any help."

Sadie's gaze dropped to my crotch. I didn't need to look to know my erection was on display, but I did need to go do something about it.

I was walking out of the kitchen when I heard her start to laugh.

"Laugh now, Sadie, because tonight you're gonna learn the meaning of orgasm denial."

"Ha! Joke's on you; my sex life as a whole has been one giant lesson in orgasm denial," she mumbled her off-handed comment at my back.

I stopped mid-stride and looked over my shoulder.

"Say again?"

"You heard me."

Now that I was looking at her the teasing and bravado in her tone had slipped away and so had her smile.

Fuck, yeah, I heard her. Her sex life had been shit. Which meant I was the lucky bastard who got to show her the good stuff.

"Are you smiling?" she snapped.

"Fuck, yeah."

"Glad you think my lack of orgasms is funny."

"About as funny as you knowing I'm gonna go jack off before my dick confronts the real possibility of serious damage. And you think it's funny because you know I've been hard since last night. And you coming out in nothing but a tee, swaying your ass, was to tease me. Well played, Sadie. So, tonight I'm gonna get mine back and that's gonna start with me taking my time and you're not gonna come until I'm ready. But by the end of the night, after I show you what you've been missing, you'll understand why I'm smiling."

I turned, leaving her in the kitchen with wide eyes and her lips parted.

"Oh, and one more thing," I continued. "I know it's early in the morning and you've expressed your disinterest in discussing buttplugs before coffee, but later this afternoon I'm gonna need you to give that some thought."

I made it down the hall, but instead of going right into the hall bathroom, I went left into Sadie's bedroom. Not even seeing the room devoid of furniture—something that irritated the fuck out me—made my erection soften in the slightest. I strolled into her bathroom, left the door open, and stripped off my clothes.

I was naked in the shower when Sadie came in.

"Seriously?" she huffed.

"Yep."

I had my head tipped back under the spray, hands up, washing out the soap, cock still rock hard.

"I have a glass shower door, Reese."

"Yep."

"I can see you."

If she meant to sound annoyed, she missed the mark. Even over the pounding water, I could hear the whine in her voice.

"Tonight, you're gonna see a lot more of it."

"Reese!"

"Relax, I'm just taking a shower."

"What about..."

If I wasn't afraid of what would happen, I'd make her finish her question. Talking about me jerking off, hell even her watching me, did not embarrass me. But me shooting off simply from hearing her talking about it would not be good.

"Changed my mind."

"*Can* you change your mind?"

I righted my head and looked through the slightly foggy glass.

"Why wouldn't I be able to change my mind?"

"It looks...because it's..." She stumbled and lowered her eyes. "Standing straight out."

That *it* was. It was also painful as fuck but switching it up and dishing out some payback was almost worth the pain. Seeing her eyes glued to my dick was very worth it.

"Finish getting ready."

Sadie jolted out of her trance; her gaze slowly traveled up my chest. She took her time fully taking me in, and when she was done, a wicked smile tugged at her lips.

That smile filled me with dread.

But it was the wink and shrug she threw my way before she turned that made me brace.

"You mentioned tonight," she started conversationally as she picked up a tube of mascara. "Just so you know, the bakery closes at six today." Sadie came up on her toes, leaned in deep bringing her face closer to the mirror, and when she did her tee pulled up, exposing the barest hint of her ass.

I'd been outplayed. Again.

My gaze stayed riveted on the swell of her ass as I fought the urge to reach down, take my cock in hand, and start pumping. In order to resist, I snatched the bar of soap from the ledge and lathered, studiously keeping my hands above my waist.

Sadie's right hip hitched up, taking her even closer to the mirror, her lips slightly parted, and she kept brushing shit on her eyelashes.

"I have to come straight home after that," she continued and moved to the other eye.

I'd never, not even with my wife, watched a woman put on makeup. Thus, I didn't know how long it took to apply, though I did know my ex took a year to get ready and the end results of her efforts didn't hold a candle to Sadie's natural beauty.

"The guest room furniture sold," Sadie went on and straightened.

Although the hem of her tee fell back to mid-thigh the sight before me was no less sexy. Her statement however pulled my attention from her fantastic ass, my throbbing cock, and the plans I'd been making for that evening, and I focused on what she'd said.

Guest room furniture sold.

My teeth clenched until the muscles in my jaw ached.

———

AFTER MY SHOWER, I followed her to Treats.

It was early, the shop didn't open for another hour, and her first employee didn't start for thirty minutes. That gave me plenty of time to look over her security system and cameras. The alarm would do. The cameras were shit. I made a list of what I needed to bring back from the office and went in search of Sadie.

I found her where I'd left her, in the kitchen.

A kitchen that smelled of cinnamon and apples.

Sadie also looked relaxed in a way I hadn't seen her before. She was totally in her happy place, so it sucked I was going to pull her out of it with the air perfumed by freshly baked muffins.

"I'm done," I told her.

Without looking up from pouring batter into the tray in front of her, she said, "Okay."

"Babe, look at me."

She stopped pouring and looked up.

"Last night you said you were moving. We didn't get a chance to talk about it."

Every bit of tranquil and calm seeped out of her.

Fuck.

"Where and when are you moving?"

"Um..."

Um? What the fuck?

"Sadie," I prompted.

"I'm moving at the end of the month, and I don't know where."

"End of the month is in three weeks."

"Yeah."

"And you haven't found a new place?"

Then in the silence, it hit me—why she hadn't found a new place to live. And that sour in my gut was back. In three weeks, she'd be homeless.

Fucking homeless.

She'd gone from having eighty-five K in the bank to being on the verge of losing her business and her home.

That shit was whacked.

Totally fucking whacked.

And it wasn't going to happen.

"Got shit to do." I broke the silence. "I'll be back in a few hours. Your screen's shattered but the phone's still useable. Call me if you need me." I paused then clarified. "That means you call me if you catch sight of your brother or any of the Horsemen. Or if he tries to call you."

Sadie stared at me with a look I did not like. And the longer she held my gaze, the more doubt I saw creep in.

"Reese."

My name came out as a plea, and I knew what was coming next—excuses. She was gearing up to tell me all the reasons why she and I weren't a good idea. And all those reasons were going to be centered around her money problems.

So I cut her off at the pass.

"Don't, Sadie."

"Don't what?"

"We have a deal. Last night you agreed. Do not go back on that. Don't use the time I'm gone to build those defenses back up. Open and honest. If you've got something to say that doesn't have to do with the problems you got right now, I'm all ears. We'll talk it through. But don't put money between us. Don't let what that fucktard Nate did to you stop you from moving on."

"It's not that easy."

She was right, it wasn't. Sadie had weight bearing down on her on two fronts—losing everything she worked hard for and trusting me after what her ex did to her. I had that same baggage, only mine was nearly two decades old. So it wasn't lost on me I was asking her to get over something that happened to her six months ago, when I'd been nursing my hurt for years.

"It's not easy. What it will be is worth it."

Sadie's eyes followed me as I rounded the long metal table she was working at. When I got close, my hand went to the side of her neck and I gently squeezed.

"You want something to think about while I'm gone?" I asked. Sadie nodded and I continued. "Think about waking up next to me. Think about you coming into your kitchen and finding me there drinking coffee. Think about me in the shower and you at the sink getting ready. And while you're thinking on that, think on this—I have not slept next to a woman in so damn long I didn't remember what it felt like. But I will never forget what it felt like waking up to you sprawled out over me. Never, Sadie. I'll remember that feeling for the rest of my life. The first morning in a very long time I woke up and the first thing I felt was happiness. And from there my morning got better. Coffee with you in your kitchen while you were teasing the fuck out of me. Straight up, Sadie, I figured this morning I'd have to push back the panic of starting something with you. It might sound fucked-up, but I spent a lot of years giving my bitch of a wife free rent in my head, and I figured this morning after we agreed to more, to explore things with us, those old fears would pop up. They didn't. All I felt was relief I wasn't going to waste another day fighting my feelings for you. Think on that. Think about what you felt and know from here it only gets better."

Sadie's face lost the unease and worry. Along with that, those pretty blue eyes went from stormy to serene. She'd told me she didn't want to get lost in me. I didn't feel the same. I wanted to drown in her, in those ocean-blue eyes. I wanted to wrap myself around her and absorb all that she had to give.

"Your ex-wife is an idiot, Reese."

"I know, baby."

"Okay. I'll think about this morning. But I might not be able to search my feelings about it because you in my shower is pretty much burned into my brain and that's all I can remember."

I knew my smile was smug when her brows pulled together.

"Cocky," she mumbled.

"Baby, what did you expect? You just admitted all you remember about this morning is my big dick."

"I didn't say it was big."

"If it wasn't big, it wouldn't be all that memorable," I pointed out.

"Whatever."

I leaned forward, kissed the corner of her mouth, and straightened.

"Everything's gonna work out."

"If you say so."

Since I'd said it and I meant it there was no need to argue my point.

"I gotta hit the road."

I dropped my hand and stepped back.

Sadie's eyes narrowed and she asked, "That's it?"

"What's it?"

"No kiss?"

Damn, if the woman didn't want me smug, she needed to stop.

"Didn't miss that move over the sink."

"What move? I was just putting on mascara."

And if she wanted me to believe all she was doing was putting on her makeup, she needed to not smile while she lied.

I focused on her lashes rather than the blue of her irises. Indeed, she had put on mascara, but nothing else. No shadows or liner. None of that powdery shit I'd seen women blot on their faces. Sadie's skin was naturally flawless, and there was a glow to her cheeks that couldn't be artificially manufactured. In a nutshell, she was beautiful. But that dark mascara did draw your attention to her eyes and enhance their attractiveness.

"You're beautiful."

Sadie's head jerked back, and her eyes flared.

"No, I'm—"

"You are beautiful," I repeated. "Top to toe, baby, absolutely *beautiful*."

"Thank you."

Barely a whisper.

"Now, like I said, I got shit to do at the office. I'll see you in a few hours."

"Okay."

I was at the swinging door that led to the front of the bakery when Sadie called my name.

As soon I turned to look at her she launched in, "I liked waking up next to you. I liked you in my kitchen first thing in the morning drinking coffee. And I liked you in my shower. Not because I got my first look of all that is you but because I liked knowing you were watching me. You make me feel what you said, beautiful, and I've never felt that before. You also make me feel sexy and ditto on never feeling that. But I was also happy and as you can imagine, *I* haven't woken up in a very long feeling that."

Good goddamn that felt good.

"Don't know how that's possible. But you'll be getting that from me."

"Getting what?"

"Everything. Every-fucking-thing you need so you'll never doubt you are so beautiful sometimes it takes me by surprise just how pretty you are. And there is something about you that's so goddamn sexy it's like it rolls off you. It's not that you have the best ass I've ever seen, it's not your long legs, it's not that your tits are arguably better than your ass. It's none of that but all of it. It's you. It's this sweet and bashful thing you got going on that makes a man wonder how much work he's gotta put in to make you ignite. And just a reminder, I'm looking forward to putting in the work, baby. So that's what you're gonna get from me. And you're gonna get so much of it you'll never again doubt how beautiful and sexy you are. But you're also gonna remember you're a badass—tough and strong and smart as hell. See you soon, Sadie."

With that, I pushed through the door.

She again called out, but that time it was to tell me she'd left a caramel macchiato and two lemon-poppyseed muffins on the counter.

I didn't stop to thank her. I didn't break my stride as I walked by, snatched the bag and the to-go cup. I wasn't being a dick, but there was only so much a man could take. And after the morning she'd given me, I needed to leave and regroup.

Not to rebuild my walls.

Not to rethink my decision.

To ponder the speed at which I was falling for her.

Though, I already knew I wasn't going to do a damn thing to slow it down. I just needed to make sure she was with me for the ride.

13

I WALKED into the office and found Brasco and River in the reception area. They turned to look at the same time and smiled.

Shit.

"Guess you were right," River tossed out. "Never seen it done that way but can't argue the outcome."

"Seen what done, what way?"

"Foreplay. I thought you were a little outta practice when I first met you and your brothers were giving you shit about Sadie. Never thought of coffee being dumped on my head as foreplay before and at the time I thought my game was just better than yours. But I guess I was wrong."

At the time that conversation had taken place I was being a dick. Pushing Sadie while holding back. It wasn't foreplay, it was fucking torture.

"Right," I clipped.

"For a man who spent the night at the woman's house he's been after for months you seem a little...*off*," Brasco joined in.

I was unclear how Brasco knew I'd been going back and

forth with Sadie for months. However, asking him would prolong the flow of information. And I needed information like yesterday.

"Have you ever heard of TJ Gayle?" I asked the detective.

"Yeah. How do you know him?"

"Sadie's ex took off with a shit-ton of her money—all of it, to be precise. She said she reported it but also hired this TJ guy. From what she's told me I'm not getting a good vibe but before I talk to him it'd be helpful to get your take."

The humor went out of Brasco and he bit out, "Her ex took off with her money?"

"Only thing Gayle confirmed was that the name Nathan Mallard was bogus and the ID he gave Sadie when she hired him was also fake. I didn't get into Nate's social and banking info and if she direct-deposited his pay or if he got paper checks. I can find that on my own, and the less I drill her about the situation the better."

"Who'd she report it to?" Brasco went on.

"Don't know. Didn't ask the detective's name or what precinct."

I'd liked Jet Brasco the minute I'd met him and the more I got to know him, the more I liked him. But seeing him pissed and the level of that anger about a woman he barely knew getting fucked over only proved what I already knew —he was a good cop and a damn good man.

"TJ means well. I wouldn't say he's totally inept but he's only good at one thing, taking pictures of cheating spouses. Beyond that, any real investigation work, he doesn't have the skills. He's not out to screw people over, but he won't turn down a job even if it's above what he can deliver and that's not because he's an asshole, he just has a family to feed and isn't smart enough to recognize his limitations."

That was both good and bad. The good part was, Sadie hadn't been taken for a ride. The bad news was I'd been looking forward to getting in Gayle's face and demanding Sadie's money back. Though, he'd fucked up so that might still happen.

Wilson walked around the corner and motioned for us to follow.

"I'll be right in," Brasco said and jerked his head toward the hall. "I'm gonna see who took Sadie's statement and get the report sent over."

"Appreciate it."

I headed in the direction Wilson had disappeared and River silently followed. When we hit the conference room Wilson was back in his chair. Asher, Cole, and Jack were also seated.

"Davis will be in later," Wilson started, leaving out that Davis had sat outside Sadie's house all night awake and needed to catch up on sleep. "Rhode's in his office going over a new case. Cole needs to get on that with Rhode but I wanted him briefed on this first."

In other words, there was no time to fuck around. We had an active investigation going on that was punted to us by the US Marshals and lives were on the line.

"Thanks for joining us," Wilson went on, his gaze stuck on River. "Where's Jet?"

"Making a call to get Sadie's file sent over."

River's explanation was barely out of his mouth when Brasco came in.

"File's being sent to me now. Detective Winegarner was assigned. Brent's a good guy. If there's been no movement, it's because he's hitting roadblocks, not because he's not working."

That was also good news though not the news I wanted.

"Is he gonna have a problem with me looking into this?" I asked.

"No. I'll see him when I get to the station and have a word."

More good news. Not that it would've stopped me if he did take issue, but it was always better to keep the line of information flowing without hard feelings.

"I know you two have to get to the station, so I'll make this quick." Wilson's gaze darted between River and Brasco. "I reached out to Butch. I'm not getting a good vibe. Something's changed with Zeus. And it's not just he's taken over Tug's stable, which I'm still shocked about mainly because Butch was adamant when we met that Zeus did not want the trouble of running women. Too many variables. Now he's selling ass and not doing a damn thing to hide it. But it's the new attitude that worries me. So, I asked you here to ask, is there something we need to know that you haven't told us?"

When Wilson was done, neither man spoke. But River clenched his jaw and Brasco looked uncomfortable.

"Nothing solid." Brasco broke the silence.

"What's that mean?" Asher joined the conversation.

"It means there are rumors, but nothing to substantiate those rumors and until there is, we wait."

I looked over to River. Jaw set, deep scowl, hard eyes holding mine.

He was bound by oath, but he wasn't feeling the same level of patience as Brasco.

His loyalties were split. His woman was best friends with Rhode's woman. He'd worked a case with us involving some seriously sick shit linked to children that got Letty kidnapped. Letty's sister had been mixed up with the Horsemen so there was no love lost there. He also wasn't happy the DEA had Butch on the inside and none of us could make moves to take down known criminals, but River had been a cop long enough and had worked with the Feds enough to know sometimes the better play is to wait. But there was something more; he looked *pissed*.

"What's the chance of getting Sadie's brother to flip?" Brasco went on to ask.

"None," I answered. "The guy's an idiot moron. Anyone approaches him with an offer he'll run straight to Daddy Zeus. He's gagging for the clout being a Horsemen will bring. Plus, he's neck-deep in running the women, so he's got free pussy clouding his already limited judgment."

I hoped to God Sadie never found out what her brother was doing for the Horsemen. Not that dealing drugs or transporting guns was any better. But Josh Pierce was a sick motherfucker.

"When those rumors are substantiated or disabused, I'd appreciate a call."

Wait, what?

That was all?

Wilson never gave up on a thread until it unraveled.

Brasco looked visibly relieved. River looked more ticked.

"As soon as I have something to tell you, I'll call."

"Right, thanks for making the time to meet with us."

That was Wilson's polite way of dismissing the detectives. Neither of them missed it.

"Reese, I'll be in touch by this afternoon."

"Appreciate it. River, good to see you."

River jerked his chin, silently returning my sentiment. I took no offense; the man's teeth were clenched so tightly it was likely he couldn't speak in fear of spilling the truth.

I heard the front door open, then close, as well as felt my phone vibrate with an alert. I sat with the rest of my team.

"Dirty cop," Jack muttered, and Cole nodded his agreement.

"Gauging by River's reaction that'd be my first guess," Wilson confirmed. "But there's other viable options. The Horsemen aren't the only club in the area, and they're not the only club who wear a one-percenter patch, they're just the biggest. Zeus could've easily made alliances with another club or clubs, and he's stupid enough to think there's safety in numbers."

"And now that he's running girls there's more money coming in," Cole picked up that vein. "More money, more responsibility, more members means he can run more products which means, even more money. But, that last meet, he looked like he had an ace up his sleeve. He wanted it clear he had nothing to do with Letty being taken but he also made it clear he didn't give the first fuck if we believed him or not. And when Reese stepped up and told him that Sadie was under our protection and his, Zeus shrugged. Then the asshole grew some big balls and to our face told us Sadie was a Horsemen due to Grinder's affiliation. And last night, someone going into Sadie's house, taking the money that Reese got from Grinder...that doesn't say he's got more dickhead biker back-up—that fucking screams he's got someone who he feels has a bigger dick at his back."

I didn't want to think about Zeus's smug bitch ass telling me Sadie was under Horsemen protection. I saw red then, and if I didn't keep a lock on it, I'd see red now. I couldn't fuck the DEA's case.

"River's off-limits," Wilson announced. "He doesn't need any of us putting pressure on him. He's struggling with what he knows. He's family, so we put him at ease and let him do what he needs to do. Let's break this down quick. Reese, fill us in on what's up with Sadie."

I did a quick rundown of what Sadie'd been struggling through and how she'd been trying to raise capital to keep her business afloat. Throughout this, Asher, Cole, and Jack scowled. Wilson had leaned back in his chair and crossed his arms. But I had more to tell them beyond her money troubles.

"Sadie had a friend in high school named Lori. Zeus violated this girl. Josh knew because he saw firsthand the aftermath. He also knows his sister is terrified of Zeus. So scared, he's the only reason she agreed to take a loan from me. Swear to God, she would've gone down fighting, but she would've gone down. But once Zeus was in play and offering to find Nate, something snapped in her and she agreed to take my money. I'm not gonna tell her that me paying off her rent isn't gonna stop Zeus. But we know, he's gonna continue. Whether that's to pull Grinder in deeper and make him more loyal, or so he has a debt to hang over Sadie. I don't know. He wants Grinder in deep, I don't give a fuck. He thinks to fuck with Sadie, him and I are gonna have problems in a way that I forget the DEA's making a case."

"She's selling her stuff?" Cole sneered.

"Yep. Clothes, shoes, furniture, whatever she can sell to make money, she's doing it. I also found out last night she's moving. Though this morning I found out she doesn't have a place lined up to move into, which means she's not looking because she can't afford a new place."

"What the fuck?" Asher exploded.

As Wilson had pointed out last night, everyone on my team liked Sadie. It was hard not to like a sweet, shy woman who baked like a goddess, had a great smile, and a body made for sex. But there was just something about her that drew you in. She was shy but still friendly. Timid at first but once she got to you her wicked sense of humor came out. Sadie was not overly outgoing, she wasn't loud, she didn't flaunt her curves, yet you couldn't miss them in a reserved sort of way.

Thinking back, I couldn't remember if there'd been a day that had passed since we'd come to Idaho that one or more of the guys hadn't gone into Treats. Someone from my team had seen her every day. Which meant she'd also seen them, and in those months, she'd become friendly with all of them. But in her own shy way I was the only one she'd flirted with.

Damn, I was stupid as fuck.

"She can stay with me," Jack piped up.

Wilson snorted, Asher chuckled, and Cole straight out smiled.

"She's staying with *me*," I corrected.

"In your cabin?" Jack grunted. "Dude."

He let that hang.

My cabin wasn't like Rhode's A-frame cabin on the top of a mountain in Sandpoint. His was big, open, rustic, and seriously fucking cool. Mine was a six-hundred square foot log cabin with a loft bedroom. It was no less cool than Rhode's but nowhere near the size. It was also temporary until I found a property I wanted to build on.

"Yes, my cabin."

"There's barely enough room in there for you. The two of you will be on top of each other." Jack pointed out.

That's the plan.

"Does she know she's moving in with you?" Cole asked.

"Nope. And I'm not asking."

All three men outright laughed.

I sat back in my chair and watched, giving them time to burn themselves out. When they were done, Cole went on, "You know she's gonna have your balls, you move her into your cabin without asking, right?"

Oh, Sadie was going to have my balls all right, but it was a calculated risk. In this case, asking for forgiveness was easier than asking for permission. In three weeks, she'd be homeless, and I was not spending the next three weeks arguing with her about moving in with me when in the end, she'd be moving in no matter what. I was saving both of us the hassle and drama.

"She doesn't have an alarm at her place and she's right, it would be a waste of time and money to install one. River and Letty just got settled in their new place; Letty would have no issue with Sadie staying there and neither would River, but Sadie would never do it. She's got way too much pride. So for the same reasons, Rhode and Brooklyn are out. I know Mrs. Simpson would take her in, and Sadie might go for that only because when the old woman speaks you listen no matter how much pride you got. But with the Horsemen sniffing around, Mrs. S is out. And there's no way in fuck my woman's staying with any of you. She's got—"

"Whoa. *Whoa*. Whoa," Jack cut in. "Your woman?"

"My woman."

My confirmation was met with Jack's narrowed eyes. And I couldn't say I was pleased with my friend's reaction.

"No disrespect but are you sure you're ready for her? And I'm asking not only for her, especially after the story you just told us about her ex. She's gotta be raw after that. And you've made no qualms about how you live your life. Again, no disrespect, you don't make promises and you don't fuck over women, but that's my point—you don't do commitment and promises."

Unfortunately, what I'd filled the guys in on wasn't a story, it was Sadie's reality. And I wouldn't ever make a promise I didn't know I could keep.

"You know me better than that, Jack. And it's been near twenty years since Ellie fucked me. It's past due I let that go and move on."

My friend's narrowed eyes turned into saucers. And I understood why. He'd known me for years and I'd never once given any indication I'd ever commit to another woman. But Sadie was Sadie.

"Do not carry a burden of wrongful deeds by someone else in your mind. Forgive and forget," Cole recited from memory.

"Confucius?" Jack inquired.

Cole gave a slight jerk of his head. "Buddha."

"Right," Jack drawled.

Cole quoting Buddha or Confucius or Tao was not uncommon, though sometimes I was still taken aback by the sharpness of his memory.

"Something like that," I mumbled. "All I know is it's time. If I don't move the fuck on, I'm gonna lose a chance at something and I'll regret it."

"Well, friend, you might regret moving her into your house without talking to her about it." Cole circled back. "She might be on the shy side, but she's got some bite to her."

I was looking forward to testing Cole's observation. But he did have a valid point, Sadie had a temper on her. Something to think about. I'd test the waters, feel her out, and if she was vehemently against living with me, I'd put an alarm in at the cabin and go stay with one of the guys.

"Noted," I told Cole then looked at Wilson. "Sadie's got blind spots, including the sidewalk in front of the bakery.

Would you mind me using what we have in stock? I'll make a list and you can invoice me."

Wilson's studious gaze came to me. Moments later it looked thoughtful, so I braced.

"Take what you need, make a list so I can replace it. No invoice."

"I should—"

With a sharp shake of his head, he cut me off, "No invoice."

Whatever it was my boss was going to say, he'd obviously changed his mind. Cameras and invoicing were not what was on his mind. But Wilson shared when Wilson felt like sharing. And seeing as we had work to do, I was grateful he'd decided not to impart wisdom that would delay that.

"Fill me on the case the Marshals sent over."

Wilson didn't immediately fill me in, he stood and made his way to a whiteboard that had been flipped so the information was hidden. He turned it around and pointed to a picture of a very well-dressed, clean-cut older man.

"This is Marco Kelly. Mother's Italian, father's Irish. So he's got strong ties to both countries. He's also got family in both places. Blood family and *famiglia mafiosa* kind of family. He's been in the States for about thirty years. Two years ago he moved from New York to Malibu." Wilson dragged his hand along the board and pointed to an enlarged map of the area and a picture of a house taken with a telephoto lens. "Eleven thousand square feet of oceanfront views, nine bedrooms, a walk-out basement which, according to the original house plans, adds another six thousand square feet and could be finished off with an additional living room, kitchen, and four more bedrooms. The property is forty acres and the last of its kind backing up to the Point Dume State Park."

"Jesus, I bet that cost a fortune," Cole muttered what I was thinking.

"Twenty-nine million."

I let out a low whistle and looked back at the picture of Marco. The man looked innocuous, like a very wealthy grandfatherly type. But he was anything but harmless. If his picture had made it to our whiteboard that meant he was into some seriously bad shit.

I learned a long time ago not to judge someone on appearances. Marco Kelly and Trevor Lawrence were worlds apart financially, yet they were the same—low-life criminals. The only difference was one committed his felonies in an MC cut and dirty jeans and the other in a twenty-thousand-dollar suit.

"What does the SOIB have on Kelly?" Cole continued.

In recent years the sex offender investigative operations branch had taken on a new role to included sex trafficking. The team the Marshal service had put together had a seventy percent success rate of recovering victims. Which was far higher than regular law enforcement. Add in force multipliers like Takeback and a handful of others who did what we did, which was to assist in the investigation and takedown of traffickers, they're now at eighty percent. Still not good enough but better than rescue rates in the past.

To be fair, the Marshals had dedicated teams devoted to human trafficking. Most police agencies did not have that kind of manpower, especially those in rural America.

"Still new, they've only had the case a week. But it looks like he's running a sex club out of his Malibu mansion."

"Sex club? Since when do we investigate sex clubs? As long as there's no prostitution, forced sex, or underaged participation they're not illegal."

Jack wasn't wrong. But they weren't exactly legal either.

They fell in a weird gray area of consenting adults partici-
pating in sex. The key was consenting and the second
caveat was adults.

"That state park?" Wilson went on. "Lots of hiking and
horseback riding going on. But also, lots of acres between
state land and Kelly's house. There's a fence that circles the
property and a ten-foot-high gate at the entrance. The
house is tucked nicely in the canyon, hidden. Neighbors
haven't heard or seen anything. But someone out riding
their horse saw a woman running near the gate naked.
Report says at first the rider ignored the woman. It's private
property, people can run around naked all they want when
they live in that kind of seclusion. But when the woman got
closer to the fence, it became clear it wasn't a woman. It was
a girl and she had lash marks crisscrossing her back and legs.
When the rider called out to the girl to offer help he says
she ran away from him back toward the house."

Fucking disgusting.

"Police went out, interviewed Kelly's staff, and they told
the police no one had been on the property. Kelly himself
was in New York at the time. No warrant so they couldn't
enter. One of the detectives had a bad vibe, didn't like the
feel of the staff, so he took it upon himself on his time off to
sit at the bottom of the canyon and catalog who went in and
out. During the day, the staff only. Late at night, lots of cars.
Expensive. They stay about four hours then they leave. Not
one at a time, en masse, like an event just let out. Weeks he
watched. Same cars, same nights, same time. Instead of
going to his leadership, he gave the intel to a buddy of his
who works fugitive apprehension and it made its way up
from there."

"Sex clubs a jump," I noted.

"That detective got license plates. When the SOIB took

over, they ran them, got names. No warrant means they can't go deeper, but Shep can and he did. Banking records show all of them made hefty payments to a corporation Kelly owns called Joi. No pretense, no hiding, straight out public record."

Shepherd Drexel was a hacker for hire. He also liked to give you the runaround. He wasn't what one would consider a "good guy." He dealt in a gray area, doing bad things to stop bad people. But when it came to sex trafficking and sex offenders, he lost all subterfuge and did anything he could to help.

Maybe I'd been wrong and Kelly was just a kinky old man who ran a not-so-legal-but-not-illegal sex club.

"Rhode's looking over the SOIB's proposal now, but it looks like they want someone going undercover."

"I'm in." Jack immediately volunteered.

"If needed, Asher and Cole head to California," Wilson corrected. "Asher will go in, Cole as cover."

"Is this because Asher spent that summer in Amsterdam?"

I couldn't stop my lips from twitching. Asher hated when Jack busted his balls about that trip. We all knew there was zero chance Asher had participated in legal prostitution, but Jack loved to push buttons, and since there were pictures of Asher and his buddies in the Red Light District, Jack brought it up whenever he could.

But before Asher could respond, Wilson did.

"No, it's because if you go in and see something that should not be going on, you'll lose your shit and burn the house down. And don't deny it. Asher's the only one with the disposition to go in."

That was factual. Asher was the most levelheaded and Jack had the worst temper. It wasn't a lack of control, it was a lack of tolerance. He'd seen too much over the years, and the more he was exposed to it the less he attempted to control his reaction to it.

If there were underaged children and any sort of abuse going on, he would not think twice about pouring gasoline on what I was sure were marble floors and lighting a match. *After* he escorted all the innocents to safety.

"Wait, what makes the SOIB think Asher will be able to get in?" I inquired.

"The intel from Shep came in ten minutes before you got here so I haven't looked, but according to Shep, if you know where to look, the club isn't a secret and neither is Kelly being the owner. What's not disclosed is the location of the *soirées* as they're called. He's confident once Asher's given a new identity, he'll get in."

"That's a clear indication that the club is what it says it is. If Kelly was trafficking women or whoring them out, the vetting process would be exhaustive and information about joining wouldn't be easily found," Jack pointed out.

Incidentally, I agreed.

"The SOIB wants to be sure, so we'll insert Asher. He'll get a look around and if something feels off, we go deeper. If it seems to be what it claims to be, then we punt it back to SOIB and move on." Wilson concluded that topic and moved to the next. "Jack and you, Davis, are gonna back up Reese. I want the three of you to find out what you can about the rumor Brasco referenced. Rhode is going to dig into Nathan Mallard. Reese, I'm going with you to talk to the PI Sadie hired."

"Brasco said TJ Gayle means no harm, he's just not very good at his job," I relayed.

"Good, then he'll have no problem refunding Sadie whatever she paid him."

I sure hoped not, but if he did, he could bitch and moan all he liked, just as long as he wrote her a check.

"Grab what you need to upgrade Sadie's system," Wilson went on. "I need a few hours, then we'll pay a visit to Gayle. Get the file he has Nathan and a check for Sadie. That should get Rhode started while he waits for Brasco to get the file the CDAPD has from Sadie's report. That work for you?"

"Yep."

"Good." Wilson's fist rapped on the table twice and he stood. But after that, he pinned me in place with that same thoughtful stare from earlier. "My two cents. With this, to get her safe, don't ask. Do whatever you need to do to get her in your house but do that smart. Do it quick and effectively. If she gives you shit and refuses, I'm taking an extended business trip and she can do me the favor of housesitting my condo."

Wilson was full of shit. He didn't have a business trip, but if it meant Sadie had a place to live and she wouldn't stay with me, he'd find somewhere to go.

That was Wilson. He'd literally give you the shirt off his back—or in this case, his condo.

"Appreciate it."

"Got shit to do."

So did I.

And I'd only left Sadie an hour ago and I was already jonesin' to get back to her.

I pushed out of my chair but stopped when Asher called my name.

"Lunch?"

"Yeah. Early before I go with Wilson to meet Gayle."

"I'll be here."

I made it to the door when Asher called out again.

"I mean that, Reese, I'll be here. Whatever you need, yeah?"

Christ.

I had a brother and three sisters. None of whom I was close to. Not for any reason other than time and distance. They had their families and were scattered around the country. I had a job and before that, I was in the military. But there was still love there, plenty of it. But not closeness. Not shared experiences. Not understanding born from a different kind of brotherhood.

That was what Asher, Davis, Rhode, Jack, Cole, and Wilson gave me—brotherhood.

The real kind.

"Yeah, brother, I know."

I rushed through grabbing the shit I needed to expand Sadie's security cameras, made a list of what I took, and I was out the door.

Not once did I think about how far I was gone for a woman who was going to kick me in the teeth a time or two before she believed in what we could have. I didn't think about how badly that was going to hurt. I didn't once wonder if I was crazy for starting something with her, knowing she was going to be stubborn.

She was worth the effort it was going to take to win her.

And that was what her love was, a prize to be won.

A prize that would be mine.

14

"SADIE, Mrs. Simpson is here to see you," Kat called back into the kitchen.

Shit.

"Thanks, I'll be right there," I called back then added, "If you would please get her a table and whatever she wants to drink."

"Already done," Kat chirped.

Of course it was. I wasn't the only one afraid of Mrs. Simpson.

Maybe fear was a stretch, but not by much. Mrs. Simpson was a stickler on manners among other things. She was also like a human lie detector. I knew she sensed something was wrong last night at book club, that was why I'd dashed out of there as quickly as I could.

Now I was going to have to lie. Or attempt to lie, at which time, Mrs. Simpson would know and she'd be mad and hurt that I tried to pull a fast one on her.

Gah.

I finished placing the newly decorated cupcakes on a tray and sucked in a fortifying breath. If I was brave, I would call Letty and Brooklyn to come in and rip the Band-Aid off. But I wasn't brave and I was still holding out hope when I placed the tray of cupcakes in the display case that Mrs. Simpson was just visiting for a coffee and a natter.

I glanced around the full bakery, found the beautiful older woman sitting in the far corner—eyes on me. Posture perfect, hair neatly styled, heavy makeup, jewelry at her ears, neck, and wrists, dressed to the nines. That was Mrs. Simpson—always. Growing up, my mother had never dressed like Mrs. Simpson. She would on occasion throw on a dress and do herself up if that occasion was special. But for the most part, she was casual both in clothes and in her general appearance and she'd passed that down to me. I wondered if Mrs. Simpson's daughter was like her—a striking beauty who looked runway-ready at all times.

I knew I was taking too long arranging the goodies in my case when I glanced back at Mrs. Simpson and she was scowling.

Shit.

As gracefully as I could, knowing she was watching and would correct my carriage if my shoulders slumped, I walked to her table.

"Good morning, Mrs. Simpson. You look lovely as always."

"Thank you, Sadie. Please sit with me."

I bit my lip to stop myself from smiling. I didn't miss that she had not returned the compliment. Not that she would; Mrs. Simpson didn't blow sunshine. She said what was on her mind and didn't hold back. Thus, I knew she was not impressed with my ponytail or the jeans and Treats t-shirt I was wearing. And she likely hated my sneakers more than my clothes.

I took the chair opposite her.

As forementioned, Mrs. Simpson didn't beat around the bush; she also didn't waste time.

"Perhaps you were unaware of my business dealings with Mr. Johnson."

Mr. Johnson?

My landlord.

Dread seeped in and my spine went straight.

Oh, no.

"I was...not aware, no."

"My portfolio is diverse. A smart woman knows how to maximize and manage her wealth."

Oh, no, no, no.

"I wish you would've come to me," she softly informed me.

Oh, shit.

"Alas, you did not. However, since I own a thirty percent share in this building, Mr. Johnson made me aware of the situation. Normally, I do not get involved in daily or even monthly operations. I have people who do that for me, advisors who then meet with me personally to discuss anything that needs to be discussed. This is not because I do not understand the businesses I am involved in. It is simply because there are so many, it would take all my time, and I quite enjoy my time free. However, with this, I contacted Mr. Johnson directly and inquired about your delinquent rent."

Delinquent rent.

That made my tummy coil and churn.

"That debt has been cleared by me personally. Further, the next six months have been paid in advance."

I needed to say something. Unfortunately, all the oxygen had crystallized in my lungs, and I felt dizzy.

"I have not and will not discuss this with Letty and

Brooklyn. I do not participate in tasteless gossip. However, I'd like to know why you have not gone to your friends and asked for help—and that includes me, lovely."

That debt has been cleared.

Six months paid in advance.

My lungs unfroze. Sadly, that meant I was now panting. "Sadie, child, calm yourself."

I would never be so disrespectful to ask myself if the old woman was crazy—but was she *crazy*?

How was I supposed to calm myself when I wasn't sure if I wanted to sob in relief, scream in frustration, or hide from the embarrassment.

A smart woman knows how to maximize and manage her wealth.

I didn't have wealth, but I hadn't protected my money.

So stupid.

And now Mrs. Simpson knew.

She was waiting for an answer so I gave her the truth.

"I didn't want to be a burden."

In a very unlike Mrs. Simpson fashion, she sucked in a breath then wheezed out, "A burden?"

My breathing wasn't yet under control, so I nodded.

"That is appalling you would allow yourself to feel such a vile emotion. You, my lovely, are not a burden. Friends are not impositions. They are gifts. And when a friend is struggling and you are given the opportunity to lend a hand—whether that be by listening, advising, or offering financial help, that gift blossoms into something richer. You've denied them something special, Sadie. They are good, strong women, they should be your foundation, your sounding board, or as these youngsters who lack a proper vocabulary call it—your ride or die."

Hearing the prim and dignified Mrs. Simpson say the

words ride or die sent a laugh I couldn't hold back ricocheting around the room.

"Yes, I can see how you would find that amusing, however, it does not answer my question."

"I have a brother," I told her.

"I know that, dear. He is in desperate need of a shower and haircut."

Ohmigod. She'd seen Josh.

"Actually, he's in desperate need of morals," I corrected. "He's been..." I trailed off, not wanting to use profanity but not coming up with something suitable to replace dick.

"A pain in the ass," Mrs. Simpson supplied, and I felt my eyes round in shock.

Still unable to curse in front of her I agreed, "Yes. He's been that his whole life. And the older he became the worse it got. My parents, they are good people. Great parents and I watched them wonder where they went wrong with him. I watched my mom get her feelings hurt over and over. So many times, I saw her crying. My dad was hurt, too, but his hurt turned into anger. He loves my mom and didn't like to see her in pain."

"And you were the good child. You caused no harm," she surmised.

"Yes. I grew up watching what I said and did. I got good grades, I didn't give them any hassle, I worked hard and saved to open my business. I've never asked them for anything. I never treated them like a bank like my brother did. I've never yelled at my parents. I've never called them names. I'm the one they can count on. I'm the self-sufficient one."

"You're the blessing, not the burden." Once again Mrs. Simpson guessed correctly. "And that has transferred to Letty and Brooklyn. You don't want to be what you consider a drain on the friendship, so you've kept your problems a secret."

And that was why I'd avoided Mrs. Simpson for as long as I had. She was far too wise.

I squirmed in my seat and started to sweat in places I shouldn't be sweating. My stomach was still flip-flopping and not in the exciting way it did when I saw Reese. All the churning and roiling was making me feel sick.

"My parents love me," I blurted. "I don't want you to think badly of them. They never put pressure on me. They've always been supportive."

"I would never think such thoughts. As parents, we do the best we can. There is no one-size-fits-all when it comes to raising children. However, sweet girl, sometimes we unconsciously put undue stress on our children. No loving parent purposefully sets out to encumber their child with unnecessary expectations. Regrettably, we unwittingly saddle our children with these expectations, and they turn into obligations. I don't doubt your parents love you deeply. However, you being you, that is to mean—sweet, loving, kind, and thoughtful—have turned unspoken expectations into duty. It is not your responsibility to be perfect. If you listen to nothing else, hear this—you are not perfect, you never will be, and it is a goddamned waste of energy to endeavor to be such. You are Sadie. You are all that you are, but you are also human. You will fail. You will stumble. You will need help. You will make all sorts of mistakes in your life. What you will never be is the perfect mother, the perfect wife, the perfect citizen, the perfect businesswoman. There are many ways to fail in this life. However, the most egregious of these failures is when you fail to love yourself enough to acknowledge that perfection is not obtainable."

I was wrong. So very, very wrong. I should've gone to Mrs. Simpson and told her everything. Right from the very beginning—the day Nate left, I should've run to Mrs. Simpson and soaked up every bit of wisdom and kindness she was willing to share.

"I need to talk to Letty and Brooklyn," I admitted.

"Indeed you do."

"And we need to talk about my rent." I paused and gathered myself. "I didn't say thank you. I apologize for that, I was in shock. But I appreciate your help more than I can express. So, thank you. I want you to know, I also appreciate Mr. Johnson's kindness and understanding. I have been doing my best to raise money to pay my bills. Recently Reese has become aware of my situation and the money that Nate stole from me. He offered me a loan. After being stubborn about accepting, Reese lost patience and made it clear it was no longer an offer but a demand. I gave in, not because I'm smart, but because my brother is now involved with some scary people, and I don't need them in my life."

I sucked in a breath and continued. "After selling some furniture, clothes, and such, I have almost six thousand dollars. I was going to give that to Mr. Johnson this week, however, I will write you a check today to start paying you back."

When I was done, Mrs. Simpson was staring at me. Not with her normal, kind, compassionate eyes, but with a fury I didn't think a woman of her age could pull off.

And while she was staring at me, I heard the front door open. I didn't need to turn to see who it was. Just like all the times before when Reese entered my sphere, I felt him. Only this time with my stomach still feeling sick, I didn't get to experience the pleasure of the butterflies his presence invoked.

"My apologies, I must've heard you incorrectly. Did you say, Nathan stole money from you?"

Oh, no.

That was as close to Mrs. Simpson spitting out words as I'd assume she'd allow herself. Seething might've been a good way to describe her tone. Though there was more bite than mere seething.

"Yes," I confirmed. "That is another reason I didn't say anything. I created my own problems. As you said, a smart woman manages her money. I didn't do that. I trusted Nate to pay the bills. I gave him access to my accounts."

"Bull pucky!" she exploded. "Utter rubbish."

"What's going on here?" Reese boomed.

Mrs. Simpson tore her gaze from mine. Then she looked up and up and farther up until I suppose she locked eyes with Reese.

"I'll tell you what is going on, Mr. Turmel. Sadie and I are having a discussion. I have just learned that her money was stolen. That is not me gossiping, I assume since you're here you have finally awoken and have come to see the woman that Sadie is. However, my question to you is, what are you doing about this?"

"Mrs. Simp—"

"Quiet, Sadie," Mrs. Simpson rudely interrupted. "I want to know immediately what you and the rest of the gentlemen are doing to recover Sadie's money."

I was not over the shock of Mrs. Simpson's impolite interruption, but I still didn't miss the curt, brusque manner in which she spoke to Reese.

"It's being handled, Mrs. Simpson," he gently told her.

My gaze shot to Reese.

Patience and understanding.

Not that I thought he'd be an asshole to an elderly lady,

but I was still a little surprised at the tenderness he used to address her. Equally as surprising was how soft his face was.

"I would like the details of how this situation is being handled," she pushed.

"I can understand you wanting that." Reese continued with a gentle tone, but a firmness had crept in. "But that's not gonna happen. Sadie has cupcakes to bake and a business to run. You have books to sell and women to keep straight. Let me and the guys handle how Sadie's money will be recovered."

Without missing a beat Mrs. Simpson narrowed her perfect kohl-lined eyes on Reese and blasted him.

"That is sexist and frankly offensive."

"No, what it is, is me giving my woman some peace after she's been stressed and worrying about how she'll keep her business. And it's me sparing you the unpleasantries of my job. What it is not is me belittling two women who mean something to me. Sadie will be kept up to speed on what's happening. If she chooses to inform you or the rest of her friends, which I hope she does, then she will. But just to put your mind at ease, I will tell you; we will find Nate. And when we do, he will be paying back what he stole."

The anger was swept clear away but that didn't stop Mrs. Simpson from injecting a healthy dose of mock annoyance into her tone when she said, "I wish you boys would come up with something befitting a beautiful young lady. *My woman* sounds barbaric and uncivilized. What will happen next, Mr. Turmel? Will you club Sadie over the head and drag her into your cave?"

"No, Mrs. S. This is where I toss her over my shoulder, take her to my cabin, and show her how a real man worships *his woman*. And do not pretend you don't know what I am talking about. Only a well-loved, cherished woman behaves like you do. Mr. Simpson loved you well and thoroughly, enough that it filled you up and overflowed, enough that in his absence it still pours out of you."

Mrs. Simpson sniffed and corrected her posture.

What she didn't do was correct Reese for calling her Mrs. S., which she despised.

"Indeed, you are correct. Now, please escort me back to the bookstore. As you pointed out I have books to sell. And there is no telling the trouble Letty and Brooklyn will get up to if I am not there to supervise."

Reese graciously held out his hand and helped Mrs. Simpson stand. Once she was on her feet he leaned down and brushed his lips over her cheek.

My silly heart swooned.

"Be back, baby."

My heart swooned again.

"I'll be in the back. I'll let Kat know, just go through," I told him and looked over at Mrs. Simpson. "I'll be over with a check."

"Nonsense. That is a discussion for later. In the meantime, I do not want anything from you except for what Reese here said—peace. Use this time to regroup. There is no rush."

I fought back the tears threatening to burst out of me at any moment.

I shouldn't have been such a coward.

"Babe?"

"I'm okay."

Reese's brow lifted in disbelief.

I shot him a smile that was mostly fake but a whole lot grateful.

Grateful for him, grateful for Mrs. Simpson, grateful for the wisdom she shared.

15

"I HOPE you know how special she is," Mrs. Simpson remarked as soon as we were on the sidewalk.

I knew this was coming.

So I was prepared.

"I know how special she is."

"I know men like to believe they can do everything on their own. And men like you, like my husband, like to believe that they shoulder the lion's share of life's strife. Men like you who are strong, protective, fierce sometimes can forget that a lioness is vicious in her role to provide for her pride. Do not forget the strength your lioness possesses. She will instinctively fulfill her role and in doing so she will feed your soul. She will strengthen you. She will hunt for and find your demons and she alone will banish them. She will soften your heart and in doing so she will protect it with the same ferociousness she hunts. Do you understand what I'm telling you, Mr. Turmel?"

Fuck.

I was wrong. I was not ready.

Still, I answered, "I understand."

"Strong men need stronger women. But do not forget there is a fragility that needs to be cared for. She will forget. She'll go to battle day in and day out. She will strive to be the strength you need. She will need to be reminded, sometimes daily, sometimes multiple times a day, her worth does not come from winning battles. It will come in the form of deeds. Big and small. She will judge her worth on her victories and she will scoff when she fails. It will be up to you to remind her worth comes from the inside, what she gives the world—a smile, a kind gesture, thoughtful words, caring about those around her. Sometimes those are not reciprocated and that's okay. True kindness isn't given with the thought of getting something back in return. Do you understand?"

"Yes," I pushed out.

"Good. And lastly, you were correct; my husband gave me more than I needed during our lives. He did that because he loved me. He did it because I gave the same to him. He did it because he knew I need it to heal deep hurts. There are times when a marriage is unbalanced, the same is true in a courtship. One takes, the other gives. The scale will never be truly equal. It's not meant to be leveled, it's meant to be forgotten, so forget it now. Take what you need from her now while she is struggling while your instincts are telling you to wrap her in cotton and hide her away. It is only in hardship when a woman or a man can prove their mettle. Teach her how strong she is by laying what's been holding you back at her feet now while she is in the midst of turmoil. Our Sadie will not let you down. She will rise up to the occasion and she will shine. You will give her that even as you are taking what you need. Do you understand?"

Christ.

Not once in my life had someone so easily read what was weighing on my mind.

But her advice was a day late. I'd already laid out what had been holding me back. Though my need to protect Sadie from what was going on around her was spot on. And Mrs. S. could say what she wanted, but she felt the same way.

But her point was made, and I understood.

"Last night, I told Sadie why I was holding myself back. And she now knows how I feel about her. But, yes, I understand what you're saying, and I appreciate you sharing your wisdom with me, and I will not forget what you've said."

"How do you feel about her?"

Nosy.

But I wouldn't have it any other way. With Sadie's parents in Florida and her brother being a monumental douche it was good she had someone looking out for her.

"I enjoy spending time with her."

"Men." She ridiculed and lifted her chin in what was meant to be patronizing and she didn't care that I knew she was mocking me. "It is okay to express your emotions. It does not mean you have a small penis."

My step halted, the muscles in my neck contracted, and I had to adjust before I tripped and took the old woman down with me.

"Please don't ever say penis in front of me again," I begged.

"I wouldn't think a man of your size would be easily affronted."

Was she referring to my height or my *size?*

I violently shook that thought out of my mind before I could contemplate it any further.

"And I wouldn't think a woman with your class would say penis," I volleyed.

"Silly, *silly*, man. You mistake class with experience."

I wasn't thinking about that either.

"This conversation is over."

"Prude."

I looked down into a pair of eyes that had turned hazy with years. A gentle, wrinkled face that had once been line-free and youthful. She was no less beautiful at ninety than I suspected she was in her twenties, though her beauty was now the true kind that came from within. At thirty, she would've been a knockout. High maintenance all the way. Then and now.

"I'm going to have a talk with Letty about the types of books you're reading."

"If you think my experience comes from the pages of a romance novel, Mr. Turmel, you are mistaken. There is nothing in those books that could begin to compare to what my handsome husband gave me. There is a reason I am partial to the plundering Vikings in those historicals. There is nothing more exquisite than a predatory man on the hunt when his intentions are pure of heart. I simply wish in your marauding you'd come up with something more fitting than *my woman.* Perhaps when you conquer you should refer to her as *your prize*, seeing as that will be what she is. A prize —and if you're lucky and cherish your spoils, she will be that for the rest of your life. Then you will be well and thoroughly loved as well until it spills over for you to share with the next generation."

I wondered about the rubric Mrs. Simpson used when deciding between calling me Reese and Mr. Turmel. I did this as an evasive maneuver so my mind wouldn't accept that a sweet old woman would say things like plundering

Viking or predatory man. Nor did I want to think about Mrs. S. talking about me conquering Sadie and cherishing my spoils. Though I was going to cherish the fuck out of her, and part of me cherishing her would be me doing filthy things to her body so one day she'd extol the exquisiteness of the predatory man who loved her so hard he did so in both deeds *and* orgasms.

"Sadie's more than a prize. She's everything."

"Proof you can teach an old dog new tricks. I take that to mean you're falling in love with her."

I waited for the wound in my heart to start leaking poison. The toxicity of that word was so ingrained I never thought there would come a time when I could hear it directed at me again. And I never thought I'd ever consider feeling all that word entails—not ever again.

But the toxin didn't spill out and pollute my blood. The nausea didn't come.

"I won't fight against it," I admitted.

"Very well. That's a start. Now open the door like a gentleman. I must get to work."

Thank fuck.

I walked Mrs. S. in, escorted her to the checkout counter, waved to Letty, and got my ass out of there before I was sweet-talked into moving boxes. Though Letty's idea of sweet-talking came in the form of a demand.

When I got back to Treats, I was pleased to see there was still a steady stream of customers even though the morning rush was over.

I made my way to the counter where a very bubbly twenty-something greeted me. "Hey, Reese, Sadie said for you to go on back."

"Thanks."

"No probs."

Probs?

Fuck, I was getting old.

Sadie was basically in the same spot I left her in a few hours before, except there were now fresh-out-of-the-oven cupcakes covering the stainless-steel worktable instead of muffins.

"Those smell good, baby."

"They'll taste better after they're frosted," she said and pushed a naked cupcake my way. "But you can have one now if you want."

I snatched the treat off the table, peeled back the pastel green paper, and took a bite.

Lemon.

My favorite.

I chewed, swallowed, and shoved the rest into my mouth.

Throughout this Sadie watched—eyes dancing, a bright smile on her lips.

Damn, she was gorgeous.

"Good?"

"Delicious."

I didn't miss the way her chin dipped at my compliment or the way her smile got bigger.

"We got a problem, Sadie."

Her smile vanished and her shoulders hunched forward. "What now?"

"Not sure I can find more hours in the day to hit the gym," I started. "Means I'm gonna need an alternate way to burn off the copious calories and sugar I'll be consuming when you bring home the leftovers from your case."

Her lips twitched.

"I think maybe we might be able to come up with an at-home workout plan."

Yeah, we would.

"I got the cameras I need, are you gonna have a problem with me working out front when you have customers? I won't make a mess, but I'll be drilling. Didn't think about it before but if you'd rather I wait, I'll come back later."

Sadie's nose scrunched.

"You care," I muttered. "No worries. Is there a time when you're not busy?"

"Between two and three is usually dead. A few stragglers here and there. But I don't pick up again until after three, then until close is busy again."

The doors were open from seven to six—eleven hours with only one of those hours being slow.

If that motherfucker hadn't taken her money, she'd have no worries.

"I'll be back at two," I told her. "What were you and Mrs. S. talking about?"

To my surprise, Sadie didn't make me work for it.

She told me everything they'd spoken about right down to Mrs. S. scolding her about not telling Letty and Brooklyn.

"She's right about Letty and Brooklyn," I told her.

"I know. I was going to go over to Smutties once I get the cases full for the afternoon rush."

"Good."

Sadie bit her bottom lip and fidgeted with a spatula she was using to scrape the sides of a bowl of what looked like chocolate frosting. Though Sadie didn't do something as simple as plain old chocolate so I knew it would be flavored. From experience, I'd guess raspberry.

"What's on your mind?" I asked.

"She covered my rent," she whispered. "The rent I owed plus six months in advance."

Shit. Maybe that wasn't enough to get her caught up.

"If you still need money, my loan's still on the table. I'll float you whatever you need to get back on your feet."

"It's not that," she whispered. "I should be able to start building back up. I'll talk to her about a payment plan. And really, it was the back rent that was killing me. If I can stretch that out over a few months, make small payments, it will help huge."

"Okay. So what's got you tweaked?"

"Mrs. Simpson paid it."

She said that like it was morally imperative I understood but I wasn't tracking.

"She likes you."

"She more than likes me."

Ah, I got it.

"Yeah, Sadie. She cares about you. So do I. So do Letty and Brooklyn. Rhode, River, Wilson, hell, all the guys. None of us would let you fall. Not individually, not collectively. One way or another we're gonna pull you through this."

That was the wrong thing to say. Or maybe it was the right thing.

Sadie bowed her head and her shoulders trembled in big racking shakes.

I moved around the table, pulled the spatula out of her hand, tossed it on the table, and scooped her up.

By the time I made it to her office, Sadie's face was shoved against my neck, my skin was wet, and she was shuddering.

I spun her office chair around, planted my ass in it, and prayed it didn't collapse under our weight. I gave her a few minutes of silence before I spoke.

"I take it you're finally seeing it."

She nodded her head but didn't speak.

"That's good, baby. Real good."

I waited longer. Then, because she'd opened her eyes to the people around her, I decided to push.

"I want you to think about moving in with me." I felt her body jolt, then she went solid, but I soldiered on. "If you don't want me there, I'll go stay at Asher's place. But I want you at my cabin."

"Reese."

"Don't answer me now, just think about it. You need to save money while you're getting back on your feet. You can stay there a month, three, six, whatever you need."

"Okay, I'll think about it."

Christ.

Mrs. S. was a miracle worker.

"Thank you."

There was another bout of silence. This time I didn't try to fill it. I simply sat in a too-small chair, holding Sadie in my lap, thinking about how good she felt.

How right.

Then I let my mind wander to something Mrs. S. had said.

Our Sadie will not let you down.

I let that wash over me, allowing those words to replace years of cynicism. Not every woman was my ex-wife. Not every woman cheated.

Sadie deserved a clean slate, she shouldn't pay for someone else's mistakes.

Fuck, *we* deserved a clean slate.

Both of us.

Starting new, starting fresh, starting now.

"I need to talk to my parents," she mumbled, misery clear in her tone. "They're not going to be happy I've kept this from them."

I bet they won't be.

Since she hadn't asked a question there was nothing to say so I gave her a squeeze.

"Should I tell them about Josh?"

I couldn't think about how fucking good it felt she was asking my opinion about what to tell her parents or I'd be swept away with emotion. It wasn't because I was asked my opinion; I get asked and give my input daily. But my team asking me about a case and Sadie asking me were two vastly different things.

"No. One thing at a time. Wait to tell them about Josh until I have more information for you to give them. Besides, there's nothing they can do for Josh. He's made his choice."

"Okay." Another beat of silence. "They're gonna be so pissed I didn't tell them sooner."

"Probably. And you're gonna have to give them that. They love you. You've been struggling and they've been living their life in Florida, they're gonna feel some parental guilt for that. They're gonna be upset you didn't give them the opportunity to help you. But in the end, they'll get over it. They'll understand."

She nodded and pushed her forehead deeper into my neck.

"Thank you for listening."

Shot. To. My. Heart.

"Anytime, Sadie, yeah?"

"Yeah."

I dropped my lips to the top of her head and left them there.

Lemon and sugar with a hint of vanilla.

In the quiet of her office, Sadie in my arms, breathing her in, I felt the undeniable connection that had already clicked into place, lock.

Sadie could call this off tomorrow, she could end us before we really had a chance to start and walk away. The thought terrified me. Down to my bones scared the shit out of me. If she left, she'd take a piece of me. A piece that was far bigger than the one the woman I'd married had taken. It wouldn't be my trust she'd shatter—it would be my heart. It wouldn't be my manhood that would take a hit—it would be my soul.

I lied to Mrs. Simpson at least in part. The truth was I wasn't going to fight falling in love with Sadie—I was going to actively pursue it. I was going to drag her along with me until she was in just as deep as I was. Then I'd do what I'd never done before and beg her never to go.

16

"AND THAT'S EVERYTHING," I finished.

"Um..." Letty trailed off and glanced over at Brooklyn.

It was later. I was at Smutties and I'd just given my friends the condensed highlights of the last two years of my life with a heavy emphasis on the last six months. Throughout this neither interrupted, at least not verbally. But their facial expressions had said it all. Both were angry. I wasn't sure if that was directed at me since I hadn't told them what was going on or if they were pissed at Nate. Maybe a mixture of both.

"Oh," I continued. "And Reese asked me to move in with him. Well, not *move in* move in, but move in until I can get on my feet since I'll basically be homeless in a few weeks."

"Basically?" Brooklyn sputtered. "Is there a different shade of homelessness I don't know about? I think it's like being pregnant—you either are or you aren't."

Well, in my case, I could sleep in my office at the bakery so I wouldn't actually be homeless in the sense I'd be sleeping on a park bench, but I would be without a home.

However, with the stink eye Brooklyn was tossing my way I did not explain the difference.

"We'll get to Reese in a minute. Let's go back to Nate and what the fuck?" Letty spat. "What the fuck, Sadie?"

The repeat of "what the fuck" was a clear indication there was no maybe about it; she was pissed at me.

"Letty," Brooklyn murmured.

"No, Brook. Just no." Letty's hand came up, halting her best friend from saying more. "Do you not like us?"

"What?"

"Do you not like us?" she parroted.

My heartbeat quickened to a painful staccato.

"I love you two."

"Then why? If you loved us, the moment, the very *second* you found out that stupid fuck stole your money you would've been over here or on the phone so fast your hair would catch fire."

"I know. I was wrong. I'm sorry. I thought I was doing the right thing trying to fix everything myself. But that wasn't right. I see that now and that's why I'm here."

"Well, fuck a duck." Letty threw her hands in the air. "Now I can't be mad. And I really want to be mad because I'm so freaking hurt you didn't come to us. And now I can't be mad because you apologized."

It wouldn't be a stretch to say that Letty was a tad bit dramatic. Okay, it wasn't a stretch at all, it was just the way it was. She could be over the top about the smallest of things. But this wasn't small, I'd messed up big. Letty and Brooklyn were best friends, sisters of the heart, but that didn't mean they didn't welcome others into their circle. They did. And once you were in, neither of them made you feel like an outsider. Their friendship that had started from practically the womb (their mothers were best friends as were their fathers) didn't overshadow their friendships with other people.

But along with the drama, Letty could hold a mean grudge and it seemed she wasn't going to do that. Relief and guilt mixed together.

"I really am sorry," I whispered. "Everything came bearing down on me and I didn't know what to do so I shut down. I went into survival mode. Then embarrassment set in, and I was so humiliated I didn't want anyone to know. Unfortunately, that wasn't all. Shame turned into stubbornness and when Reese found out and tried to offer me a loan I turned him down—for a week. I was going to lose Treats because I couldn't get over myself. I had a bunch of stupid excuses that were total lies, but I was so scared I was trying to self-sabotage.

"But when Reese told me about Trevor getting involved and then my house was broken into, a new fear took over. The kind that has nothing to do with losing my business. The kind that makes me afraid Trevor will find Nate, make him pay me back, then want some sort of payback from me. So, I accepted his offer in hopes Trevor wouldn't continue to try and solve my money problems. But as I told you, Mrs. Simpson paid my rent, so I don't need the loan."

"But you still want Reese?" Brooklyn asked.

No, I didn't *want* Reese, that wasn't a strong enough word. He was a necessity, a craving, a basic need for survival.

"She wants Reese," Letty answered for me. "It's about time the two of you stopped dancing around each other."

Brooklyn's head bobbed in agreement.

"Right. He was getting grumpy and that's not like Reese. He's the one who's always optimistic. Well..." Brooklyn drew that out then finished, "He always has a positive attitude about work and his friends, but the man has serious issues with women. *Damn.*"

Brooklyn abruptly stopped and slapped her hand over her mouth.

"I know about his ex-wife," I told her. "I also know about his commitment issues. Trust me, they became clear after we had sex in my office and he essentially told me he wanted to have sex again but there would be nothing more."

"You what?" Letty screeched. "You left that part out."

"It wasn't pertinent to the story."

"Like hell it wasn't. That's the whole plot," Letty announced, and I braced from the drama that was sure to spill and Letty didn't disappoint. "Fuck Nate. Fuck him so hard I hope when Reese and the guys find him, they beat him up before they get you back your money. Nate's the villain. Villains suck but they're necessary to the story. But the hero...now, that's where it's at. And Reese, all tall and pretty with just enough issues to make him interesting... that, my good friend, is the real story. So you had sex. When, where, was it good, is he good? Wait, I don't want to know, I have to look at him. Never mind, I wanna know."

I was blinking rapidly, wondering how the topic of conversation had changed so dramatically.

Drama Queen Letty, that was how.

"Good Lord, Lets. Nosy much?" Brooklyn half-heartedly admonished.

"Please, like you don't want to know. I bet he's good. He has to be; no way is God so cruel He'd give Reese all the goods and have him suck in the sack."

"You're going to hell," Brooklyn groaned.

"Don't say that!" Letty fumed. "I'm a good person."

I sat nestled back into the overstuffed bean bag that Letty called a Love Sac. It was so comfortable I could fall asleep in it and wake up the next morning well-rested and ready to take on the day. Though I could also do that in my bed sleeping next to Reese, which I much preferred.

"It wasn't good." I cut into their staredown. Their heads snapped in my direction. "It was in my office in the middle of a fight. I jumped him. It was quick and rough and he's bossy. Super bossy, and I think he's taken lessons on dirty talk. Which, we need to find where those classes are taught and post about them on Facebook, Insta, Twitter, and TikTok. All men should enroll and learn the art of giving women orgasms with words."

Slowly, they turned to look at each other, then after a beat back to me.

"But it wasn't good?" Letty asked disbelievingly.

"In all the words in the English language and others besides, there isn't one to describe what it was. It wasn't good. It wasn't great. It wasn't even life-changing. It was something else. It was me feeling powerful. Beautiful, sexy, desired. It wasn't about sex; it was more than that. It was like I needed to be connected to him in a primitive way or I'd die. I said I jumped him—maybe attacked is a better description. I was pissed and we were arguing and suddenly there was this clarity that I was looking at the man who, I don't know, I was meant to be with. But I couldn't say that so I did the only thing I could do."

"Holy shit," Brooklyn wheezed.

"But then after it was over, the depth of my feelings scared me so bad I told him to leave. And when he told me we'd be doing that again, I denied it and told him we wouldn't. And we haven't. I mean, the sex, that hasn't happened again."

"Are you cray-cray?" Letty asked.

Yes, I was totally crazy.

"I told you my head was messed up."

"But it's straight now?" Letty went on.

"Last night after the break-in I was feeling a little raw and I woke up in the middle of the night. Reese was supposed to be sleeping on the couch, but when I went out to check, he wasn't there, and I panicked. He was just in the bathroom." I waved off Letty's big eyes. "But Reese, he saw it and took me to my room and got into bed with me. He told me he wanted to be more than friends, more than just sex. It took him a little bit to get me to agree, but he promised it wouldn't get messy and I believe him. He didn't say he'd be patient with me but he didn't have to because over the last week he's proven he will. Any rational man would've run a mile, but Reese stuck it out, so how could I not get my head straight?"

"Reese slept in bed with you?" Brooklyn asked, then her eyes darted to Letty.

"Yeah."

"Like, all night?" Letty joined. "He didn't, let's say, climb in, talk to you, then climb out and go back out to the couch to sleep?"

"I'm getting the sense this means something. But you've lost me."

Brooklyn leaned in and with a conspiratorial whisper that she didn't need since we were the only ones in the bookstore, she told me, "Rhode told me that Reese doesn't spend the night."

"Okay."

"No, Sadie, he doesn't spend the night at women's houses, and they don't spend the night at his. Not since he divorced his wife, and that happened in his early twenties and he's now forty-one."

"Reese is forty-one?"

"Focus, Sadie. He spent the night with you."

I was getting it. To them, this was a big deal and I understood why it would be. But for me, it felt natural. Reese didn't belong to those other women. He belonged to me. He was meant to be in my bed.

"He told me this morning he hadn't woken up to a woman in so long he couldn't remember what it felt like, but he'd never forget what it felt like waking up next to me. And he told me that this morning was the first time in a long time he woke up happy."

Brooklyn jumped up so quickly I jolted in surprise. When she was on her feet they started to shuffle in what looked like was supposed to be a dance but instead, it looked like she was having an epileptic event. I wasn't sure if I should laugh or call an ambulance.

"Reese *loves* Sadie," she chanted. "He *loves* her. He wants to *keep* her."

"And everyone says I'm dramatic," Letty huffed and swept her hand in Brooklyn's direction.

I wasn't sure about love. But according to Reese, we were going to find out. Not that I was going to fight it. I was all in to see where a relationship with him would go.

"*Hello*, we haven't discussed me moving in with him," I called out.

"Why would that be a discussion?" Letty asked.

"Because I have to give him an answer."

"The answer," Brooklyn started, "is yes. Hell to the yes. So much *yes* don't let the door hit you on the ass when you move what's left of your shit into his cabin, *yes*."

I couldn't stop my smile.

Not that I tried all that hard.

I'd been scared for nothing. I should've known Letty and Brooklyn wouldn't judge me. They gave me support in whatever form I needed. That was what friendship was about. An ear to listen, advice to be given—or not, depending on what was going on—smiles, celebrations, crazy dances.

I guess I was moving in with Reese.

But I knew that before I'd wandered over to Smutties to convene with my girls.

Their agreement was just icing on the cake.

"I think you're rubbing off on her," I told Letty.

"Tell me about it. The heifer is trying to home in on my act."

The drama that Letty dished out was no act, it was just her.

Which made her one kick-ass mama jamma.

17

IT WAS NEARING two and I had to get back to Treats.

Lunch with Asher had turned into lunch with Asher and Wilson. After that, the three of us went to TJ Gayle's office. He was exactly what Brasco had said—a decent guy who lacked skill. I couldn't say he was decent enough to write a check without grumbling about it, but we left with a five-thousand, one-hundred-and-thirty-dollar check and a promise it would clear.

So there was that.

However, that was where the good ended.

Gayle had looked into Nathan Mallard. He'd found the few things he could, but not a lot. Definitely not five-thousand, one-hundred-and-thirty-dollars' worth.

"The guy's got means and connections," Wilson said and looked up from the bank statement he was going over. "Driver's license, not too hard. Clean social, harder. But Nathan Mallard's got records that would pass a standard employment background check from one of those online places. Either he's got the knowledge, or he knows where to go to find someone who does. And he'd have to have the money to pay before he fucked his next mark. And that doesn't come cheap."

Wilson of course was correct. Mallard had a bank account in his name, his social was clean, so when Sadie had started paying him nothing pinged on that end. Driver's license to match. School records to back up the story he'd given Sadie. Credit history, utilities in his name, lease agreement. A whole life, but it only went back a year.

Asher set down the stack of papers I'd printed from the email that Brasco had sent.

"Detective Winegarner doesn't have much, and not from lack of trying. No one else in the area has reported the same kind of scam. He called every station in the panhandle, police, sheriff, FBI field offices. He hasn't branched out to Washington yet. But he has no leads. A general description from Sadie, the dates the money was withdrawn—"

"The bank." I reached over the table and grabbed one of the statements and continued. "They have cameras."

"Winegarner tried that. Manager wants a warrant," Asher told me.

"Shep doesn't need authorization," I pointed out.

"If you can get him to help you without making you jump through his hoops."

Wilson wasn't wrong. With something like this Shep would be a pain in the ass, and his fee would be a hell of a lot higher than Gayle's.

"I'll email him. We also have the bullshit, creepy-as-fuck resignation letter to dust for prints, but it's been handled so many times I'm not holding out hope. We need a picture of this guy."

"Agreed." Wilson tidied the papers in front of him before he said, "Got a meet with Butch tonight. I'm taking Davis with me. Asher and Cole need to get ready for their trip. Rhode doesn't pull watch anymore. So, tonight, you got Jack sitting in his car in front of Sadie's."

That was something else that had been discussed at lunch; the SOIB decided they wanted to send Asher in. He and Cole were headed to California to set up and get ready in case his application to join Joi was approved. Which Shep had said wouldn't be a problem. The man was scary good at what he did, so if he was giving his guarantee I wouldn't bet against him.

"I don't think I'll need Jack."

Asher barked out a sharp laugh. Wilson smiled. But it was Rhode who spoke from the doorway.

"Heard some things today," he joined. "Got an excited call from my girl. According to her, you've pulled your thumb out."

Sadie had texted me when she left Treats and when she'd returned. However, she didn't tell me the extent of her conversation with her friends. Nor had I planned on asking. Women had shit with their girls that was just between them. It wasn't my business unless Sadie gave it to me, or in this case, Rhode, since his woman had shared with him.

"I thought I already made myself clear where I was at," I returned.

"You did," Rhode confirmed. "Now I got it from Brooklyn, and like I said, she's happy."

"Glad to be of service. Though your woman's always happy, so that's nothing new."

Rhode flashed an arrogant smile. He knew he made his future wife and son exceptionally happy.

"Got Asher and Cole on a flight out of Spokane for tonight. Hotel's set up until the house is ready for them to move in. Should only be a few days. Shep's sending their new identities to Cali. Those will arrive day after tomorrow."

When Rhode was done Wilson looked over at Asher. "Tonight good for you?"

"Yup."

"Did Shep get the list of members?"

"Oh, yeah." Rhode's face lit. "He's sending it now. But he said there were some interesting people on the list. A-list celebs, a few tech giants, wealthy socialites among the ordinary ultra-rich. Fifty thousand a year to join is nothing to sneeze at, but there are extras tacked on to that. Private parties that can run twenty-five thousand for the night or upward of seventy thousand if it's a weekend event. And not all parties take place in Malibu. Paris, New York, Dubai. You know, all the usual spots."

Well, that list would be interesting to go over.

Rhode's gaze came to mine and he went on. "I went over the report from Gayle. The guy's half-moron. There's not much to go on, but damn if he didn't try very hard. I was thinking, and I hope you don't mind, but I asked Shep to get us the security footage from the day Mallard went into the bank to sign the documents to be added to Sadie's account."

One step ahead.

That was typical Rhode.

"We were just discussing that very thing," I told him. "Appreciate you asking. Saves me the hassle."

"Yeah, well, Shep likes me. He said give him a day or two, he's got some other stuff going on that requires his attention."

If waiting meant we'd eventually have answers, then wait I would and I'd do it happily. Besides, if I'd contacted Shep directly and it didn't involve a trafficking case, he'd make me answer a minimum of five stupid riddles that I'd have to ask Cole to solve for me, then Shep would require I send him payment in some new form of cryptocurrency which would also delay getting what I needed. The man prided himself on being a pain in the ass.

My phone chimed with a text. I leaned back to pull it out of my pocket, then engaged the screen.

Sadie.

I read the message then read it a second time before I smiled and looked at Wilson.

"I don't need Jack."

"Damn, brother, you got a way," he returned.

I didn't have any sort of way. What I had was Letty and Brooklyn at my back. I didn't doubt one or both of those women urged her to take me up on my offer.

"The girl posse," I remarked then added, "And that posse now includes Mrs. S, and she can be persuasive."

"Tell me about it," Rhode muttered. "Last week she made me, and I mean, *made me*—I had no choice in the matter if I wanted to live—read about a cold case of two missing teenagers who disappeared twenty years ago. The case is from Florida. I'm not sure what she thought I was going to do, but you better believe my ass sat in Letty's office and I read the article she had pulled up."

"At least she didn't speak to you about penises and insinuate her husband took her like a pillaging Viking. So, I'd say you got off damn easy."

"Fuck yeah, I did. I'd ask if you were serious but I do not want to know why Mrs. S was talking about..." Rhode trailed off and made a disgusted face.

"Seeing as Mrs. S was banging on Letty's door while River was banging on something else, asking if everything was okay, I'd say River wins," Asher chided.

Hell, yes, River won.

Hands down.

"Forgot about that. Remind me to bring it up the next time we get together for a poker night." Rhode laughed.

I glanced down at my watch and noticed I was running late.

"Gotta get back to Treats," I said and stood.

"You mean, you gotta get back to Sadie," Asher corrected.

"That, too."

"Mind if I head over with you? I want to grab the letter Mallard gave her. I'll dust it while you're installing her new cameras."

"Don't mind at all."

I started for the door then stopped.

"If I don't see you before you leave, have a good trip and don't get used to sunny SoCal weather."

"It's not the weather I'm worried I'll get used to." Asher wagged his eyebrows and smiled. "All those tanned, toned bodies, makes a man believe—"

"In plastic surgery," Rhode cut in.

"Nothing wrong with a nip and tuck here and there," Asher drawled.

"Right. Be safe out there."

"Always."

With Wilson following, I continued out of the office thinking about Sadie's text. Short and to the point.

I'd like to move in. Thank you for the offer.

18

I WAS PACING MY OFFICE. I should've been filing the invoices I'd just finished paying but I was too nervous.

I sent Reese a text fifteen minutes ago telling him I was going to move in, and I hadn't heard back.

Maybe I should've waited until he came back and told him face-to-face. The problem with that was I was equal parts excited and anxious. The excited part was obvious, I was going to be staying with Reese. This meant lots of time to get to know him. Lots of time being spent together. The anxious part was much of the same reason I was excited— lots of time spent getting to know each other. Only, he'd be getting to know me better, and what if he didn't like what he found? Oh, and there was a healthy dose of worry that I would forget the move was temporary, just until I got back on my feet, and I would get too comfortable. Then when it was time for me to move, it would be awkward, possibly because I would be so comfortable and want to stay living with him so badly, I'd overstay my welcome.

God, that would be embarrassing.

There was a knock at my door. I turned but didn't get a

chance to open it before Reese walked in. He didn't slow his stride as he closed the space between us. Not that there was much of it, my office wasn't that big. But when he got to me, he didn't stop either. One hand lifted, curled around the side of my neck, and the pads of his fingers dug in as he yanked me to him. His other arm went around my back, then up and diagonal until I was anchored to him.

All of this shocked me.

All of it was sexy as hell, especially the neck grab.

But I didn't get a chance to luxuriate in the feel of him manhandling me. Nor did I get a chance to think about why I liked Reese doing it but if another man tried it, I'd kick him in the balls hard enough to ensure children were not in his future.

Reese's mouth came down on mine, mine automatically opened, and our tongues met.

This kiss was not like our first. It was nowhere near last night's. It wasn't frantic but it was borderline desperate. The kiss was meant to convey something, and Reese was desperately trying to convey it. There were no dueling tongues—there was no battle or struggle for dominance. Reese took control and he guided the kiss to deep and wet while managing to keep it sweet. He tasted good, his hard body felt good pressed against mine, and both of those were made better when he growled.

Good Lord Almighty.

I was on the verge of attacking him again when he broke the kiss and rested his forehead against mine.

"Fucking hell, Sadie."

I felt my smile form and I allowed it to get bigger, hoping he wouldn't see it.

"Pleased with yourself, are you?"

Maybe I should've been ashamed of myself for letting

his out-of-breath-turned-on panting go to my head, but I was not. And suddenly I understood why he was so arrogant when he knew he did something that made me want to squeeze my thighs together.

"That was a good kiss," I explained.

"No, baby, that was all you."

Well, if he wanted to think that, I wasn't going to argue.

"Thank you," he whispered.

"You kissed me. I should be thanking you."

"Thank you for saying yes and moving in with me."

I couldn't stop that fluttery feeling I got in my belly from flickering to life.

"I'm the one who should be thanking you for that, too. You're doing me a favor letting me stay with you."

Reese pulled back and stood to his full height, which meant I had to tip my head back to look him in the eyes.

Green and brown merged together into the most complex shade I'd ever seen.

"You're not staying with me."

His statement came out rough and scratchy.

"I thought you offered to let me move in."

"Yes, move in. You're *moving in*, Sadie."

I was confused. Whether it was from our kiss, or from staring into his eyes which never failed to dazzle me senseless, I was lost.

"Okay," I slowly said. "I'm moving in."

"Right." He dropped a closed-mouth kiss on my lips and told me, "Wilson's here to pick up the letter Mallard gave you."

Wait. That was it?

Just "right," then we move on? I wasn't well-versed in caveman, but Reese's "right" sounded an awful lot like a decision had been made. The problem was, I didn't know what we were deciding.

"What does *right* mean?"

"What?"

"I said I was moving in and you said *right*," I explained. "What does that mean?"

"It means you're moving in."

At that juncture I was so thoroughly perplexed I decided to drop it.

"The letter's in the safe. I'll get it for him."

Reese nodded then glanced around my office. When his gaze landed back on me, I noticed his smirk.

"Don't you have cameras to install?" I asked.

"Yup."

"I think before we have sex in my office—the sequel, you should get on that. And you know the original's always better."

"Wouldn't be a sequel. It'd be the prequel to a brand-new book, with unwritten chapters, and an unknown story-line. But mark this, baby, it'll be an action-adventure, and the ending will have a twist you never saw coming."

With that, he walked out.

Did he just say that?

Unwritten chapters?

Unknown storyline?

A twist I never saw coming?

I think I swooned.

I wasn't sure, I'd never done it before, but I think it just happened.

Just to be sure, I'd ask Letty. She'd know.

———

"PACK MORE," Reese instructed from the bed.

My bed, where he was sitting as I packed a bag to go to his house.

After I'd given Wilson the letter and Reese had finished installing the new cameras—with Wilson's help they were done in less than thirty minutes—we had discussed coming to my place after I closed. First, because someone was coming over to pick up the furniture they'd purchased. An added bonus of Reese coming to my place to help me pack—which apparently really meant oversee and boss—he helped me carry the bedframe and bigger dresser out to the garage. Not that it mattered all that much if strangers came into my house since I'd no longer be living there—as of tonight. I'd reminded Reese I had three weeks until my notice was up. He reminded me I didn't have an alarm. It must be said, I was over the word *alarm*. But more I was over thinking about why I needed it.

Freaking Josh.

And speaking of Josh, I hadn't heard from him. I also hadn't heard any motorcycles driving down the street in front of Treats or seen any Horsemen. But according to Reese *and* Wilson, that didn't mean anything. As mean and criminal and stupid Trevor was, they communicated then hammered home he wasn't stupid in the sense he was dumb. He was a criminal, had been one for years and was walking the streets free, thus not stupid.

So I was moving into Reese's cabin immediately.

But he lived fifteen minutes away in Hayden, not in another state, so I didn't understand why I needed to pack more. I still had to come back and move the rest of my belongings into storage. Thankfully, I had a friend who was going to let me put my minimal stuff into their unit, so the rent wouldn't be too bad.

I still needed to save and get back on track.

"Reese, I only own three suitcases."

"Do you have trash bags?"

I poked my head out of the closet and gave him my best "what the hell are you talking about" scowl. Then just in case he wasn't clear that his suggestion was boneheaded I told him, "I am not putting my clothes in trash bags. I'm not fleeing the country. I'm moving."

"Fine."

Fine?

He was giving in that easily?

I didn't ask.

I moved on, coming out of the closet with the last of my t-shirts that I'd be able to fit into the third suitcase—*if* I sat on it and Reese zipped.

I tossed them on top of the neatly-folded jeans and looked over at Reese.

"Everything okay?"

"I don't like being here."

Welp. That was honest. It was also harsh.

"What?"

"No, I *hate* being here."

"That's kinda—"

"I look around and see this room empty. Your guest room, your dining room, empty. And I know why they are, and I hate why. I hate looking around knowing you were in a position where you had to sell your stuff. It fucking guts me. I fucking hate it so bad it burns my chest. But I admire the fuck out of you that you are all that you are. That you are the kind of person who does whatever needs to be done. Love that about you, Sadie. But it doesn't quell that burn. So, no, everything's not okay. But at the same time, it is because I know you're gonna be okay. And not because

Mrs. S paid your rent or you're moving in with me. One way or another, you would be okay because *you* would make that happen."

I thought he was done so I started to say something but stopped when he continued.

"And everything's not okay because I want to be the one who makes everything okay for you. I want to be the one who you need. And that's not you. You don't need me to do a damn thing for you and I don't know what to do with that."

I loved he thought that. I loved it so much my breath whooshed out and I was left speechless.

Reese sat on my bed, such as it was nothing more than a box spring and mattress on one of those metal frames, since the fancy bedroom set was the first thing I'd sold. It was only a few years old and since I'd taken good care of it, I sold it for almost what I'd paid for it.

When I was done taking in his grumpy pout I glanced around the room. It was most assuredly empty. No dressers, no nightstands, no lamps. Just that box spring and mattress, my suitcases on the floor, and Reese.

"It's just stuff," I started. "And before you say anything, no, it didn't feel good to have to sell it. But it's stuff. One day, I'll be back on my feet, and I'll buy more *stuff*. And I like that you think that I don't *need* you. But you're thinking about it all wrong, Reese. I might not need you to fix me or my problems. Though it's important to note, you are. If it wasn't for you, in a few weeks I would've been sleeping in my office. But I do need you for all the important stuff. The stuff that matters."

Reese held my eyes and I hoped I was giving him what he needed. Even though I wasn't entirely sure what that was. I was not a doormat. I didn't ever want to need a man in the sense that I had to rely on him to make me whole or fix things. I wanted to enter a relationship on equal footing and remain there. That wasn't to say, I wasn't so naïve I didn't know there were times when compromise came into play and the other person might get more of what they wanted. But it was vitally important to me that I bring just as much to the table as the other person. Because there would come a time when I'd have to be the one to step up and be the strong one. And I couldn't be the sort of woman who let her man down thinking it was his "job" to always be the rock.

And the longer Reese was quiet the more I started to get worried he was the type of man who needed a woman to need him in ways I was not capable of.

"You said you didn't want me to get lost in you," I reminded him and hated how weak my voice sounded.

"I don't." Reese surged to his feet, skirted the suitcases, and stopped in front of me. "I want you exactly as you are," he confirmed.

Relief swept in but I was still unsure.

"Then why is everything not okay?"

"Because I'm not used to this. I've never been with a woman who is so damn strong and impressive and resourceful. I spent my relationship, then my marriage, breaking my back trying to accomplish the impossible feat of making an insecure, miserable woman happy. The only part of that relationship that made sense to me was that she needed me. You don't. My marriage failed. I spent years blaming myself. Then I spent years letting her fuck with my head when she wasn't even part of my life. I met you and honest to God, my eyes opened. You are the opposite of her in every way and I feel so much for you, instead of letting those feelings take root I fight them. Not because I don't want you, but now I'm back to blaming myself. How in the fuck could I have been so blind and stupid to marry that woman? It is an uncomfortable realization when a man has to face how badly he fucked up."

I was rejoicing in the fact Reese thought I was the opposite of his ex-wife. I didn't want to bear any resemblance to the type of woman she was.

"Why would you go back to blaming yourself?"

"Because she wasn't you."

Thank God for that.

"No, she's not me. But I still don't get it."

"Sadie, she is not *you*. She was never meant to be the woman to stand at my side. First, because she doesn't know how to be at a man's side, she needs to be on his back like a lead fucking weight because she's too weak to *stand*. But more importantly, she was not *you*."

Was he saying he thought I was the woman who was meant to stand at his side?

"Now you're getting it," he said softly.

"I don't think I am."

I didn't want to get my hopes up only to have them crash and burn in a fiery ball of hell.

"Baby, you are. I just saw it happen. The moment you understood exactly what I'm telling you. And my fuck-up was not blaming myself, hell it wasn't even marrying that leech. It was thinking that my manhood had something to do with the woman in my life needing me to fix her. Mixing up what love is. Thinking that love is a *because* when it's really a *regardless of*."

"A regardless of?"

"I'm not falling in love with you *because* of the way you make me feel, that's selfish. Life's life and one day shit's gonna get tough and when it does all those becauses have to mean something. And I need you to fall in love with me regardless of shortcomings, regardless that one day I might need you in a way that's gonna feel heavy, but you'll stick with me, regardless of the hard times or the easy times or arguments and fights. I'm falling in love with you knowing that the becauses are really, *regardless ofs*. So there's my fuck-up, thinking my whole life that love was selfish, not understanding that when the right woman, the one who was meant to be there, you love each other regardless of anything that's thrown in your path."

When he stopped speaking, I didn't need to phone Letty to ask her what it felt like to swoon. I knew I was well beyond that. I didn't feel faint and lightheaded. I felt stronger than I'd ever felt in my life. I felt like I could jump off a skyscraper and fly. And since I'd been inching toward the edge since the first day I'd met Reese, I decided it was time to jump. Not off a tall building but into the unknown. Into the chapters of our story that had not been written yet but would be an action-adventure with a twist. I trusted that whatever that twist was, Reese would make it good. He wouldn't catch me as I fell—he knew I didn't need that—he'd just fall by my side.

"Will you please kiss me?" I asked.

"No."

"No?"

"If I kiss you then I'm gonna want to fuck you. And for the five millionth time, the next time I have you I want to take my time. I also have retribution to dish out, meaning the time I was going to take has doubled."

That made fire tick up my back and wetness flood my panties.

"Then why are we still standing here?"

"Babe."

"Don't babe me. Snap, snap, get to work zipping up that case, and start hauling them out."

"You're bossy when you're horny."

I scrunched my nose and shook my head.

"Don't say that word, it's gross."

"Horny?"

"Ugh. Yes. It sounds like something that would be said in a bad eighties' porn."

Reese smiled and narrowed his eyes.

"There's nothing bad about eighties' porn, Sadie. Though, I'd like to know how much of it you've watched."

"Enough. And the eighties were not kind to women. I mean, leg warmers and teased-out hair while getting...you know."

Reese's smile went electric. It was so hot I was worried he was right; I was horny.

Gah!

"I'll give you the leg warmers, but the big hair? Sexy. Women in the eighties were women. Real, unaltered women."

"Thank God you don't have a leg warmer fetish—"

If I was going to say more, I didn't get it out. Reese slammed his mouth down onto mine and kissed me. The best part? He was laughing while he did.

19

"*REESE,*" Sadie groaned.

My hands on the inside of her thighs pushed, rolling her ass off the bed, my lips pulled off her clit, and my tongue speared inside her pussy.

"Reese!"

That was a frustrated growl. She was close. Had been for the last ten minutes but every time I heard the hitch in her voice I pulled back.

Even if I wasn't exacting revenge for the t-shirt, I wouldn't have let her come. She tasted too fucking good. She felt too good. She sounded like a wet dream, moaning and groaning with every lick and suck. And she looked like a fantasy come to life naked in my bed.

After our first encounter ended with her calling herself a slut—and it must be noted I seriously fucking hated that word—I was a little worried I'd have to take some time coaxing her out of her shell. That was not the case. She stripped out of her clothes, climbed onto my bed, and waited for me to join her.

No hang-ups about her nudity.

She did not hide her reaction to me. Her eyes blatantly roamed my body. She took her time taking her fill and she did it with lust-filled eyes and a smirk.

No hang-ups with my nudity.

When I told her to spread her legs, she spread them. When I'd crawled between her legs, my intentions clear, she spread them farther. When I took my time kissing the inside of her thighs, she squirmed. When I'd taken more time than she liked, she begged. And when my mouth made it to her center, she was dripping wet.

In other words, I could spend all night eating her pussy, edging her to orgasm, and pulling back, only to start all over again.

I heard her phone ringing from somewhere downstairs, ignored it, and swirled my tongue around her opening, lapping up more of her excitement.

"I'm gonna die," she panted.

I felt her hand slide into my hair until she had a fistful. Her other hand went between her legs and she started working her clit.

Hot as fuck.

"Oh, God."

I gave her a few moments, mainly because I seriously got off knowing she had no issue playing with herself while my tongue was in her pussy. Either she was so far gone, reaching for an orgasm I'd denied her for the last half hour, or this was just her—hot and wild with no hesitations. Whichever was fine with me.

The ringing finally stopped and the only sounds that filled my small cabin were her moans. She was close again. Her thighs tensed, her hand in my hair held me where she wanted, and she ground her pussy into my face.

It was time.

I lifted my head, glanced up, and nearly shot off at the sight. Sadie's head was tipped back, her breasts that were too big to be perky were trapped between the insides of her arms, her nipples were pebbled, her knees high and wide.

"Move your hand."

She kept at her clit.

"Sadie. Move your hand."

She slowly righted her head, then equally slowly opened her eyes. Oh, yeah, she was gone.

And damn beautiful.

"My turn, baby. Move your hand, I want at your clit."

Her hand moved and a sluggish smile tugged at her lips.

I now understood the meaning of premature ejaculation. I was dangerously close to coming on the sheets. From a smile and the taste of her on my tongue.

Her phone started ringing again, and again I ignored it when I lowered my head and wrapped my lips around her clit.

All it took was a few flicks of my tongue. Her legs tensed and her hips jerked.

I continued to give her my tongue until some of the tension ebbed, then I could wait no more.

I surged up. Her hand fell away, I moved beside her, rolled to my back, and tagged a condom off the nightstand. I had that fucker rolled on in record time. Rolling again, I plucked her out of the bed and pulled her over me.

"Sit up, Sadie."

"Hmm."

"Up, baby, ride me."

Her head lifted off my chest, but she didn't sit up.

"Can I kiss you first?"

"I taste of you."

She seemed to contemplate that for a moment before

she shrugged the best she could considering her position on top of me.

"I've never tasted myself."

Why the hell did that turn me on so damn much?

"Then kiss me but do it climbing on."

The wicked smile she gave me contrasted with the soft, serene look in her eyes.

"In a hurry?"

"I'm not, but you should be. Last chance to climb on."

"And if I don't?"

Fuck. She was killing me.

"If you don't then I'm flipping you over and taking control. I'm giving you this so you control the pace. You wanna play, we'll play. But warning, Sadie, your pussy in my mouth, listening to you for the last half hour was so goddamn hot, I'm not gonna be able to hold back."

"That doesn't sound—"

"Sadie!" I growled and she moved.

Her lips came to mine and they didn't disconnect as she adjusted herself over my lap. I let her take what she wanted how she wanted it. If she changed her mind about kissing me, I wasn't going to push it. But when she groaned as she slid her tongue against mine, I knew she not only didn't mind, but she liked it.

I broke the kiss to order, "Reach down and put me in."

I felt her fingers graze my shaft, not tentatively, not shyly. Not my Sadie. She wrapped her hand around my cock and started to jerk.

"You wanna give me a hand job later, I'm game. Right now, you need to stop jacking me off and line me up."

Thank fuck she did what I asked.

I fisted the sheets in an effort not to grab her hips and

slam her down when the head of my cock slid in, and she took only a few inches.

"You're in control, Sadie. As hard and fast as you wanna go. But, honey, I need you to move."

"Maybe you should be on top."

That was the first time since we'd gotten into bed that I heard uncertainty in her voice.

My hands came off the bed, went to her thighs, and with more control than I knew I possessed, I slowly moved them up to her hips.

"I want you on top. Whatever you do will feel good. Can you take more of me?"

Sadie nodded and slid me in a little more.

Jesus.

Even through the latex, her pussy was hot. I had to force myself to stay still and let her go at her speed.

She lifted up, glided back down, still not taking me fully, then back up until she just had the tip.

Now it was my turn to bang on death's door. She was going to kill me. I was using all of my concentration trying not to blow or alternately not flipping her over, so I was not prepared when she dropped down fast and hard, taking all of me.

"*Fuck.*"

Sadie's hips swiveled and her tongue plunged into my mouth.

The uncertainty was gone.

There was no more hesitation as she fucked my mouth and my cock.

She rode me hard. She rocked and bounced and ground down. All I could do was hold on for the ride. She was totally in control—not something I normally enjoyed or allowed—but with Sadie, I fucking loved it. Loved how she was getting off, moaning louder, taking what she wanted, not giving a fuck about anything but what her body needed.

She wrenched her mouth off mine, sat up, and fucked me harder.

"Lean back more. Put your hands behind you on my thighs."

"Reese, *baby*," she groaned.

Baby.

Fucking hell. That was the first time she'd called me anything but my name. And I wasn't sure which I liked better—her moaning *Reese* or a breathy *baby*.

"I got you."

My hands left her hips. One snaked between her legs, the other cupped her tit, and I rolled her nipple between my finger and thumb.

"Harder," she begged.

I added more pressure to her nipple and rubbed her clit faster.

Her head dropped forward, her eyes closed, and she stopped sliding up and down and started rocking faster.

Good Christ.

Hot, wet, snug pussy hugging my cock.

Tits swaying, strong, thick thighs cradling my lap, beautiful brown hair spilling around her shoulders.

I could take no more.

"I'm gonna come, Sadie."

Her eyes shot open, she looked at me from under her lashes, and her fingernails dug into my thighs.

Those blue eyes were dark with lust, but there was something else and I hoped it was what I thought. I was not a man who needed the words, I love you. Words were empty. But what I saw shining in her eyes was not. And I needed her to see the same in me. I needed her to know that even though I might not say those words to her, I felt them.

My ass clenched, my muscles tensed, my world narrowed to my cock, and I blew into the condom. The only thought I was capable of was taking her with me. My fingers tightened around her nipple, my thumb at her clit worked faster until with a final roll of her hips, her pussy spasmed.

Neither of us made a sound. Our gazes remained locked as the pleasure of our releases washed over us. No moans, no groans, no words. In the silence, a thousand emotions were exchanged. Everything that needed to be acknowledged was now branded. It was blistered onto my heart. The scar would remain long after my death. A mark I would wear for all of eternity. Knowing that, the enormity of what that meant didn't scare me. The significance of it soothing. After years of being aimless, my life was set back to right.

I had not yet recovered from my orgasm when my phone started ringing. I hadn't come to terms with what we'd shared when the shrill sound yanked me from a dream-like state to the harsh reality of my job.

"Fuck," I grunted. "I would not move if I didn't have to. That's Wilson's ringtone, so I gotta get it."

Sadie slowly slid up, taking her time before she lost me.

Fuck, but I liked that.

But I liked the softness in her eyes and the low, nearly inaudible moan that accompanied a look that said she hated that I had to get up as much as I did.

Whatever Wilson had to say, better be good.

She swung her leg over, dropped to her hip, and curled on her side. I leaned over and gave her a quick kiss before I rolled the other way and got out of bed.

By the time I was finished in the bathroom my phone

had stopped ringing. I was halfway down the stairs when it started again.

This meant I quickened my step.

I found my phone in the kitchen where I'd left it after tossing our dirty dinner dishes in the sink before I carried Sadie up to the loft.

I answered the call just before it went to voice mail.

"What's going on?"

Wilson didn't bother with pleasantries, he launched right in.

"Sadie's house was broken into again."

The first vestiges of anger seeped in.

"Say again?"

"Neighbor was coming home, saw someone looking in her front window. Didn't like what he was doing so he called it in. Cops rolled out. When no one answered their knock, they did a walk around. Found a window broken and called in a possible break-in, found out who lived at the address, tried calling her. Since she didn't answer and Brasco had been asking about Sadie Pierce, they called him. He called me, I told him Sadie was safe with you. I met the cops on scene and let myself into her house. Place has been ransacked. As much as a mostly empty house can be, anyway. Boxes in the closets opened, the contents dumped on the floor. But someone was in here looking for something."

Traces of anger were a thing of the past.

I was fuming, fucking *pissed*.

"Did the neighbor give a description?"

"No. It's dark as fuck around her house. All they saw was someone looking in a window."

My jaw clenched and I had to remind myself she was no longer living there. And if she ever thought to move out of my cabin, her next house was going to be lit like a mother-fucker. Moose be damned.

I heard Sadie padding down the steps and my irritation grew.

One more fucking thing for her to deal with.

"Do the cops need her to come there?"

Her sharp inhale made me turn to face her.

Gone were the soft, sated eyes.

Stress and fear were back and that pissed me off more.

"No. Brasco said he'd meet her here tomorrow."

She mouthed the word "Josh" and I shook my head.

"Hold on, Wilson, Sadie just got up."

It was cute as fuck the way her eyes narrowed but not enough to cut through the frustration.

"No easy way to tell you so I'm gonna say it and remind you that a few hours ago, you rightly set my ass straight about stuff being stuff." She nodded so I continued. "Someone broke into your house. Wilson's there now. Obviously, he can't know if something's stolen so tomorrow after work, we're gonna met Detective Brasco there and he'll take your statement."

She just stared at me with wide eyes. No other reaction. Her body didn't grow tense, her shoulders didn't sag, she almost looked like she was indifferent.

"Sadie?"

"Why would someone break into my house two nights in a row?"

"Don't have an answer to that."

"Do you think Josh would come back? He already took the money. Which meant he was in my house and saw that there wasn't anything of value to steal. I mean, is the TV still on the wall? That's the only thing in there that's worth anything. I don't even have a computer at the house."

That was a good fucking question.

"The neighbor didn't report seeing a motorcycle," Wilson said in my ear, obviously hearing Sadie's question. "But I'll go over there and ask before I leave. And the TV's still on the wall."

"TV's on the wall," I relayed. "Has Josh ever asked you to store something for him?"

"No."

"What do you keep in the boxes?"

"Boxes?"

"Hang on," I told them both. I pulled the phone from my ear and put it on speaker. "Wilson, where are the boxes?"

"Guest bedroom and garage."

Sadie scowled and her head twitched.

"Nothing worth anything to anyone but me. High school yearbooks and trophies were in the garage. I think my cap and gown from graduation was in one of the boxes. Old pictures of friends, family. Literally nothing of value. In the guest bedroom, I stored old CDs and DVDs." She paused to think then went on. "I think there are photo albums in there. Books. Knickknacks from the shelving unit that used to be in my living room. But again, nothing worth anything. In the last few months, anything that was worth any money was sold."

Fucking hell.

"Those people come to your house?"

"Yeah."

Jesus.

"Where'd you sell the stuff?" Wilson asked.

"Market Place, Craigslist, and there's a local CDA website I posted on."

Not good.

"And they came to your house to pick up the stuff?"

At Wilson's question, she jolted. The first sign that she understood the danger she possibly put herself in.

"Well, yes and no. They came to the house but never into the house, just the garage. And when someone came over, even if it was just a woman, I wore a fake wedding ring. And I made sure to talk about my husband."

At least there was that.

"What about the furniture? No one came inside to move it?" Wilson pushed.

"No. My friend Joey helped me move it into the garage. Actually, he was there once when a couple came to pick up my bedroom furniture and helped them load it onto the trailer."

"Joseph Bramble?"

"Yeah."

"That's the neighbor who called the police," Wilson announced.

"He would. He and his wife are good people."

"Anything else stored in those boxes?" I asked.

"Not that I can remember."

"What about jewelry? Anything special that you didn't sell?" I went on.

"No. I'm not a jewelry person. And the fake wedding ring I wore was a gold band I bought at Walmart."

I hated what I had to ask next, despised it down to my core, but I had to know.

"What about Nate? Did he leave stuff at your house?"

"No."

"Nothing?"

"No, Reese, nothing."

The part of me that was Sadie's man liked that answer. The investigator side of me wished he'd left a toothbrush.

And it was that side of me that was pissed at myself for not thinking about it earlier.

"Now that we're on that topic," Wilson said, "what about at the bakery? Did he leave anything there?"

"Like what?"

"Anything," I told her. "A t-shirt, a toothbrush, a comb, anything."

Sadie looked startled for a moment then she slowly started to nod.

"Actually, yes. He had this leather case. It has a tooth-brush, comb, and razor in it. I forgot about it."

"Where is it?" Wilson clipped and Sadie stiffened.

"At the bakery, under the sink where he left it."

I moved around the two-seater dining room table that separated us and tagged her around the waist, bringing her flush to my side. Her arms wrapped around me and she held on.

"We'll get it in the morning," I told her.

She nodded against my chest and nuzzled in.

For a smart man, sometimes I was dumb as fuck. I shouldn't have waited to hold her. Now that I was, I felt the slight tremble in her body and Mrs. Simpson's warning came rushing back.

Strong men need stronger women. But do not forget there is a fragility that needs to be cared for.

Sadie was so strong, and I had to look so hard to find the fragility it was easy to overlook it.

Yeah, I was a dumb fuck.

"I'll meet you there," Wilson told me. "Cops are dusting now. I already sent the prints out I pulled off the letter but those will be a few days. Tomorrow we'll see if we can get DNA from the kit Mallard left behind. In the meantime, I think you should work from Sadie's office."

It was good my boss thought that, since I was going to tell him that was what was going to happen.

"Appreciate it. I'll stop by the office in the morning and get what I need before we meet you at the bakery."

"What time should I tell Brasco you'll be at the house?"

I tipped my head down to look at Sadie but she was burrowed in and I couldn't see her face.

"Sadie?"

"Six-thirty," she mumbled.

"Done."

With that, Wilson disconnected.

I waited for her smart-ass comment about Wilson hanging up without saying goodbye.

It never came.

"Let's go back to bed."

She let go and stepped back. I followed her up the stairs, watched her climb into bed, then I turned off the light and did the same.

Before I could shift her into me, she rolled and rested her head on my chest.

"Wanna talk about it?" I asked her.

"No."

"If something's scaring you or bothering you, it's best to get it out."

"I'm not scared, and it sucks someone went through my stuff, but I wasn't there so it really doesn't matter."

"It does suck, it's a huge invasion of your privacy. Don't let—"

"Reese, I'm fine. Totally fine. I'm here with you safe and I know you'll keep me that way. So what if someone found my high school yearbooks and DVD collection? It's not like I was hiding something super-secret or someone found a box of kinky sex toys and porn. At most they now know I have an addiction to spicy romance novels and I'm a packrat who still has DVDs even though all the movies I own are now on Netflix and Hulu. What do I care? *It's stuff.*"

I'd pretty much stopped paying attention to what she was saying after she said she was safe and she knew I'd keep her that way.

Maybe from her, I needed the words. Or more to the point, I needed to say them to her because I love you was on the tip of my tongue.

I didn't say it.

But I hoped she understood what I was saying when my hand went under her chin and I tipped it back to kiss her. With every glide of my tongue, every soft touch of my lips, I was saying the words that I wasn't ready to verbalize. It was not the type of kiss that was the prelude to sex, it was slow and gentle, and never in my life had I shared a better kiss.

When we broke apart and she snuggled in deeper I knew she felt the unspoken words.

"I told you I needed you for the important things."

I had nothing to say to that but there was a lot to feel.

So many emotions were coursing through me they were ripping me apart—tearing at the muscle, slicing the scar tissue, feeding, repairing, putting me back together.

Everything all at once.

Another *because* that was really a *regardless of*.

20

"DOES he really have to be here?" Letty asked.

I was behind the counter, the morning rush was over, and Letty had come in under the guise of needing coffee before she opened. She didn't know about my second break-in in two days—I mean, who does that happen to? So I knew her complaint was because she wanted details on my first night living with Reese, and with him sitting in the bakery, even tucked into the back corner, she couldn't ask what she really wanted to ask.

That was why I leaned in close, lowered my voice, and gave her what she wanted so I could give her what I needed.

"Last night was the best night of my life and it had nothing to do with the sex. Though that was spectacular. Something kinda clicked, for both of us. He'd already been honest with me and told me he wanted us to take a shot at being more. I'd already committed to doing that. So it wasn't that. It was bigger. It sounds silly and dramatic, but it doesn't make it any less true. I could feel his thoughts, like he was willing me so hard to hear them and I did. I tried to do the same. I'm not ready to say the L-word. Hell, I don't think I want to ever say it again. But with Reese I don't have to say it or hear it—I feel it. And to me, that's all that's important."

"Yeah, Sadie, that's all that's important," Letty softly said.

"I feel a little crazy," I admitted.

"Crazy's relative." She smiled. "Crazy in love, even if you can't say it, is a far cry from crazy around the bend stab someone."

"Funny you should say that. My house was broken into *again*. So this morning I'm feeling both kinds of crazy. Not that I'd actually stab someone but I'm seriously thinking about it."

"What?" Letty shrieked.

I glanced to the back corner and found Reese staring at us.

"Shh. I think people in Bonners Ferry heard you."

Thankfully, Kat was on her fifteen-minute break and she was in my office enjoying some downtime after being slammed for three solid hours.

"I don't give a rat's rear end who hears me. Someone broke in? What'd they steal?"

That was something I'd been thinking about all morning and I still couldn't think of anything worth risking breaking in for.

"I don't know. I haven't been there yet. But honestly, I didn't catalog my DVDs and CDs. So unless my Maroon 5 CD is gone or my *Fast & Furious* one through nine are gone I probably wouldn't remember. I've lived in that house three years and I've never heard of any of my neighbor's houses getting broken into, but mine's down twice in two days. I hate to say it, but I think it was Josh looking for money or something he could hawk."

Letty flinched and I wished I would've kept my trap shut about my brother. The bad-news sibling connection hit close to the bone with her—as in straight into the marrow. Though, her sister ended up being a hero, mine was applying to be a bigger shithead than he already was. That was what prospecting was, applying to be part of a criminal gang.

Who did that?

Josh Pierce, that was who.

Or I suppose I should start referring to him as Grinder.

Gag!

"I can't believe he's part of the Horsemen," she mumbled.

"You and me both. He's never been right. But this is a whole new level of bad."

"Wait a minute," Letty drawled. "Does River know about this?"

Oh, shit.

"Probably not. It happened last night late."

Letty's eyes narrowed and I made an effort to do some damage control.

"Seriously, Letty, it was late. I'm sure he didn't find out until he went into work today and he loves you so he wouldn't call you to tell you your friend's house got broken into again. He'd wait until he could swing by Smutties and tell you face-to-face, so he'd be there in case you needed him. And remember, I wasn't even there so it doesn't matter. I'm just telling you because I needed to vent about it, not because I'm worried. Reese is handling it. Well, Reese and Wilson. The only reason why he's even taking me over there tonight is to see if I can note anything that's missing. Like I told Reese last night, I'm not scared, and it might sound strange, but I don't care. Hell, I spent months selling all my shit. It's like I've totally detached from stuff."

Some of the peeved look left her eyes but she was still cautious when she asked, "You're really all right?"

Thankfully, she'd dropped the topic of River.

"Yep. Totally fine. Oh, and in other news, which I'm thinking of as a silver lining, is last night while Reese and Wilson were asking me questions about the break-in, it led to them asking me if Nate had stored or left anything at my house, which led me to remember he'd left a case under the sink in the bathroom here that had a toothbrush and razor in it. Reese is hoping he used one or both and they can pull DNA. I feel stupid I forgot but it could be the break they need to find him. Though I'm not sure what good that will do. I did put—"

"Stop. Don't go down that road. It doesn't matter if you added him to your account, that doesn't give him the right to empty those accounts. And what will happen when the guys find him is he'll be walking with a limp as they escort him into the police station."

Oh, yeah, my friend was still so mad that she was imagining Reese and the guys breaking his legs.

Glad I wasn't the only one.

"And now you're caught up on my drama. What's new in *Casa de Kent*?"

"River is getting impatient and says if Brooklyn and Rhode don't get married in the next month, we're getting married first and he doesn't care that Brooklyn will pitch a holy shit fit."

"Why don't you have a double wedding?"

Letty glanced down at the rock that she calls a ring and smiled.

"That might work."

"It would be awesome," I corrected.

"I need to get back to the store. Mrs. S is there alone."

That reminded me, I needed to look at my finances and come up with a figure I could afford to start paying her back.

"I'll stop by this afternoon."

"Kisses."

Letty blew me a kiss and picked up her coffee off the counter.

"Kisses back."

I checked the back corner and once again met Reese's stare. I smiled, he returned it, and that flutter in my belly made itself known.

Only now that I wasn't trying to deny it was there, it fully unfolded, and it felt damn good.

———

REESE WAS DRIVING us to my house, or my old house as it were. I was zoning out the window looking at nothing when he said, "I forgot to ask, what did Mrs. S say to you when you two went to Letty's office?"

"She told me to stuff it."

Technically, she told me to stuff it up my rump which shocked the hell out of me, and I decided if a woman as classy as Mrs. Simpson was using such profane words it wouldn't be smart to push her. So, I didn't.

"She told you to stuff it?"

"Yep. She wouldn't hear of discussing a payment plan. Before she told me to stuff it she explained that she didn't need the money and it was more important to her that I get on my feet and get caught up with the rest of my vendors."

"Kindness," he mumbled.

"Indeed. She is the definition of kindness."

Reese turned down my street and I immediately went on alert and started looking for...shit, I didn't know what I was looking for. A car I'd never seen, a motorcycle, a Horsemen, my brother.

"Sadie," Reese rumbled.

"Yeah?"

"Baby, look at me."

I stopped scanning and looked at him. His eyes left the road, and like he had superpowers that would allow him to ascertain my wellbeing in a split second, his eyes roamed over my face before looking back at the road.

"You're safe," he told me.

"I know. I was just looking around."

"You were looking for something or someone out of place."

Apparently, he did have superpowers.

"Fine, I was, but not because I'm scared."

I saw Wilson's black SUV parked in my driveway and two cars parked at the curb. One was a police cruiser, the other a bland sedan that I guessed was Detective Brasco's.

Reese pulled in next to Wilson and shut down his Rover.

"We'll make this quick then go get dinner, yeah?"

"Sounds good to me."

Reese did another perusal before he smiled and got out. I followed suit, including the smile so when Wilson was in my space as soon as my door opened, I was smiling up at him.

He registered my smile, and in return frowned.

What was that about?

"Hi, Wilson, long time no see." I attempted to joke.

"Hey, Sadie."

Still no smile. Not even a hint of one.

"Everything okay?"

"That's what I'm trying to figure out."

"Huh?"

"You're smiling." He pointed out.

"There's a lot to smile about."

Wilson's gaze went over my shoulder, and a moment later I felt Reese's arm slide around my shoulders.

See? Lots to smile about.

"Brasco in there?" Reese asked.

"Yeah." Suddenly, Wilson shook his head and cleared his scowl. "Cops last night left a mess, there's fingerprint dust all over."

"Are you worried that will freak me out?"

"I'm not sure if there's anything that *could* freak you out, Sadie."

With that, he turned and made his way up the path to the front porch.

Thankfully, Reese hung back a minute, which gave me the chance to ask, "What was that about?"

"He's worried about you."

"Why?"

Reese's head twitched. Not much, but enough that I noticed.

"Baby, after months of struggling you come out from under that to having your house broken into, *twice*."

"Is he worried I'm gonna crack?"

Reese barked out a rough laugh before he leaned down and kissed me.

"No, he's not worried you're gonna crack. He's just worried because he cares."

Well, hell, that felt nice.

"I'll tell him I'm okay."

"You can do that, but he'll still worry. That's just who he is. When he cares, he does it deeply. And since he cares about you, he'll worry no matter what you tell him."

That felt even better. Not as good as knowing that Reese loved me, regardless of the fact he hadn't said it.

And since I'd given it a lot of thought throughout the day, I'd concluded that was what we'd told each other last night. That was what that something big was. And I adored that neither of us had to say it out loud to know.

Reese thought that love was the *regardless of*, and he was right. It was also in the silence. It was the stillness of the moment. In the quiet when two souls communicated with emotion instead of sound.

"Baby," he groaned.

Yep, he felt it, and I didn't need to say a damn word.

"Let's get this over with so we can start our night. I'm thinking it's my turn to torture you with my oral skills."

Reese's lips quirked up.

"You good with your mouth?"

I had no idea if I was or if I wasn't. I'd given a blow job before, but it wasn't like I'd asked for a scorecard rating my performance.

And since I didn't want to oversell a bill of goods I simply shrugged, then added. "Maybe torture means torture as in you'll be in extreme distress, and it'll be horrible. Or maybe it means torture in the sense that it'll be so good you'll be a one-pump chump as soon as I get my mouth on you. You'll just have to wait and see."

"Christ, you're fucking cute."

"I'm a badass, baker, business owner. I am not cute."

"You're right, you're fucking adorable."

He started moving us to the front door when I told him, "You say fuck a lot."

"Yep."

"That's it? Just yep?"

"Not sure what else there's to say except, yep."

I guess he was right, there wasn't anything else to say because he didn't say anything else.

We crossed the threshold, Reese's arm still around my shoulders, only now it felt like he wasn't simply walking next to me, he was offering me his strength should I need it.

But when I looked around the space, I felt nothing.

I wasn't numb. Logically, I knew someone uninvited had been in my home. I just didn't care.

"Is it unhealthy I feel nothing?" I asked. "I'm trying to. I'm not in denial. But looking around..." I trailed off, not knowing how to finish.

"It's not unhealthy as long as you're not closing yourself off."

I nodded and gave the room another look. There was black dust on the countertops. I felt nothing. My couch cushions were askew. I felt nothing. Detective Brasco was coming into the living room from down the hall, and it didn't even feel weird he'd been back in one of the bedrooms.

"Sadie. Reese. Thanks for coming."

Even that, the detective greeting us like we were visiting him in his home instead of mine, didn't make me feel anything.

"Brasco," Reese returned. "Any luck today?"

The detective's gaze shot to Wilson's then back to Reese.

What was that about?

"Unfortunately, nothing solid."

"But you have something flimsy?" I asked.

"I'm sorry?"

"You said you didn't have anything solid which could be interpreted as you have something but it's flimsy. So, do you?"

Detective Brasco smiled and chuckled.

"Yes, Sadie, we have something flimsy. However, due to an ongoing, unrelated case, I'm not at liberty to discuss it."

"With me," I added.

"Yes, with you."

"But you'll discuss it with Reese?" His smile died and I rushed on to explain, "That wasn't me being snarky. I totally understand you not being able to talk about certain things with me. I was asking to confirm you'll discuss it with Reese, meaning you'll keep him in the loop."

Reese gave my shoulders a squeeze. I took that as confirmation even if the detective wasn't at liberty to tell me that either.

"You have my word, Reese and Wilson will be kept in the loop."

"Perfect. Shall we start in the bedroom or the garage?"

Out of the corner of my eye, I caught Wilson's lips twitch. His head was bent and he was studying the floor before he smiled.

"The bedrooms."

"I'll follow you."

The detective went back down the hall. Reese gave me another squeeze before he dropped his arm and held out his hand.

I glanced down at it, then back up at him and smiled. After that, I laced my fingers with his and he trailed behind me as I made my way to the guest bedroom.

Disaster.

It was an utter disaster of a mess.

CD cases opened, ditto with the DVDs. Papers were

strewn all over the room, photo albums were haphazardly thrown about.

I knew how to feel about that.

Pissed.

"So, the albums seriously make me mad," I proudly announced.

I was so busy taking in the mess I hadn't realized Reese had gone stiff beside me.

"What's wrong?"

He didn't answer me. Instead, he asked his own question, "The garage look like this?"

Wilson jerked his chin and Reese's jaw went tight.

"What's. Wrong?"

Reese turned until he was facing me. He released some of the tension in his grip and I knew it cost him when he spoke in a gentle, even tone.

"Whoever was in here was looking for something."

My gaze went back to the pile of open cases.

"Obviously."

"No, Sadie. This doesn't say robbery. This." He stopped and pointed to the chaos. "Says someone was looking for something in particular. Something important that they want. A thief doesn't open every CD case. A thief doesn't leaf through photo albums. They grab shit and go. Are you getting me?"

The lack of the word fuck scared me. I heard Reese mad, homicidal even, the fucks came more frequently than normal and the absence of them now made me think he'd stepped over mad and had gone straight to furious.

"I'm getting you."

"I know I already asked this, but I need you to think hard. Has anyone ever asked to keep something at your house?"

Since this was important, I decided to think hard and not point out that his tone was borderline condescending.

So, that was what I did. I took a moment and thought back over the last three years since I'd moved in. No one had asked me to keep something at my house. Then I thought back further to when I lived in my last apartment. Still, I was coming up blank. I couldn't remember anyone asking me to hold on to something for them and I didn't think that was something I would forget.

"No. No one's ever asked."

"When Nate was over, was he ever in this room?"

Sweet Jesus, I would be happy when that name was never spoken again.

"I don't know. Possibly, but I don't have any direct memories of him in here."

"But he spent the night."

"Reese—"

"I wanna know this shit less than you wanna tell me. But it's important we understand how much access he had to your house."

"Nate's been gone for over six months. Gone, Reese. Poof, up in smoke. Do you think after he got away with all my money, he'd take the chance and come back here?"

"If he left something important enough, yes."

"Now I'm freaked out, pissed, and it's worth the repeat —freaked the fuck out. For some reason, a stranger in my house rifling through my shit doesn't bother me. Nate in my house, that's infuriating."

"Sadie—"

I didn't let Reese finish.

"Yes, he was in my house unattended. Yes, he spent the night. No, I never stayed at his house. And I'm not gonna go back to blaming myself for being stupid. I was dumb, I paid for it, I've dealt with it, and now I'm moving the fuck on. I'm so fucking sick of thinking about him. You have no idea how happy I'll be when I never have to hear the name Nate Mallard again. Actually, starting now, no one fucking mention his name to me. If he was in here looking for something, I do not want to know. Keep that shit between the three of you and do not loop me in. I'm done dealing with this, Reese. I need you to take this. If I have to hear about him any fucking more, I might hunt him down myself and poke his fucking eyeballs out."

When I was done ranting all three men were staring at me like I had a screw or fifteen loose. Which was probably accurate. It was not the stress that had done me in, even though at times I felt like quitting, I never did. It wasn't selling my stuff. It was the mere thought that Nate would have the audacity to come back into my home. Even if it wasn't him, the thought of it sent me over the damn edge.

"That's a lotta fucks, baby."

I transferred my glare from the piles of shit strewn about the room to Reese.

"If you wanna be a wise guy, I know a fuck that's gonna be off the table for a long *fucking* time."

"Right." He smiled and winked then turned to the detective. "This is gonna be a wash. No way to tell if something's missing. We'll look in the garage before we go, but if it looks like this, then that'll be a bust, too."

"Figured as much."

We all exited the room and I glanced in my bedroom. My mattress was pushed off the box spring and my clothes were all over the floor.

I clenched my jaw until it ached.

"Can you do me a favor and ask one of the guys with a truck if they'll take my bed to a vacant lot? I wanna burn it."

Burn away every last memory of the idiot who shall remain nameless.

"No, but I'll get Davis to come get it and take it to the dump."

"But I want to burn it."

"Won't work, baby. I tried it. Took all of the shit Ellie left behind out into the backyard and lit it on fire. Watched it burn until it was nothing but ash. Didn't make me feel any better, didn't make me any less pissed. All it did was fuck up my grass. He's gone. You've given it to me, so now he's nothing to you. Not even a memory. Leave it at that, do what you said you were doing, and move on."

It sucked that he was so smart.

As we all walked through the kitchen, I ignored the black dust and the open cabinet doors.

Instead, I asked, "Did you really burn all her stuff?"

"Yep."

"I thought you left her."

"I did. Then she moved out of the house. The problem was, she wasn't only a liar, she was a lazy bitch, too. And since I didn't want my credit jacked, I had to clean out the shit she left behind. So, I burned it."

I shouldn't have thought it was funny but I kind of did. Only because Reese was a good man, and even if he wasn't, there was never a reason to cheat. So in the end, she deserved to have her shit burned, even if it was stuff she didn't want. I wished it had given Reese some peace but he'd moved on so it no longer mattered. And I was moving on, too.

The detective went first, then Wilson, and Reese held open the door for me as I stepped into the garage. More of the same. Stuff everywhere.

I let go of Reese's hand and walked to a broken trophy. I picked it up off the concrete and held it out.

"I'm really extra mad about this being broken." I shook my third-place state championship trophy. "I swam my ass off that year. I was at the pool at four a.m. before school every morning for months, training. Countless hours in the pool after school. I swam until my shoulders ached so bad I wanted to cry. Now look at it, it's broken. Fucking asshole."

I could tell they thought another screw had come out.

I did not give one shit.

I loved this trophy. Out of all of them, this one meant the most to me.

No one said anything so I continued.

"I'm not saying his name. But if *he* hid something important in my house, wouldn't *he* know where it was? *He* wouldn't need to break my damn trophy to find it."

There were a few beats of silence before Wilson answered.

"Yeah, he'd know. And it's possible he went there first and didn't find it, thought you had and moved it, so he tore about your house to find it. Could also be he hid it in one of the pieces of furniture you sold, so he went through the boxes hoping you packed it away when you emptied out drawers. Or it could be that we're wrong, and it wasn't him. We won't know until the prints come back. That is, if he wasn't wearing gloves. Good news; the toothbrush in the kit had been used and the razor had hair in the blades, so that's been sent off. Now, you got what you need. The rest is for Reese."

I nodded because he was right, the rest was for Reese.

And I knew to my core, if there was something vitally important, he'd tell me. If not, he would handle it and leave me out of it.

"Awesome. Great. Perfect. I don't mean to sound like a whiney cow, but can we please leave now?"

"Wilson. Brasco. We're out."

"Sadie, sorry to drag you out here."

"Please don't apologize, Detective. You didn't do this to my house. I appreciate you giving me last night and going out of your way to come back."

More goodbyes were exchanged, the men shook hands, and traded strange looks. I didn't study those too hard; I didn't want to know what they were silently communicating.

When we got out to Reese's Rover, he pressed my back to the door and kissed the ever-loving hell out of me.

After that Reese took me to dinner then we went home. *Home.*

To the cabin I shared with Reese.

And just like that, my life had changed.

21

I WATCHED Wilson make his way through the crush of people. Treats was wall-to-wall packed for the morning rush. If I hadn't already known, coming to work with Sadie for the last week would've told me how tough she was. But seeing her in action day after day had sealed it.

The woman didn't stand still.

If she wasn't at the counter helping make drinks and ring people up she was in the back baking. I now understood why it had been so important for her to fix the broken oven. She had three in total, and all three were in use all day. If she wasn't filling the cases, she was filling orders—birthdays, anniversaries, weddings, job promotions. If there was something to celebrate Sadie could bake a cake for it.

She didn't dally, she barely sat down, and when she did it was in her office to pay bills or print out invoices. It was exhausting watching her. I was also afraid she was pushing herself to the breaking point. She had one full-time employee and two part-time. She needed to hire one more part-time employee and take a day off before she burned out. Which was something I'd been meaning to talk to her about but hadn't had the time in the last week.

Working in the back of a bakery had proven difficult. Ninety-nine percent of the cases Takeback was involved in were classified. Sadie's internet connection was not secure, which meant I couldn't check my email or download case files.

"We got a break," Wilson said as he sat across from me.

Fucking finally.

"Cali case, the break-in, or Mallard?"

Asher and Cole were in California soaking up the sun waiting for Asher's application to be approved. Cole had reported he was bored as fuck and hated the sand—too many memories of his time in the Middle East and Asia. I felt that down to my soul, I had zero interest in visiting the beach. I much preferred dirt over sand. Freshwater lakes over the ocean.

"Break-in and Mallard. Met with Butch. As you know, he had to cancel last week. He confirmed Grinder broke in that first night. Came back to the clubhouse with the money. But his story is, he went by his sister's, you were there, and you gave it back to him not wanting trouble."

I felt the muscles in my neck contract and my fists clenched.

"I'm tired of that asshole running his mouth, talking shit."

"Yeah, well, you're not the only one. Butch said that Grinder's not well-liked among the members. Talks like a tough guy, never backs up his shit talk, and kisses Zeus's ass. And if you can believe this shit, some don't like Grinder taking freebies and fucking the girls up. Butch isn't sure if he'll be patched in. But they're expanding and that might work in Grinder's favor. Even if the majority don't want him, he's still a body to handle business. The second break-in wasn't Grinder. He left that morning on a run to Montana and didn't get back until the next day."

Not surprising. The second night wasn't about Grinder being pissed at his sister. It reeked of desperation.

"Good to have that confirmed but we already figured that. Brasco get the prints back?"

"Sadie's, yours, and the neighbor Joey's."

I wasn't sure how I felt about that. Three people, one of them Sadie, one a married neighbor who was only there to help move furniture. The other me. There should've been more. But she'd been too busy stressing out and hadn't had time to have friends over.

I was wrong. I knew how I felt about that. I was just trying to shove the anger down and stay on topic.

"DNA came back. No match in any database."

Fuck!

"Good news is we have it," Wilson finished.

"We have it, but we don't have him. No prints on the letter. The cameras from the bank were a bust since they don't keep backups over six months. Mallard electronically transferred the money to his account and promptly moved it to crypto. He didn't have to leave Sadie's office to fuck her over and steal her money."

"I got nothing to say to that, because you're right. The only thing we can do is be patient. Rhode's still searching for open cases that fit, you are, too. You talked to Sadie's employees and they gave you the same vague description. No one at the bank remembers him. The address on his application was bogus. His school records and previous employers and references were fake."

Previous employers.

"I didn't ask Sadie if she checked his references."

"Shit," Wilson grunted. "Just saw the report that both the detective and Gayle called the numbers, and they were dead ends. Didn't think to ask her."

My gaze went across the room. She was slammed busy with a line ten deep.

"I'll ask her after the rush."

Wilson nodded and his brows pulled together. I couldn't read the shift in his mood. Could be he was pissed we'd overlooked something so basic, or it could be he was worried about something else.

"Tell me," I demanded.

"Butch had more to share. Zeus's attitude change."

Fuck.

"And?" I prompted.

"He's working someone in the sheriff's department. It was a setup. New, young deputy out on his night off with some buddies. Zeus sent in one of his girls, and I mean girl. She's fifteen but looks twenty-one. I've seen pictures of this girl and no joke, I wouldn't have guessed she was fifteen and she was in a bar being served. This deputy is twenty-three; taking home a twenty-one-year-old would be the norm for him. Went to her place, Zeus had the room wired with cameras. Caught the whole thing. Butch relayed that there was nothing kinky, straight-up ordinary sex. The problem is, sex is anything but ordinary when it's an adult with a fifteen-year-old. Now Zeus has this deputy by the balls. He goes up the chain, explains what happened, he's going down for statutory rape. He keeps it quiet, he's Zeus's bitch. So far, the deputy's kept it quiet and Zeus is feeling cocky, working to set up a few more cops."

Sick fuck.

"He needs to go down."

"DEA's working on it. But Butch has a problem.

Someone fucked up and ran with some intel that Butch reported and now Butch is on the hook. That's why he had to cancel last week. The intel he reported only Zeus's lieutenants knew about, and Butch is one of the four people. Now Zeus is questioning all of them wanting to know how the feds knew about a warehouse that was only a month old. And it was the first time drugs were stored there."

Holy shit, that was a huge fuck-up. Butch didn't just have a problem, he would be fucked—the kind that meant he stopped breathing if anyone found out he was undercover.

Wilson wasn't done. "From now on, all of us are carrying burners. Butch has those numbers programmed in his phone. No one is to answer them, for any reason. If he runs into an issue and he can get a text out he will. He won't text that he needs help or a location. It will be a number. Any number to any of our phones."

That was smart.

"Is there a reason he'd text one of us and not the DEA?"

"Butch isn't feeling love for the DEA right now. No one wants this shit done more than him. But in their impatience, someone's getting sloppy. And it's not the DEA who's gonna pay, it's Butch. And we're local and he trusts we'll have his back."

Damn right, we will.

"Are you gonna tell Brasco and River you know about the deputy?"

"Haven't decided yet. Some lines have to be respected. This might be one of them. Though something's not sitting right. Butch said this deputy is scared shitless and hasn't talked. Brasco said there were rumors. One and one's not equaling two. And I'm not sure how I feel about helping a man out of a jam when he took a fifteen-year-old to bed."

I couldn't stop my wince. Wilson had a valid point. We helped put sex offenders behind bars. We didn't exonerate them.

"Fucks me to say this, brother. Actually makes my stomach churn, but if the girl looks like you says she does, was in a bar, and this deputy's on the up-and-up, no prior run-ins with minors, no fucked-up kiddy fetish, seems to me both the girl and the deputy are victims."

Wilson sat in silent contemplation for a few moments. Before he stopped contemplating and scowled.

"I want this motherfucker put to ground."

Now we're talking.

"I do, too."

"He's getting the young ones plastic surgery. Has some hack surgeon in Montana giving these girls implants."

And it just keeps getting more and more disgusting.

"What's Butch's take? He ready to jump ship? We can step in and start dismantling the Horsemen at any time."

"He's not ready yet. But I think he's getting close. We have dirt, but not enough. I think it's time we start digging deeper."

"Agreed."

"When Asher and Cole get back from California we'll hit it."

What my boss left out was that he was down three men. Asher and Cole and me.

"Appreciate you being cool about Sadie's situation."

"There's nothing more important than taking care of your woman."

The way Wilson said that made me wonder if he had personal experience with taking care of a woman. He was a closed book. We all knew about his military service, his stint at Homeland, and the work he'd done with the Marshal Service, but his personal life was off the table.

"You ever been married?"

Complete closedown.

"For fifteen years."

Wilson had been married for fifteen fucking years and he never mentioned it?

"Why'd you get divorced?"

"Didn't. She's dead."

Totally devoid of emotion. And if I didn't know the man better, I'd think he didn't give two shits his wife was dead. But I knew Wilson; he hid it, but out of all of us on the team, he felt the deepest. I saw it with every rescue we'd participated in. Each one cut him, leaving him with a new scar. His wife of fifteen years dying would mark him in ways I couldn't imagine.

"Damn, brother, I'm sorry. Truly fucking sorry. How long ago?"

"Nothing to be sorry for. Took me a long time to understand why she did what she did. I find no peace in her suicide, but I sure hope to fuck she has."

It was not understanding I saw in his eyes, it was guilt, and not a small amount of it.

"Wilson—"

"Don't, Reese. I know you got good intentions but don't feed me a line of bullshit. It's been twelve years. I feel the way I feel and that's not gonna change. So do me a favor and drop it, yeah?"

Hell, yeah, it was guilt I saw. And what he was saying was he blamed himself and always would.

"I'll drop it for now only because we're in a crowded bakery. But if you think I'm gonna sit around and pretend I don't know you're blaming yourself and suffering then you don't know me. You're always on the rest of us not to internalize what we do, what we see. And there you are internalizing big shit you need to talk about. That shit's not on, brother, and you know it."

"It's not the same," he argued.

"Bullshit. It might not be about the job. But it's about family. It's about the team. It's about our leader suffering in silence and him keeping the rest of us in the dark when we've all laid our shit on you."

There was a loud crash. Wilson was up and I wasn't far behind, both of our hands automatically going for our weapons.

"Sorry! Sorry!" a haggard-looking woman with a toddler shouted over the noise. "I'll clean it up."

I glanced down and saw the broken plates and pastries mixed with coffee.

"No worries," Sadie said, coming out from around the counter. "Go find a table. I'll clean this up."

Wilson was already on the move to help. I needed a moment to calm my racing heart and clear my head.

This shit needed to end.

A week ago, she gave me a gift—her trust.

She'd openly given it in front of Wilson and Brasco. That night when we got home, and every night since then, I'd done my best to show her exactly how I felt about that gift. And I knew she read my message loud and clear. Irrevocably proving showing is more important than telling.

22

"SADIE."

Reese's growl sent shivers down my spine.

I sucked harder.

"Gonna blow in your mouth, baby."

That was what I was going for though I couldn't tell him that with a mouthful of cock.

I swirled my tongue around the tip, then went lower to the part just under the head. The place I knew drove him wild before sliding down his length and taking him to the back of my throat.

"Jesus, fuck, baby."

As it turned out, I could torture Reese with my mouth. Thankfully, it was the good kind of torture that normally led him to yanking my mouth from his cock so he could flip me on my hands and knees and take it home.

But right now I didn't want that.

I wanted to give him this. I wanted him to blow in my mouth, something he'd only done a few times.

With that in mind, I added my hands. One wrapped around his shaft, and I started stroking in time with my mouth. The other went lower and cupped his balls. I'd never done this—held a man's balls. I wasn't exactly sure what to do with them but when Reese's hips jerked off the bed and he hissed out a groan I figured he liked it.

But again, a mouth full of cock meant I could ask.

Luckily for me, Reese was good at giving direction.

"Slow your mouth, Sadie. I wanna enjoy this another minute."

I did as he instructed.

"Want your ass up here where I can reach it. Don't lose my cock, baby, but shift up here."

I wanted to deny him, give him this without getting anything in return. But if Reese wanted something while we were in bed, he got it. Period. That didn't mean he demanded I do things I didn't enjoy, it meant that he controlled the pace, the positions, and the orgasms. And since his control meant I was having the best sex in the history of sex, I gave him whatever he wanted.

He dropped one of his bent knees, so I could maneuver over it and scoot my knees next to his chest. I managed to do this without losing his cock, but my rhythm suffered, and I lost purchase on his balls.

Once I was settled, Reese lifted my left knee and placed it on his chest.

"So fucking wet, it's dripping down your thigh."

I had no doubt. From the moment my lips had wrapped around his thick cock I felt the wetness between my legs. That was what made sucking him off so hot. While I was torturing him, I was torturing myself. I was pretty sure if Reese gave me enough time, I could orgasm just from blowing him—that was how much it turned me on.

"Hand back to my balls."

I cupped his balls just as he pushed two fingers inside of me. My hand reflexively squeezed a little too tight.

Reese grunted and I moaned.

"A little less than that but more than before. Roll and tug."

Roll and tug?

I could've figured it out if his fingers weren't curled inside of my pussy rubbing the special spot that never failed to send zaps of electricity throughout my body.

But I was willing to give it a try. I rolled gently but when I tugged, I gave them a soft squeeze.

"Exactly fucking that, baby."

I found a new rhythm and added more suction, loving the sounds he was making. Grunts and groans that catapulted me closer to my orgasm. I licked on upward glides, sucked hard on the way down. I got braver and tugged harder. He adjusted his hand and went after my clit, making me lose my concentration.

"Change of plans," he growled.

Before I could protest, his hands went to my hips, he jerked me up and settled his mouth on my pussy.

There was no build-up. No slowly allowing me to get acclimated to the new position. He sat me on his face and ate. Teeth and tongue and lips.

And from there it was a race to the finish.

He won. Not that I had a chance of winning. He was so good with his mouth and his control was such that he could hold out as long as he wanted. It would've been annoying if it wasn't so damn spectacular.

I moaned my orgasm around his cock. My thighs trembled, my back arched and locked, and white hot pleasure seared through me. I was still panting the last spasms of my orgasm when Reese rumbled, "Lose the hand and finish me off with your mouth."

I unwrapped my hand and bobbed faster. I now understood why when Reese was done going down on me he licked his lips and told me he loved the way I tasted. I never in a million years would've guessed I'd think that was sexy. But more, I never thought I'd agree. I was addicted to the way he tasted. Not only the way his cock tasted but his mouth and his skin. I could and had spent time licking and tasting his skin. Everything about him was perfect because he was mine.

"Fuck, Sadie, your mouth is so damn sweet."

I loved that he thought that.

"Gonna come, now."

I felt the first hot jet and slid my lips to the root and swallowed. I swallowed more and more and with each swallow, I continued to massage his balls.

"Baby," he groaned. "Fuck, don't stop."

His hips jerked up again and he kept spilling into my mouth.

By the time he was done I swallowed what I could and the rest leaked down my chin.

I felt his body go from taut to limp. I slowly started sliding my mouth up and down, not ready to lose him completely.

"Can I tell you something without you getting pissy?" he asked.

That was never, *ever*, ever a good way to start off a question with a woman, and especially not in bed. But still, I nodded.

"By and far, you've got the best mouth I've ever had. Best pussy. Best lay. Never had better. You've given me some great blowjobs, baby. But that, hands fucking down was the best blowjob I've ever had. Thought I was gonna pass out, it felt so good."

Well, I didn't necessarily like the reminder he'd had other women but I wasn't a virgin when I met him so what could I say? And the flip side to that was I was reaping the benefits of his experience, so in the end, I was coming out on top, so what the hell did I care?

I smiled around his cock before I pulled off.

I couldn't stop myself from squirming, seeing it still semi-erect resting on his belly.

"You want more, baby?"

I always wanted more.

"I always want more."

I knew he caught my meaning when he softly said, "I know you do, baby."

A few minutes later he set about giving me more.

More of himself and more orgasms.

———

I WAS DRAPED OVER REESE, my head on his chest, and I was drifting off to sleep.

My body felt like a wet noodle and I was so tired I was dreading going to work tomorrow. Not because it was late. Reese was always mindful of my schedule and made sure that no matter how creative he got with our lovemaking we were done early enough for me to get a full eight hours of sleep. So it wasn't a lack of sleep; I was running on empty and I had been for months. I couldn't remember the last time I took a day off. And now that I was thinking about it I was wide awake.

"I think I need to hire another employee," I said into the dark.

Reese's hand on my hip stopped gliding. But it started moving again as he said, "I was thinking about that this morning. Meant to talk to you about it tonight. But we'd already talked about..." he trailed off.

I didn't need him to remind me who we'd talked about. And I also didn't want to remember how disappointed Reese looked when he had to ask me if I'd checked references and previous employers of the idiot who shall remain nameless. I had checked his references and past employers, which made Reese's eyes light up when I told him. So I took that as a good sign, moved on putting the nameless idiot out of my head, and went back to icing a wedding cake. Reese went into my office and shut the door. I figured he did that because he was making calls he didn't want me to listen to. I was a-okay with that.

"What did you want to talk to me about?"

"Just that, you hiring someone so you can take a day off. You work your ass off and I know you enjoy what you do, you like working hard. But there's hard, and then there's burnout. You need a day off, baby. And not just because I like having a lazy morning with you and a full day to take you somewhere. Straight up, you need a break to refill your reserve."

In many ways, it was great having a man who was astute and watchful. Bossy only in the best of ways. Controlling when it meant orgasms were involved. Protective, but with a mind to my feelings.

But the very best part of Reese was him wanting to take care of me. As the days slid by, I began to grasp what he'd meant when he told me he'd wanted me to need him. He'd explained it then, and we'd hashed it out, but he'd been wrong and he didn't realize it. He didn't need me to need him in the ways he said. He wanted to take care of me.

That's what he needed. And in return, he needed me to take care of him. He needed us to be a united front, he needed to know he could count on me. I needed that, too. And I wasn't taking care of him by working eighty-four hours a week, week after week. I had a business to run but I still had a life to live and a man in my life who deserved my time.

"I'll ask the girls if they know anyone who needs a job. If they don't, I'll put an ad out in the paper. And before you ask—which will not be asking but telling me—yes, I'll have you run a background check on them. And while I cannot legally discriminate, I will do my very best to hire a woman."

"Good."

That was all he said.

"Thank you for taking care of me."

"My pleasure, Sadie. Never doubt that, yeah?"

It would be impossible for me to doubt it. Every day, multiple times a day he shows me.

"You know it's my pleasure to stand next to you," I whispered.

"I know."

Then I used his word and settled in.

"Good."

In the warm cocoon of Reese's arms, I fell asleep.

23

SADIE HAD JUST DROPPED her purse on the couch when there was a knock on my door.

"Are you expecting someone?" she asked and yawned at the same time.

It was the day after she said she was going to hire someone new. It was after she'd worked a twelve-hour day and she looked dead on her feet. And it was then I realized I'd been a selfish asshole bringing her home after she'd been on her feet all day, feeding her, then spending hours inside of her instead of letting her get extra sleep.

"No. But I'm sure it's one of the guys. Why don't you go up and take a bath?"

"A bath? We haven't had dinner."

There was another knock, this one louder.

I gave up talking her into relaxing and moved to answer the door. I checked the window and saw Wilson and Davis on the porch. Davis had two pizza boxes in his hands.

So much for getting Sadie to relax.

I opened the door and without waiting for an invite, Davis stepped in.

"Hope two's enough. I'm starving," he said.

Wilson was slower to enter and at least had the manners to apologize for the intrusion.

"Sorry to barge in on you. We need to talk and now was the only time."

Wilson's gaze went over my shoulder, and he narrowed his eyes.

"Darlin', you need a day off."

I was momentarily stunned. I'd never heard Wilson address Letty or Brooklyn by anything other than their first names. And he certainly had never slipped into a southern drawl.

"You hitting on my woman?" I asked, half teasing.

"I think he's trying to politely tell me I look like shit."

"I'm not sure *you* could ever look like shit, but you do look tired."

"Now I know you're hitting on her," I grunted and contemplated kicking him out.

"Brother, he's paying her a compliment," Davis said from the kitchen. "And since she's yours I reckon you've noticed she's hot. But just because you've somehow managed to hook her doesn't mean the rest of us lost our eyesight."

"How about we stop talking about how hot my woman is?"

I might've been magnanimous enough to form my demand as a question, but it was no less a demand.

"Sure," Davis agreed. "Besides, I wanna talk about why we haven't had a poker night in forever."

"I've given up gambling," I reminded him.

"Quitter," he grumbled and shoved a piece of pizza in his mouth.

Yes, a piece of pizza, damn near the whole slice.

"I still owe Letty five car washes, and I swear she goes off-roading before she calls me for a wash. Now that she and River have a house, she let me off the hook doing her laundry. She and Brooklyn thought they were cute and didn't think I'd catch on that one or both of them were buying skimpy, dental floss panties and putting them in Letty's laundry. And when they didn't get a reaction out of me, they switched gears and changed to old granny panties." I turned to Sadie and finished, "That reminds me, I don't care how old you are and how many grandchildren we have, let it be known that grandma panties are expressly forbidden."

The room went deadly silent, even Davis stopped chopping on his mouthful of pizza. And Sadie looked like she was holding her breath.

What in the hell?

"Sadie?"

"Noted," she croaked. "No granny panties no matter how many grandchildren *we* have."

Hearing my words spoken back to me I understood the silence.

Fuck, maybe Sadie didn't want kids. We hadn't talked about it and I certainly wasn't going to ask her in front of Wilson and Davis.

"Yep, nothing like laying it out there," Davis piped up. "How many kids are you thinking? Remy needs some cousins, *pronto*. And brothers and sisters. Which I have on good authority Rhode's doing his best to plant another seed."

"Who raised you?" Wilson asked. "Monkeys?"

"Don't call my mama a monkey, asshole. I'm a gentleman when I need to be."

Davis was a gentleman, never. He was slightly more couth when he was trying to get laid and only marginally better when we were on the job.

"Well, I have it on good authority that Brooklyn doesn't wanna get married pregnant, so she's doing what she can to not allow that seed to take root. But as soon as the I-dos are exchanged, she wants three more kids. And I don't know how many kids Reese wants but I'm planning on five."

"Five? Jesus, woman, you know you gotta grow those little fuckers then push them out, right?"

Only Davis would call children "those little fuckers."

"I hope you never have children," I muttered.

"Planning on having a whole herd of them. I got shit to prove to the piece of shit that walked out on my mom."

Davis joked about his dad abandoning him and his mom, but he didn't find it funny. I found it repugnant that a man would leave his wife and child. I reckon he had more to prove to himself than his old man.

"A herd?" Sadie asked, not skipping a beat. "How many's in a herd?"

"However many my wife will give me. Five, six, seven. Whatever."

Sadie's mouth dropped open and she smiled hugely.

Damn, so freaking beautiful. Even dog-ass tired she was stunning.

"I'll pray for your future wife's uterus. May it be fertile and not fall out after she breeds your herd."

"Appreciate that, Sadie." Davis gave her a salute then held up his pizza. "Y'all better dig in before it's gone."

"It amazes me how you can eat the way you do and stay in shape."

Davis's lips formed a cocky smirk.

"Say one word, brother, and you'll find my boot up your ass."

He wisely didn't say anything, but he did give Sadie a wink that made her burst out laughing.

————

IT WAS after both large pizzas had been consumed and conversation had turned to the mundane. I hadn't been in the office in a week, but they'd kept me up to speed and Rhode, Davis, Wilson, and Jack had all stopped by Treats to keep me in the loop. Brasco and River had both come in as well to talk to me, but really it was to check on Sadie. Brasco because he was a good cop. River because he was a good guy and engaged to one of Sadie's closest friends.

Sadie got up from the couch, set her plate in the sink, and announced, "I think I'm gonna take my hot self upstairs and take a bath. You men enjoy the rest of your evening. Thanks for dinner."

I grunted because Davis groaned, likely thinking about my woman naked in the bath. Unfortunately, I didn't have anything close to throw at the dickhead.

Wilson attempted to hide his smile but mostly failed.

"Hate to ask, but before you go up, I need you to listen to some recordings."

Sneak attack.

I turned to Wilson and asked, "What recordings?"

"I know you want to keep her out of it, and I respect that but we need to see if she can identify the voices from the references and employers."

Total fucking sneak attack.

Wilson knew damn well that if he'd come to me before he sprung it on Sadie, I would've shut it down.

"Wilson—"

"It's okay, Reese," Sadie interrupted. "If it means giving you guys a solid lead then I'll listen. I don't just want this done for me, I want it done for you, too."

Some of the ways she told me she loved me were obvious, some were small, but I never missed them. Like now—something as small as wanting Mallard in the rearview, but pointing out she wanted that for me, too. That shit happened to her, not to me, but she'd made it a team effort. She trusted me to do the heavy lifting and trusted I'd have her back.

The hard part with that was showing her I loved her the same way, and that meant stepping back and keeping my mouth shut while she did something that I knew she didn't really want to do but was putting on a strong front.

My only solace was knowing that tonight, and tomorrow, and all the days and nights after that I'd get to be the one she leaned on when she needed it.

Davis was no longer smirking, he was watchful, keeping both an eye on Sadie and my reaction to ambush.

He needn't have worried about Sadie; her spine was made of steel. I was the one ready to blow.

Wilson had his phone out of his pocket by the time Sadie sat back down next to me. Her hand went to my thigh and she gave it a squeeze, showing me her support.

Yep.

Another show of love.

I picked up her hand, laced my fingers through hers, and rested it back on my leg.

I was so intent on studying our hands, how something as pure and innocent as holding hands could be so impactful, that I missed Wilson queuing up the recording.

But I didn't miss the voice.

I knew that nasally voice and so did Sadie.

"I know that guy, but not from calling references," she said.

Before she could go on, I added, "He comes into Treats. Suit and tie guy. Comes in around eight-fifteen every morning."

"Vanilla latte with a shot of espresso and three extra sugars."

"That's Mallard's last employer," Wilson said.

"Which one?" Sadie asked.

Wilson leaned forward and pulled a folded piece of paper out of his back pocket. When he unfolded it, I saw it was a copy of Mallard's job application.

"This one," Wilson said, pointing to a name.

"That is not who I spoke to when I called that number. That guy sounded like he smoked a pack of cigarettes a day and had a nasty cough to go with the gravelly voice."

"Is this him?"

Wilson touched his phone and a new voice played.

"Yes. That's him."

All the guy had said was "sorry wrong number" but I agreed with Sadie, the man was a smoker.

"This is the last number that was in service." Wilson played another recording.

This guy was on the line longer. He answered the phone, Wolf Construction, and Wilson was able to engage him by asking him about a new construction project. It was painfully obvious the guy knew nothing about construction or permitting.

Motherfucker.

Mallard was part of a ring.

Sadie squeezed my hand to the point of pain. And she'd gone statue-still next to me.

"Sadie, baby, do you recognize that voice?"

Her head wobbled in what could be considered a nod, but it was sloppy, jerky, and uncoordinated.

Wilson caught on and turned off the recording. Davis was up out of the chair making his way into the kitchen. I heard his plate clatter in the sink, and he was at the front door when he asked, "Sadie, sweetheart, was that *him*?"

"Yes."

It was barely a whisper, but it sounded like a gunshot.

"We're on it," Wilson said, not bothering to take his plate from the coffee table to the kitchen.

My mind, body, and heart were at war.

I didn't want to leave Sadie, but I wanted to go out with my brothers and pick up the motherfucker who'd burned my woman, made her life a living hell, and made her live under a cloud of worry. My heart wanted to be with Sadie. My body wanted to fight. My mind knew my place was beside her.

"Wilson!" I called out before he shut the door.

His eyes shot to mine.

I didn't need to say anything, he knew what I wanted.

"It'll be done, brother. Believe that."

The door slammed behind Wilson. I wasted no time pulling Sadie off the couch. I took her with me when I locked the door. She followed me with wooden steps up the stairs.

She didn't speak as I stripped her out of her clothes and helped her put on a pair of sweats and a t-shirt. Once I had her in bed, I jogged back downstairs, turned off the lights, and was back in the loft changing my clothes when Sadie finally spoke.

"Reese?"

"Right, here, baby."

Before she could say more, I switched off the light and climbed into the bed next to her. As was her way, she didn't wait for me to pull her close. She rolled into me but tonight was different. She didn't nuzzle in the way she normally did, she shoved herself as close as she could and pinned her leg over mine. Demanding closeness. Needing to hold on to me.

Good God, but I loved this woman.

"What do you need, Sadie?"

"This."

I reached down and jacked her leg up higher and held on to the back of her thigh. My other hand went into her hair and I yanked out the ponytail holder, tossed it away, and ran my fingers through her hair.

Silky and smooth, even after twelve hours of baking her ass off.

And I had the pleasure of watching her get ready every morning. I knew she did nothing to her hair except brush it and pull it up. No products, no five hours doing shit that wouldn't make her any more beautiful than she already was.

Naturally pretty.

"Thank you for taking care of me."

Direct shot to my heart.

"Thank you for letting me be me."

That knife twisted and I felt emotion clog my throat.

"Thank you for telling me you love me every day and doing it in all the ways you do without having to say the words."

I swallowed the boulder that had lodged itself in my windpipe and willed the wet I felt gathering in my eyelids not to fall.

"Thank you for knowing that's what I needed. And thank you for letting me show you. I needed that, too. I needed to show you how much I love you before I gave you the words. But it's time you get both and I hope you know that in the future I might not say them all the time and I'll never be the type that says I love you at the end of every phone call and I might not tell you every time you leave the house, but I promise I'll show you every day. I love you, Reese."

"I love you, too, Sadie."

Her body bucked, and she hiccupped a sob.

Another show.

I waited until her tears subsided and used that time to get my emotions under control. I did my best not to let my past taint the moment, but I couldn't stop my mind from casting back to Ellie. Not the fucked-up parts, but the beginning, when we met. When I'd thought I'd fallen in love. Having Sadie, feeling what she gave me, feeling what I felt for her, I knew with absolute clarity I did not love Ellie. Not even close. And the longer I laid there with Sadie in my arms the more I came to realize that there was not one thing that could taint what we shared. Not a moment, not a day, not in our lifetime.

"We're having five kids?" I asked.

"I don't know if *we're* having five kids, but I am. If you only want one there's always a donor," she joked.

"No other man's sperm will be seeding your uterus. Artificially or otherwise," I growled.

Sadie's soft giggle hit my ears and I smiled.

"So five kids?" she whispered.

"Five," I agreed.

More silence ensued and before I could ask, Sadie did what she always did, read my mood, then put my mind at ease.

"I'm fine. Hearing his voice was a shock. It didn't hurt, it was just a shock. Then honestly, I was excited to hear it because I knew you guys would get him and we could get on with our lives."

I was still digesting what she said when she mistook my silence.

"Seriously, honey, I'm fine."

"You know," I started, "you're starting to give me a complex with how well-adjusted you are."

Then Mrs. S's advice came to mind.

"I'm not fine. Your reaction to that fucker's voice gutted me. I do not like it when you go solid next to me, I don't like feeling you tremble. And when Wilson and Davis left, I wanted to go with them. For a moment I contemplated calling Jack and telling him to get his ass over here so I go could hunting with my brothers. I want to be the one to kick in his door and take him down. I was pissed at Wilson for that shitty attack, me not knowing he was going to play those voices for you and him knowing he had to go behind my back or I would've stopped him. I get why he did it and it ended in a win, but I'm still pissed. And I haven't had a drop of liquor in years. Not because I have a problem. Because when I drink, I can't control the memories of the shit I saw while I was in the Navy. But right now, I want to down a bottle of tequila. And the fuck of it is I don't know if I want to drink because I want to celebrate you giving me the sweetest words I've ever been given, toast that motherfucker's downfall, or if I want to wash the taste of bile out of my mouth that I had to swallow after hearing that dick's voice."

Sadie pressed in closer and glided her hand from my chest down my stomach and traced the waistband of my shorts.

"So breaking that down, you've got some built-up tension that you need to release."

I released her thigh and covered her hand with mine before she could dip under my shorts.

"Sadie, I just told you I don't drink because of the shit I saw and did while I was in the Navy."

"Yeah, you did. And I know better than to ask what those things are. First, because I would never want you to relive something obviously painful to assuage my curiosity. I trust that if you need to talk about it, you know I'm strong enough to hear it and you'll give it to me. But it's yours to give or not. And I know it's painful because you avoid alcohol to avoid remembering. I understand why you're pissed at Wilson. That's part of me thanking you for taking care of me. I knew you wanted to leave with the guys and you put what I needed over what you wanted. Another way you take care of me, but more another way you showed me you love me. So that leaves us with having tension you need to release and it's my pleasure to take care of you. But before I tell you I have a better option than tequila to get the bitter taste out of your mouth, I have a confession to make."

It was hard to believe that I could love Sadie more, but there it was; she'd just proven that false.

"What do you need to confess?"

"Two things. Letty's fake underwear?"

"Yeah, what about them?"

"I bought the dental floss panties."

I didn't see that coming.

I was still chuckling when she told me, "And the last time you washed Letty's car, it was me who took it to a vacant lot and did donuts in the mud."

I flipped Sadie over me and rolled on top of her.

"*That* earned you retribution. Took me four hours to wash off all the mud."

"Would it help if I said I was sorry?" She smiled.

"Nope."

"What about if I gave you a blowjob?"

"You gonna do that for four hours?"

Her lips pinched but she was still smiling.

"I don't think my jaw could handle four hours. What about if I took over the last of the car washes you owe her, would you forgive me then?"

Damn, she was cute as fuck.

"Baby, do not think I'm stupid. Letty would take her car through one of those car washes before she brought it over here so it'd be clean before *you* had to wash it. And do you really think I'd let you wash a car?"

Sadie's eyes flashed before they got squinty.

"I don't know if you can *let* me do anything."

Yep, adorable.

And seeing as I wasn't stupid I changed the subject.

"Any other confessions?"

"I know you're forty-one."

I wasn't sure what my age had to do with anything, so I asked, "Yeah, and? You're thirty-six."

"It's not polite to talk about a woman's age," she snapped.

"If I agree with you will you get to the point?"

"My point is, if we're gonna have five kids we can't wait too long, or you'll be in your fifties and we'll still be having babies. And unlike you, I can't get pregnant whenever, and then there's pregnancy and recuperation and—"

"Baby," I cut her off. "I get it. But just to say, I can't get pregnant at all."

"Don't be smart."

I dipped down and brushed my lips over her scowl until she smiled. Then I lifted my head to ask, "Any other confessions?"

"No."

"You sure? You don't need to tell me that you marked the cards and that's why I lost ninety percent of the poker games whenever Letty's around?"

"No, I didn't mark the cards."

"You didn't set up cameras and weren't secretly feeding her my cards over coms?"

"No, but if I'd known how to do that, I might've," she mumbled.

I believed she would've.

"Good. Then get naked and get on your hands and knees. I wanna taste you before I fuck you."

I didn't miss the tremble or the way her blue eyes darkened with lust.

"I can't do your bidding, Master Reese, if you don't get off me."

"Oh, yeah. Fuck, yeah, we're playing it that way tonight, Sadie."

There was another tremble but this one was more pronounced.

I got to my knees, Sadie scrambled to chuck off her sweats and panties. Next, her shirt and bra came off and she twisted so her back was to me. I scooted down the bed and she dropped to her hands, presenting me with her fabulous ass.

I grabbed two handfuls and squeezed.

"You sure you down with this, baby?"

"Yes."

"Anything you don't want?"

She took a second to think about it then said, "Take whatever you want, it's yours."

My chest exploded with heat.

And this was one of those times when I didn't need words.

I got down to the very important business of eating my woman's pussy.

24

"I'M NOT sure what I'm looking at."

At Letty's statement, I blinked and stopped putting muffins in the bakery case.

"Huh?"

"You. What am I looking at? You look different. Not bad-different. But like you're walking around in a haze."

I was totally in a haze. Or maybe it was a fog—a sex fog.

Reese and I always had great sex, but last night—end-of-the-world sex. Like when you know the asteroid is plummeting to earth and all will be destroyed so you let go of all your inhibitions, even the ones you didn't know you had, and have wild, crazy end-of-the-world sex. That was what had happened the night before.

And I was still in a fog of euphoria.

I glanced to the back corner of the bakery. Reese was there but busy on his laptop, so I couldn't see his face. But I knew he had the same hazy look I had.

"Okay," Letty snapped. "You're freaking me out. What did Reese do to you?"

"He tied me up, spanked me, and did crazy things to my

body that I'm almost positive are illegal in most countries," I whispered. "Oh, and there was a back massager involved, too, but that wasn't used anywhere gross."

Letty's startled eyes widened, then her parted lips closed and turned up, and lastly, she fist-pumped the air.

"Well, all right!" she whooped. "Good to know my girl's getting the good stuff."

I leaned over the counter farther, happy that the bakery was almost empty, and repeated, "He tied me up and spanked me."

"Heard you, doll. Am I reading this wrong? Did you not like it?"

"I freaking *loved* it. Is that weird? I think I'm ruined for regular sex. And my...you know...well, down there, I think it's broken." I leaned in even deeper and continued to whisper. "I had six orgasms. Six, Letty. Six real ones. Not aftershocks. Not mini ones. Not three really long ones. Six. I don't know what this means."

She craned her neck and looked to the back corner and said, "Girl, it means you're dehydrated. Get yourself some SmartWater and replenish some fluids. Then give yourself a few days and ask him to tie you up again. Though I don't think you'll have to ask."

I cut my eyes back to Reese and sure enough, he was watching. He was also smirking one hell of a cocky smile. I didn't bother thinking it looked arrogant; after last night and the magic he wove, he could smile any damn way he wanted. Not to mention, I'd call him Sir, Master, Captain Hot Stuff, or Superman if I was rewarded with six orgasms.

Though Letty was right; I was feeling parched and I wasn't sure if having six orgasms a day was healthy. So I'd wait a few days.

"And you're back to hazy and lost." Letty laughed.

"Sorry. I was thinking you were right, I'm thirsty. How's business? Sorry I haven't been over, but now that Nameless Idiot has been located and he and his slimy friend with the nasal issues are currently in interrogation, I should be free to move about as soon as Reese is happy with their confessions."

The call came in at three a.m. from Wilson that he, Davis, Rhode, and Jack had both men in custody and were on their way to the police station.

It was good news, great news, but it still took a back seat to wild, end-of-the-world sex.

"That was why I came over. River was getting home as I was leaving for work. I was going to congratulate you but six orgasms..." she trailed off and I was happy to have a friend who was on the same page I was.

"Sorry he was out all night."

"Girl, he was skipping in, happy as a pig in shit. He only came home to shower and change his clothes." Now it was Letty's turn to lean over the counter and whisper. "He told me that Nate was fucked up when the guys brought him in. Not only that, but he was crying. River said the guy was sobbing like a baby."

A better person wouldn't have relished someone else's misery. Especially the kind that had to do with physical violence. But I wasn't a better person and he'd stolen eighty-five thousand dollars from me. And because I was a coward who didn't know how to tell my parents even though Reese had been on me pretty much every day, I still hadn't told them and now I was avoiding their calls because I felt guilty. So I was thrilled he was sobbing like a baby since I'd cried myself to sleep on more than one night.

Prick.

Letty noted my smile with her own.

"Welp, I got books to sell," she told me. "Happy this is over for you. River told me that Wilson was confident they'd get your money back."

Yeah, that was what Reese had told me, too. Last night, when I connected the nasally guy with ass munch, it became apparent they were partners and running scams, which meant my money and likely others would be available to recover.

Praise the Lord!

I could pay Mrs. Simpson back in full. I could call my parents to explain what happened and endure their wrath for not telling them sooner, but I'd be able to tell them I got the money back.

"I'm a little creeped out that the nasal guy has been coming in for coffee."

"That's more than a little creepy. Something we'll discuss fully over a bottle of wine. But I gotta run."

"Later, Lets."

"Later."

I finished loading up the case. Jamie came back from her break and immediately grabbed a towel and spray bottle. Before she could skirt the counter, I called her name.

"Yeah?"

Jamie had been a great employee. Dependable, she never sat still, and she was sweet and polite to customers.

"Would you be okay if I took a day off here and there and left you in charge?"

Something that looked like relief passed over her face. And her words confirmed what I saw.

"Thank God. Yes, I would be more than okay. I would love for you to take a day off and more than here and there. At least one a week, two would be ideal. There are times when you're here by yourself, so don't think you need to schedule Kat or Nessa with more hours. I can handle it."

Well, then, it would seem more than just Reese and Wilson had noticed I need a day off.

"Let's start with one day a week," I told her but quickly added, "and that has nothing to do with your performance or me not trusting you. I just have to get used to taking time off."

"Totally get it, Sadie."

Kat went to clean tables, and while there were no customers to help, I walked over to talk to Reese.

"Busy?"

"Nope," he lied and looked up from his laptop and gave me his attention.

"Kat's done with her break. I'm gonna go in the back and take inventory. But I wanted to ask if you've heard anything yet."

"Nate Mallard's real name is Frederick Bateman. The other guy's name is Steve Binder. Neither of them has priors. Bateman's been charged and they're waiting to see what they can pin on Binder besides accessory. Now that Rhode has a name he's doing a deep search, so is this guy we use named Shep. Between the two of them, they'll find the money even if Bateman doesn't give it up."

"His name is Fred?"

"Yep."

"Fred? And the creepy guy who came in for coffee, he's Steve?"

"Yeah."

"Did Steve say why he came in? Was he watching me for some reason?"

"He told Brasco he came in because you've got the best vanilla lattes in CDA. That, and you're pretty to look at.

But he's not gonna admit he came in to watch you when he's steadily denying he knew what his buddy was doing."

Right.

Creepy.

Moving on.

"I'll be back out in a few minutes. I just need to check the walk-in."

Reese's lips twitched and he asked, "Have a nice chat with Letty?"

"You know I did, you were watching."

He stopped smiling and leveled an intense stare at me.

"You sure you're comfortable with everything that happened last night?"

I felt my face heat and I was sure my cheeks were bright red. Which was stupid considering he was asking about things I'd begged him to do to me.

"Yes, I'm positive."

"Even when I—"

"Yes, even that," I rushed to tell him so he wouldn't say it.

"Good."

"You seemed to, but did *you*...um..."

"Never got off so hard in my life. I didn't think you could top your last blowjob, but fucking your mouth while you were blindfolded and tied up, baby, I saw stars."

Well, that was good to know, but now my panties were wet and we still had three hours until I closed.

"Good." I winked and turned.

I didn't get two steps before he called out, "Letty's right, you need to hydrate."

I looked over my shoulder and asked, "How did you know that?"

"She was looking right at me when she said it."

"Can you read lips?"

"Yep."

"Seriously?"

"Yep."

"I feel like that's something you should've told me," I snapped. "What other secrets do you have?"

"Stick around and you'll find out."

Oh, I planned on sticking around all right.

Forever and ever and ever.

"I've got work to do."

"So, go do it."

Reese smiled and I stared.

Was this it?

Was the drama over and we'd finally just get to be us?

As if he could read minds and not just lips, he nodded.

Yeah, this was it. This was a new chapter, and even though the last one had a few bumps, it was pretty damn awesome.

I made my way through my kick-ass bakery, looking around at everything I'd created and what my friends had helped save, and suddenly it held greater meaning.

I alone was strong and capable. But with my friends at my back, we were unstoppable.

I was still smiling when I went through the swinging door into the kitchen and heard the knocking on the back door. I checked my watch again; the delivery guy was an hour early. Today was my lucky day. Maybe I could unload and put away today's delivery and leave early. Jamie was totally capable of closing by herself. I checked the peephole, saw the delivery guy, and unlocked the door.

I barely had it open before he yanked me out the door and pressed a rag against my mouth.

Self-preservation kicked in and I struggled. I mean, I

flayed and kicked, grabbed a fistful of hair and yanked, but the more energy I exerted the harder I breathed. And the harder I breathed the dizzier I became. Until lightheadedness turned into my eyes closing.

Then I felt nothing.

25

HIGH HEELS CLACKING drew my attention from my computer to a tall, slender, nicely dressed woman. Kat greeted her with a smile, then she held up a finger and went through the door to the kitchen.

Since I'd been in the bakery for a week, I knew that Sadie normally handled custom orders. I waited to catch a glimpse of my woman, but Kat came back sans Sadie and looked around the bakery.

Kat's gaze moved through the seating area and her perplexed eyes stopped on me.

That was when the first knot in my gut formed.

I grabbed my laptop and quickly went to the counter.

"Did I miss Sadie going down to the bookstore?" Kat asked.

"She went in the back to do inventory."

"She's not..."

I didn't give Kat a chance to finish. I went around the counter, pushed open the swinging door, didn't bother to look in the walk-in refrigerator or check the bathroom. I went straight to the back door and pushed it open.

Unlocked.

I glanced right and left down the alley.

No Sadie.

Fear ticked up my spine and the knot turned into a snake ready to slither up my throat and choke the life out of me.

I shifted my laptop and yanked my phone out of my back pocket and dialed Rhode.

"Hey, what's—"

"Where are you?" I cut in.

"Office. What's wrong?"

"Thank fuck," I wheezed. "I need you to pull Sadie's cameras. Back door."

I heard his fingers clicking on keys and with each second that ticked by I knew Sadie was being taken farther away from me.

Because she wouldn't leave.

"Fucking hell!" Rhode exploded.

I knew it.

Goddamn knew it.

"Is she...was she...?"

"Breathing?" Rhode supplied.

I couldn't formulate the word, so I grunted.

"Hijacked her out the door. By the looks of it, chloro-formed her, tossed her in a delivery van. By the time you get here, I'll have more."

Chloroform.

My woman was chloroformed and tossed into a van while I was in the bakery.

In the motherfucking bakery.

"Reese!" Rhode snapped.

Why didn't I go back with her? Why in the hell did I stay out front?

"Goddammit, Reese. You need to pull it together and get to the office. I have calls to make. You do not call the guys. You concentrate on driving. I'll call in the team."

Fuck. He was right.

"I'll be there in five."

"You'll be here in fifteen. Drive the speed limit and be—"

I pulled my phone away from my ear while Rhode was still speaking and disconnected. I let go of the door, let it slam behind me, retraced my steps through the kitchen, and pushed through the swinging door.

Kat immediately turned. She was no longer just scared —she looked freaked.

"You've got keys to lock up, right?"

"Yes."

"Good. I need you to go back and lock the door and close up."

"Sadie?"

I lifted my chin and clenched my jaw.

"Kat, need you to lock up, yeah?"

"Yeah, Reese," she whispered.

It was a cruel thing to do, leaving Sadie's friend standing there staring up at me with fear in her eyes, making no attempt to reassure her or explain. However, that was what I did. I went out to my Rover, got in, and drove to the office.

I didn't drive the speed limit and I didn't obey traffic laws.

It still took me ten minutes.

Ten more minutes wasted.

Ten minutes that meant Sadie was in a van passed out.

Vulnerable. Unconscious. Being taken God knows where.

Rhode met me at the door sporting a look of extreme anger.

Thankfully he didn't delay.

"Delivery van belongs to Rich's Foods. Sadie's a long-standing customer. There was a delivery scheduled for her for later this afternoon. I emailed the owner a picture of the man who abducted Sadie. He's not an employee but the owner confirmed that the van is his."

The fucking man who abducted Sadie.

"I also sent the image to Brasco. He doesn't recognize him. He's sending it to the stations to be circulated. Got a full plate number, an APB has been put out on the van. CDA doesn't have many traffic cams, but I was able to track him going north on Northwest Boulevard. He got on 95 South. The last camera I found was at the Blackwell Island Recreation Site."

"I need to talk to Grinder," I bit out.

"Before you do that, think. If the Horsemen have something to do with this, talking to Grinder tips our hand. If they're not involved, you'll be involving them. Grinder might be a dick, but Sadie's his sister; he might feel inclined to do something. Zeus *will* be involved and if he finds her, he's gonna be looking for payback. You do not want him to get it in his head Sadie owes him something. *She* explicitly told you she didn't want that."

Rhode was right. Sadie didn't want Zeus anywhere near her business, she didn't want to owe him anything. But if it was a matter of Sadie's life or me owing the motherfucker, I'd take the hit to get her home safely.

"Don't do it," Rhode warned. "We'll find her."

The door behind me slammed open. I was so lost in my head I didn't even flinch. Not when it opened and not when it slammed shut.

"What do we got so far?" Jack barked.

Nothing.

A stolen van. An unknown male. A missing woman.

My woman.

"Running facial rec right now. I also called Shep. He's better at finding cameras than I am. He's searching now," Rhode answered.

"Didn't think about this until I was parking," Jack started. "Been watching Brasco, River, and that Detective Winegarner work Bateman and Binder all morning. Both of them have their stories down, rehearsed like they practiced for the day they got picked up. Bateman is giving some bullshit about how he had a stalker back in Minnesota and that's why he changed his identity and moved to Idaho. His story is, Sadie gave him that money when she found out he was in danger. He hasn't deviated. Steve Binder's playing it like he had no idea Nate Mallard was using a fake name, just thought he needed a reference."

Rhode was following along. I was biting the inside of my cheek to prevent myself from asking if there was a point. I couldn't give one fuck what those two morons were saying. They could lie all they wanted; they were going down and Sadie's money would be returned.

"But Bateman slipped up. Brasco caught it and pushed. While he was working Sadie, he had a roommate. That was his excuse for never bringing her to his house. But he backtracked and said the buddy was only there for a weekend to visit and he didn't take her to his pad because he was embarrassed he didn't live in a nice apartment.

"Address he gave was for a building in Post Falls. Rent's twelve hundred a month. I personally went there to talk to the apartment manager. The neighborhood's nice and so are the apartments."

"Yep," Jack agreed. "But who's the roommate?"

"You think there's a third?" I rejoined.

"I think that Bateman's good-looking, well-built, but not the brightest bulb. I think that Binder doesn't have the looks to run a woman, and that voice would be a turn-off, but he's smarter than Bateman. The guy who nabbed Sadie, is he good-looking?"

I hadn't seen the video and I wasn't sure I wanted to. But Rhode had. I looked from Jack to Rhode and the muscle in his cheek was jumping.

Shit.

"Brooklyn and Letty would say he's hot. And from what I could see, he's built. He had no issue subduing Sadie— even with her fighting like a motherfucker, he didn't budge."

That settled it. I never wanted to see the video of my woman fighting a man like a *motherfucker*.

"Then my guess, my gut, both say he's the third. Two good-looking guys running women, a man behind a computer doing the banking, getting the identities, probably keeping records of the details of the mark," Jack concluded.

I'm done dealing with this, Reese. I need you to take this.

Thank you for taking care of me.

I love you, Reese.

My chest burned so damn hot it was hard to breathe.

I fucked up.

I didn't take care of her. I failed.

"Reese!" Rhode grunted. "You do her no favors letting your anger get the best of you. Clear your head of the garbage and do your damn job."

My job.

One of those assholes was in Sadie's house. They were looking for something.

Without a word, I bypassed Jack and went for the door.

"Where are you going?" Rhode called out.

"I need to talk to Bateman."

I was back on the street in front of the office when I heard them.

"I'm driving," Jack commanded. "And don't argue. Just get in and I'll take you there."

I didn't care who drove as long as I got to the station, and fast.

Jack beeped the alarm of one of the company SUVs and I slid in. Jack jogged around to the driver's side as Rhode got into the back.

I spent the time on the road thinking about Sadie's break-in. What the hell did they want? Bateman left something there. No, he didn't leave it, he hid it. Blackmail? Insurance the other two didn't turn on him? Bateman was the weak link. He stashed something at her house for a reason. One or both of the other two found out, went to her place, didn't find it, and snatched Sadie.

Why would they turn on each other now?

"Have you found the accounts?" I asked Rhode.

"I was working on that when you called. Davis got three laptops from Binder's place. Shep got me into one. For a guy who says he works at an advertising firm, his machines sure do have a fuckton of security."

"Advertising firm?"

"Yep. What I've found is Binder and Bateman have a ton of LLCs. None of them are worth anything but all of them have websites. Likely setting up fronts or leftovers from old scams."

"Any banking information?"

"I found a document that looks like account numbers, but I haven't connected anything yet."

Think. Do your job.

"They've been at this a while. Played it smart, didn't get caught. So why the hell did they stay in the area after they got the money from Sadie?"

"Unknown third's not done with his mark," Jack interjected. "Bateman was able to close on Sadie faster than the other guy. They're waiting it out until they get the money from the other woman."

Yeah, that made sense. It took months to work a mark, get a woman to trust you enough to give you access to her money or her home or her business.

"It took Bateman about eight, nine months. Three months more, keeping it legit. Then he stopped paying bills, Sadie did catch on, so he took everything and bolted. Either this other guy started after Bateman or he's not as good at working his mark. It's been six months. They need to move on. Bateman or Binder is getting impatient, putting the pressure on, maybe talking about cutting him loose."

I was throwing out whatever popped into my head. It was the only way to keep the crushing fear from taking me under. I had to keep talking.

"Or maybe Binder and the unknown were talking about cutting Bateman out, he went back to Sadie's to get what he stashed there, something that would ensure his place in the trio. Or fuck, maybe Bateman wants out and they won't let him, so again he goes to Sadie's to get whatever he hid to blackmail his way out. Sees she's sold her stuff and he tears the house apart."

"But Bateman's in an interrogation room. Would make sense if he was the one who took Sadie to find out what happened to what he hid. But the unknown took her. He has to know Bateman left something behind," Jack pointed out.

Fuck. He was right.

Jack was pulling into the station when Rhode's phone rang.

I heard him murmuring in the back seat, the muffled words not registering as I played out more scenarios in my head. We were banking on Sadie's kidnapping being connected to Bateman, but Grinder couldn't be ruled out. He was pissed at Sadie, he could've hired someone to snatch her. Or Zeus could be fucking with me, unhappy I threatened him and made it known Sadie was off-limits. He had a deputy in his back pocket. He was feeling all sorts of untouchable and his arrogance would only lead to him pushing the limits.

But was Sadie's brother so far gone, he would let Zeus hurt his sister?

Hell, yeah, he was. Josh was no longer Josh; even as troublesome as he'd been for the Pierces, he was worse now. The information Butch had relayed about Grinder spoke of a morally bankrupt man. The guy was soulless; he'd throw his sister under the bus to earn his place in the Horsemen.

"Does Zeus make his recruits prove their loyalty before they're voted in, like a gang does? Jump, kill..." I swallowed the bile. "Violate."

"Haven't heard that," Jack answered. "Don't let your mind take you there. You've been working the Horsemen as long as I have and you know damn well Zeus makes his people prove loyalty, but he keeps it in-house. He doesn't send them out on the streets to commit murder; that will only draw more attention to the Horsemen."

Right.

Jack was right.

But Zeus still could've hired someone to take her.

Jack said his gut was Bateman's crew. Mine did, too. But experience has taught me to keep an open mind and not cross a suspect off the list until their innocence was proven. The Horsemen were far from innocent.

As soon as Jack found a parking spot I was out of the SUV and jogging to the front door.

Davis was standing there, arms crossed, deep glower.

He was also barring the door.

"This a good idea?" he asked.

"Is what a good idea?"

"You being here, brother. Seeing him. Hearing the bull-shit he's spewing."

No, it probably wasn't a good idea, but it was happening.

"I'm fine."

"Reese, you're two seconds from blowing up. You know we got this."

"It doesn't matter what I'm two seconds away from doing. I'm going in there."

Davis looked to my right then my left. I didn't bother. I knew Rhode and Jack were crowding me. If the three of them thought they were going to lock me down, they were mistaken.

"Mine," I growled. "When it's your woman missing, then you get a say. But right now, it's mine. My Sadie. I get what you're trying to do. And maybe later when I got Sadie in my arms, I'll regret this. Maybe not. Got love for you, Davis, but either you get the fuck outta my way or you and me, we got fucking problems. And they're gonna start with you having a black eye and me not forgiving you for standing in the way of me finding my woman. Now, this pointless fucking standoff has wasted time Sadie doesn't have. So right now, I need you to think about how much you claim to care about her and fucking *move*."

Davis stepped to the side. I went for the door but Rhode got there first and grabbed the handle.

I growled.

He leaned closer and said, "Keep your shit. Do not go in there and get crazy. You'll find yourself in a cell and Sadie needs you out looking. Lock it down and don't fuck her by fucking up the case Winegarner's building. They're on your side."

I goddamn hated when Rhode was the voice of reason.

I nodded and Rhode opened the door.

Wilson and Brasco were standing just beyond the security door. Brasco swiped his card and the door clicked unlocked.

Brasco jerked his head to an open door to the right and we all shuffled in.

Wilson didn't delay.

"Filled Brasco in about what I knew about the deputy. I want every angle covered, including the Horsemen and the deputy." Wilson cut his eyes at Brasco. Any other time I would've tried to decipher the detective's frown but right then I couldn't care less if he was pissed. "The rumors weren't only about the deputy. Zeus has already instigated his play. It worked with the deputy so just as we thought, he's moved on to trapping other cops. Four of them. All five of Zeus's play toys are accounted for and on the job. None of them had made any moves today that could be considered out of the norm. And since the three that Brasco and Kent knew about have been under surveillance, none of them have done anything to violate police procedure."

"So you don't think it's Zeus or Grinder?" I inquired.

"Nothing points to them," Brasco confirmed.

"We're back to Bateman and his crew. The third member of that crew being the man who snatched Sadie."

"Frederick Bateman had a lease on a house in Athol," Brasco continued. "We pulled it; no other occupants listed. Steve Binder was renting, again in his name, in CDA. No other occupants were listed. Five minutes ago, Davis produced phone records and credit card statements. I cannot look at them. I can't even know where he found them. I'm going to go back to the interrogation room and watch. You four go over those records and find me a name to throw at Bateman. I think he's the weak link here. Binder's cold, calculating. Besides his looks, it's probably why he's not out working marks. He doesn't have the charisma. He's so cold, I doubt he can make any emotional connections, even with his partners. He'll let them go down and he'll roll out without blinking."

"I wanna see Bateman."

"Not a good idea, Reese," Wilson refused.

"I want Brasco to show Bateman the video and I wanna watch his reaction. I'm good at reading people; I'm the best in interrogation and you know it. I won't go in. I won't fuck the case. But I need to see his reaction."

"Fuck," Davis muttered.

"Reese's right," Jack agreed. "He's the best in interrogation. Davis, Rhode, and I will go over the intel. But Reese needs to watch."

Brasco caved. "Send me the footage. You two, follow me."

Wilson gave me a hard look before we took our leave and followed Brasco through the bullpen. The interrogation rooms were tucked into the back right corner of the station. Officers looked up from their desks as we passed but no one said a word. I vaguely wondered if one of the men Zeus was blackmailing was one of the officers watching. He wouldn't hit the brass, not at first. He'd start with patrolmen, maybe try a detective, but he'd save the big dogs for later.

Before we entered the observation room, I tapped Wilson on the arm and jerked my head back toward the bullpen. He gave me a sharp nod.

Jesus. No wonder River had looked like he was holding on by a thread when Brasco had told us about the rumors, River moved jurisdictions from Georgia to Idaho and the first precinct he gets a job in has a dirty cop—or a potentially dirty cop, when Zeus starts laying on the heavy.

Fucking hell.

My attention was pulled from dirty cops, River, and Zeus when Bateman came into view. His mouth was moving, but the sound was turned off. I reached toward the wall and hit the one-way intercom.

"I already told you," Bateman whined.

Short sandy-brown hair that looked like he'd been running his hands through it. Either that or one of the guys had grabbed a handful of hair and held it to keep his head steady while they used his face as a punching bag. Two deeply colored black eyes were forming. His lip was cut, his t-shirt had blood on it. With his face fucked up, I couldn't say if the man was good-looking or not, but what I could say was he sounded like a sniveling bitch.

Which might work in our favor.

Also, Bateman wasn't meeting Winegarner's eyes. His head was tipped down and he was looking at something on the table. A sign of guilt, something else that was good.

I took in River, leaning against the wall to Bateman's left. One knee was cocked, the sole of his boot was on the drywall, arms crossed over his chest. River Kent was a big motherfucker, standing at six-foot-three. He wasn't the tallest of the Kent Brothers. His older brother had an inch and fifty pounds on River. Echo Kent was a beast, a wall of muscle, whereas River was less bulk, but still huge.

"I bet he shit his pants when he caught sight of River," I muttered.

"His drawers were already dirty by the time your brothers brought him in," Brasco contradicted.

Good.

"Got the video. Be back."

As soon as the door closed behind Brasco, Wilson turned to me.

"You gonna be able to handle this?"

"No. But I got no choice."

"This isn't—"

"Not a good time to tell me what is or isn't my fault. And you of all people should understand that."

It was a cockheaded thing to say to my friend, but damn if I wanted to hear about how Sadie's abduction wasn't my fault. I wasn't after absolution. I was after securing Sadie's safety.

"I hear that," Wilson returned. "But to throw it back on you, I'll give you the here and now, but don't think we're not talking about this shit when you crawl up my ass to cure me of my guilt."

Confirmation that Wilson needed to unburden his soul, and more confirmation he was going to take me up on my offer.

Brasco walked into the interrogation room and all eyes went to him. Bateman was the first to look away and go back to staring at the table.

"Want you to watch something," Brasco started.

The two other detectives in the room went on alert.

Brasco didn't wait for Bateman to respond before he

stepped next to him, leaned down, and held his cellphone in front of Bateman.

I saw the moment Brasco hit play. Bateman's eyes were riveted on the screen. His demeanor went from whiny bitch to man. His brows pulled tight. His shoulders went stiff and suddenly he wasn't hunched over, playing the scared rabbit.

Frederick Bateman had shown up.

"What the fuck?" Bateman roared.

Brasco didn't move. As pissed as Bateman had become, his hands were cuffed to the table and there wasn't much he could do.

"Why don't we watch it again?" Brasco suggested. "Make sure you get a good look at what your partner did to Sadie Pierce. But this time, pay special attention to Sadie's eyes. Watch how scared she is."

"Don't show me that shit again."

Oh, yeah, the whine was gone. He sounded more like the man I'd heard on the recording Wilson had played. Voice deeper and cocksure.

"I figured you'd appreciate verification your colleague was taking out the trash for you. With Sadie out of the way, we don't have a witness."

Brasco was pushing the right buttons. But he needed to push harder.

Bateman's jaw clenched. I knew that shit had to hurt with the cut lip and the bruising, but he didn't flinch.

Brasco straightened, handed his phone off to Winegarner. And I knew that video was worse than I thought when the detective shot out of his chair and slammed a fist on the table.

"Fucked-up end for a woman you claimed to love. Said she was the best thing that happened to you. Said you cared about her and cried when your stalker found you and you had to leave Sadie to keep her safe. When we find her body, I'll be sure to tell her parents how much you love her."

I choked on the bile crawling up my throat. Wilson waited for my coughing to subside before he wrapped his fingers over my shoulder.

"You know what he's doing; it's nothing you haven't done before. Sadie was not injured in that video."

Right. She'd just fought like a *motherfucker*.

"She was the best thing that ever happened to me!" Bateman shouted. "Fucking goddamn. Fuck!"

I yanked my phone out of my pocket, not caring that Brasco wouldn't appreciate me interrupting his inter-rogation.

I watched Brasco pull his phone out of his pocket. His eyes narrowed, but he still answered.

"Detective Brasco," he feigned professionalism.

"Push him. Tell him that the delivery guy was found dead. Make him believe that his partner is unhinged, violent, and ask him if he found what he was looking for at Sadie's place."

"Right. Thanks for the update."

Brasco disconnected and looked at Winegarner. When the two detectives unlocked gazes, Winegarner took his seat and Brasco started in.

"Fucked-up way to show her how much you love her by sending a killer after her."

Bateman's gaze sliced to Brasco's and he shook his head. Bateman opened his mouth, but shut it, then started again, "A killer?"

"Listen, don't bullshit me. The van your friend stole was on route. He killed the driver, took his clothes and his van, then paid Sadie a visit. And you see the care he showed the woman you love. He practically strangled her right there in the alley."

A growl slipped out and Wilson squeezed my shoulder, "He's exaggerating."

Logically, I knew Brasco was lying, but I still couldn't stomach hearing that shit.

"Hell, Freddy, you know him. How long does he like to play with his women before he gets rid of them? How much time does the woman you love have left breathing?"

Goddamn, if I hear one more fucking person talk about Bateman loving Sadie I'm going to lose my fucking mind.

"Sam would never fucking kill someone. And he wouldn't kill Sadie. He knows I'd gut him if he touched her."

Sam.

We had a name.

Thank fuck.

River pushed off the wall and spoke for the first time.

"Seems you're wrong about that, friend. Seeing as you're locked up, Sam's decided he's not all that afraid of you. Are you sure he wouldn't touch her? Really sure? Seems to me like your buddy was just pretending to be scared of you. Do you think your pal Steve's afraid of you, too?"

"Fuck you," Bateman spat.

"Fuck me?" River laughed. "Don't get pissed at me because your buddy's got the love of your life. The best thing that ever happened to you. But, come on, we know that shit's a lie. You don't care you fucked her over, you don't care she had to sell her shit so she could eat, you don't care that right now your buddy's probably trying to get—"

"What'd you say?" Bateman interjected.

And not a moment too soon.

If River had continued with his line of questioning, I'm man enough to admit I might've puked.

"I said a lot, gotta be more specific."

"Sadie sold her shit? What does that mean?"

Honest surprise.

He had no idea she'd sold her furniture.

"He didn't break in."

"So it was Binder or Sam."

The door opened and Davis walked in.

"Rhode and Jack are still cross-referencing but we found a name Bateman and Binder both call daily."

"Sam?" I asked.

"Yeah, Samuel Barker. Rhode remembered seeing something on Binder's computer, a folder named B Cubed. There were LLC papers and an Excel spreadsheet with what Rhode thinks are bank accounts."

"Are you telling me these fuckers are paying taxes on the money they steal?"

"No idea, but B Cubed is a legit business."

"You got an address for Sam?"

"We got several."

A growl slipped out. "You could've started with that."

"And you could stand here and bitch," Davis told me. "Or we can roll out and find your woman."

"I'm staying here to watch," Wilson told us. "I'll keep you in the loop and be out as soon as I know more."

I wordlessly followed Davis and checked my watch.

Almost two hours.

Fuck.

26

I HAD NEVER in my life been involved in a physical altercation so I had nothing to compare it to, but I figured it was a safe bet getting slapped by a man hurt a fair bit more than being hit by a woman. Even if that woman was a bodybuilder. Or maybe it hurt so bad because the man slapping me was pissed as all get-out. And since he wasn't making sense, thus, I couldn't answer his rapid-fire questions so he kept slapping me.

"Where the fuck is it?"

That question was spat in my face.

I was sitting on a bed in what looked like a flophouse. The sparse furnishings made my house look cluttered. It was dingy, it was gross, it looked abandoned and unlived in. Which might be the case because either the guy hadn't turned on any lights or there was no electricity servicing the house.

I had no idea where I was because when I'd woken up, I was lying on the bed I was currently sitting on. And as soon as my eyes had fluttered open, the guy had pounced.

"Where is what?"

Crack.

The sound of his palm hitting the same, exact place he'd landed the last five smacks hit my ears before the pain bloomed.

"I know he told you."

"Who?"

Slap.

"Rick!"

"I don't know a Rick."

Big mistake. The guy's hand fisted a chunk of my hair and he yanked me to my feet. Once I was there, he kept yanking. I tried so hard to conceal my whimper, but it felt like he was ripping my hair out at the scalp.

"Nate," he snarled.

Nate.

My house.

Reese was right.

"It's...um..."

On a good day, I sucked at lying. When my face was on fire and my hair was being pulled out by the roots and all I could think about was how this guy was probably going to kill me, I couldn't come up with a lie fast enough.

"Don't fuck with me, bitch."

The guy used my hair to lean me forward. At the same time, I saw him jack his knee up, right before I felt all the air whoosh out of my lungs. I couldn't breathe. I was trying to suck in air but I couldn't. I ended up hacking and coughing which was good seeing as I was suffocating but I still couldn't catch my breath and it only pissed the guy off more.

Next thing I knew I was flying through the air. Flying. My feet were off the floor and my body was sailing across the room. My back hit the mattress; I didn't bounce because the guy was on top of it pinning me down.

"Where the fuck is it?" This time when he screamed in my face, spittle accompanied the words. Not just small specks of spit, so much of it I felt it dripping down my forehead.

Think.

Buy time.

Reese and the guys are looking.

Think!

The guest room. All the CDs and DVDs were taken out of the cases.

"You mean the CD?" I rushed out.

Nope.

Wrong guess.

The guy grabbed my shoulders and started thrashing me around.

This was not good.

I wasn't good.

I didn't have time to wait for Reese to swoop in and save me.

"I have more money," I lied. "Nate didn't take it all."

"You think I want your money? I don't give a fuck about your money. Besides, you're lying, Steve's kept an eye on your accounts."

Nasally guy was keeping an eye on me.

Creepy.

"I know it's not at your house, I checked." The guy stopped shaking me and I didn't think that was a good sign. "This will be the last time I ask—where is it?"

Yep. I was right. His calmness was a bad sign.

Fuck it.

Being compliant wasn't working.

He was going to hurt me whether I was playing along or not.

So, fuck him.

"I don't know what the hell you're talking about," I snarled. "I've told you five fucking times. Are you stupid or a fucking idiot?"

Bam.

Closed-fisted punch to the face.

That hurt so much more than a slap. So much, I couldn't control the tears as they sprang from my eyes. So much so, I couldn't control my reaction.

And that was when I fought.

I kneed. I twisted. I screamed. I struggled.

In his shock, he reared back, and as soon as he let go of my arms I attacked.

I clawed and slapped and punched.

I hit everything I could reach.

Then I wasn't hitting anything because his big hands wrapped around my throat.

My nails scraped down his face but he didn't let go.

My legs kicked and he didn't let go.

My hips bucked and I tried yanking his hair, but he didn't let go.

I heard a strange gurgling sound. I could smell my own desperation wafting through the room. My vision danced with spots.

My last thought on this earth would not be about the guy on top of me squeezing the life out of me. It wouldn't be about Nate taking my money, then my life. I closed my eyes and pictured Reese.

God, he had a great smile.

His beautiful greenish-brown eyes.

The sound of his laugh.

Big and strong and fierce and he loved me so much.

Yes, as I took my last breath and left this life, I would think about how loved I was.

The gurgling stopped. The pain slipped away, and a weird euphoria took over.

And my last thought was indeed how much Reese loved me.

27

GETTING out of the SUV and hearing Sadie's scream traveling from a quarter-mile away took ten years off my life.

But when the screaming stopped, I died a thousand painful deaths.

Sprinting the last three hundred yards was the most excruciating forty seconds of my life.

And as it would turn out, the fifteen extra seconds it took to kick down the door and enter the house would be fifteen seconds Sadie didn't have.

I hit the bedroom, saw Sam straddling Sadie, and saw red. Accompanying that sight was one of Sadie not screaming or kicking her legs. My vision hazed over.

Humanity left my soul as I yanked Sam off Sadie. The thud of him hitting the wall did not satisfy me. The blood that flew from his nose and mouth each time my fist connected with his face did not slake my thirst.

My ears roared with indecent and ruthless intent.

The only thing that penetrated my savagery was Davis calling out, "No pulse."

Instead of allowing those crippling words to take me to my knees, I continued to pummel Sam's face and torso. Every punch landed with accuracy and precision. I didn't want to knock this motherfucker out, I wanted him awake and in pain. I wanted him conscious while I broke his bones and smashed his organs. I wanted his breath and his blood and his suffering.

I heard voices shouting in the background. I felt my team moving around me. I smelled the coppery tang of blood.

But I didn't feel Sadie's presence.

I couldn't feel her heart beating.

I couldn't feel her love.

I was numb.

I felt someone jump on my back and just as I was dipping my shoulder, I heard Rhode.

"Enough!"

I hesitated and that was all Rhode needed to take me down.

"*Enough*, goddammit!" he shouted and rolled to the side, leaving me on my back staring up at the ceiling.

The fog began to lift and the agonizing noises of someone administering CPR filled the room. I looked in the direction of the sound and saw Davis performing mouth-to-mouth on Sadie as she lay on the floor. He pulled away and started chest compressions.

I had nothing to give. I was close enough I reached out and grabbed her hand.

Mine cut and bloody.

Hers limp.

Feeling that, I rolled to my side, got onto my knees, and scooted as close as I could without getting in Davis's way.

Rhode stood at Sadie's feet staring down at her, phone at his ear talking to police dispatch.

Jack was on his knees doing the same only he was talking to Wilson.

Davis worked.

Fifty-five seconds to end a life.

"Goddamn, *breathe!*" Davis roared.

I brought Sadie's hand up to my mouth and pressed my lips against the back of it.

"I need you, baby," I whispered there. "I need you to come back to me."

I wish I could say that was all she needed to open her eyes.

But it took longer. Long enough for the air in the room to thicken with grief. Long enough for Rhode to rest his hand on my shoulder. Long enough for Jack to pick up Sadie's hand and kiss it. Long enough for sweat to drip down Davis's chin.

And when the reality of losing Sadie had washed over me, in a twist of fortune, she coughed. Then she choked and sputtered and breathed. That was until her brain came back on station. Then she cried out in the most horrendous wail I'd ever heard.

Davis sat back on his haunches. His head dropped forward and his eyes closed.

I moved in and braced my hands on the floor next to her shoulders.

"You're safe, Sadie. Relax. Open your eyes."

Her mouth opened, a sound came out, but it wasn't legible.

"Don't talk. I wanna hold you so bad, baby, but I can't move you. Not until you're checked."

Sadie moved her head and yelped in pain.

"Baby, please don't move."

I felt a rush of air leave her lips and I closed my eyes.

Thank fuck for the twist.

28

TWO DAYS ago when I woke up in the hospital, which apparently wasn't when I actually woke up, seeing as after Davis had literally breathed life back into me, I woke up then. But I didn't remember any of that. I also didn't remember the paramedics coming and transporting me to the hospital. Nor do I remember the three hours I slept.

Reese remembered. Davis remembered. Jack and Rhode did, too.

Back to my point. Two days ago when I woke and saw the panic and fear in the faces of all my friends, I made the decision not to argue. Not to complain about the pain. Not to complain when Reese insisted—yes, insisted—to the point the doctor backed down and ordered an MRI of my throat and neck. That held up my release for four hours. When the MRI came back and the doctor announced I was good and there was nothing damaged, Reese had insisted on a second opinion. This led to Wilson taking him on a walk.

While Reese and Wilson were gone, Jack had a talk with me. Incidentally, he waited until Davis had gone to find coffee and had asked Brooklyn and Letty to step outside. Then Jack laid it out. He told me about Davis giving me CPR, how all of them, including Reese, thought I was dead and the only reason I was alive was because Davis hadn't quit.

Again, Davis had breathed life back into me.

So, I was not going to complain about anything.

I had a second chance at life, I wasn't going to waste any of it.

Moving on from that, Jack explained that while I was lying on the floor dead or dying, whichever way you want to look at it, Reese was beating the life out of Sam Barker. He told me that when the authorities arrived, Sam was still alive but barely. He asked me to be patient with Reese and let him be what Jack said would most likely be suffocatingly overprotective. Then Jack admitted that all the guys, including himself, would likely be suffocatingly overprotective. But it was only because the scene they'd walked into and the amount of time it had taken for me to breathe on my own had scared the shit out of them. Then he kissed my forehead.

Two days later, Sam was still in the hospital, but he was alive, and all of the guys were acting crazy.

I didn't complain.

The first night, Reese took me back to the cabin and he carried me up the stairs. Wilson slept on the couch, Davis on the floor, and Jack had stayed awake all night in one of the Takeback SUVs. Rhode went home but only because he needed to be with his wife. Who he'd clung to the entire time we were at the hospital.

Now here we were at dinner time on the second day, and everyone was piled into Reese's cabin. Which was not a cabin built for entertaining. There was room enough for two people to live comfortably. I loved it here, but if the guys were going to make a habit of hanging around we needed to move ASAP. Brooklyn had to bring over folding chairs just so everyone could sit. And no one would hear of me sitting in a folding chair. So I was tucked into the corner of the comfy couch, Letty was next to me, Brooklyn next to her. Reese in the leather chair to my left, Rhode in the matching leather chair to Brooklyn's right. And River, Wilson, Davis, and Jack in folding chairs. Four, big, oversized men in folding chairs holding plates in front of them, eating the lasagna Brooklyn had made and brought over. They looked ridiculously uncomfortable.

I didn't say a thing.

All of them had beers, including me, Brooklyn, and Letty. Reese was drinking apple juice. When my beer got low, someone got up and got me another one.

I didn't say a word—except thank you, of course.

They were all doing their best not to stare at the bruising on my face and neck even though I knew it was impossible not to notice. Still, they tried.

I kept quiet.

When Brooklyn lied and told me that the Welshes wanted some time with Remy and that was why he didn't come with her and Rhode, I gave her that and didn't call her out on it. She was a good mom; Remy didn't need to see me beat to shit. But I also knew she didn't want Remy to look at me and ask questions she thought would hurt me. So, really, she was just a great friend and I adored her.

"What's new with Asher and Cole?" River asked.

"Application is in," Wilson answered. "So now they're just waiting."

I glanced over at Reese and queried, "Application? I thought they were undercover?"

"Asher is. Cole's there as backup." Reese smiled for some reason.

It wasn't a big one like I'd imagined as I was being strangled, but it was there.

"He has to apply to go undercover?"

"No, he had to apply to be a member of the sex club he's going undercover in," Jack supplied.

"Asher is going undercover in a sex club? Seriously?"

"Yep."

I was getting ready to make a joke until I remembered what the guys did and who they worked with and how the large majority of their cases had to do with human trafficking and suddenly the joke died, and my stomach tightened.

"He's going undercover to make sure the club's on the up and up," Wilson explained.

That made me feel a little better but not much.

But when Wilson went on, I felt the tension that had become so normal I could almost forget how heavy it was, lift away.

"Talked to Brasco on the way over here. He's thinking you should have your money back within thirty days. All the accounts have been frozen. Winegarner and a dozen other detectives from other states are all getting their reports polished up and meeting with prosecutors. Idaho's got them first since they're here and the prosecutor doesn't feel like extraditing them to another state before they get their chance."

My gaze went to River, and he was smiling.

"Thank you. All of you, for everything you did."

I got grunts, but no other acknowledgments.

I didn't complain.

"I checked in on Jamie today. She and Kat were kicking

ass behind the counter," Letty told me. "I don't know if you left Kat your secret recipes, but I swear the cinnamon rolls were almost as good as yours."

The only, tiny squabble Reese and I had gotten in was when I insisted on calling Jaime. First, I wanted her to know I was all right. Then I needed to make sure she knew where I kept my recipe cards. I no longer needed them, so they were tucked away in my office.

I might've almost been strangled to death but I still had a business to run.

"She's good," I agreed. "She's been practicing decorating."

Letty scrunched her nose and I laughed. Then I abruptly stopped when my broken ribs made themselves known.

"That bad?" I asked.

"Eh. They were okay. But not Treats Bakery quality."

Oh, well. I wasn't going to complain about that either.

Davis got up and I watched him walk into the kitchen.

The time was nigh. I needed to talk to him but hadn't had a chance to get him alone all night. I scooted to the edge of the couch and Reese moved, too.

"I'm fine," I whispered.

"I'll get it," he countered.

I glanced toward the kitchen then back to Reese.

"Honey, I'm *fine*."

Reese nodded but stood to help me out of the couch.

I had just rounded the corner when Davis turned and took me in.

"You shouldn't be up."

Yes, suffocatingly overprotective.

My voice still sounded croaky and my throat hurt if I talked too much but I had something to say to Davis, so he'd have to deal with my scratchy voice, and I'd get over the pain.

"Thank you for saving my life."

Davis's eyes dropped to my midsection then went to the wall behind me.

"I hate that no one will look at me," I whispered.

"What?"

"I know it looks bad. It's totally gross—"

"Sweetheart, we're not avoiding looking at you because it looks bad. We can't look at what the asshole did to you without wishing Reese would've finished the job. We can't look at those marks around your neck without thinking about how close we came to losing you—and Reese. Make no mistake, Sadie; if you would've died, we would've lost Reese, too. None of us can look at that pretty face of yours and miss that fucker's handprint on it. We've been hit in the face before. We all know how hard he had to hit you to leave that mark."

"Thank you for saving Reese's life, too."

I was getting winded, and I knew Davis heard it when he looked at my ribs again.

So, I had to finish.

"You know what I think about every time I feel the pain in my ribs? Grateful. When it hurts to breathe, I think about how hard you worked to save my life. Every rib you broke giving me CPR means I get to be here. I'd take the broken ribs and the breath in my body over the alternative."

Davis's eyes locked with mine, but he didn't say anything.

"Jack told me what happened. He told me everyone thought I was gone but you wouldn't quit." I had to pause to take a breath. "Thank you for breathing for me when I couldn't."

I saw the flash in his eyes before they started to shine. I figured he wouldn't appreciate me watching him struggle with whatever he was struggling with, so I turned to leave.

"I'd say you're welcome, but really, it was my honor," he said to my back.

I nodded and gingerly made my way back to the living room.

Five minutes later, Davis returned.

And an hour after that, everyone left.

And I finally made the dreaded phone call to my parents. Five minutes into the conversation, Reese heard me struggling to breathe so he took the phone. Ten minutes later Reese disconnected and told me my dad was arranging flights and would be in Idaho as soon as they could.

Of course, they were on their way to me, they loved me.

———

REESE WAS in the bathroom getting ready for bed.

Something he hadn't done since I'd moved in. He'd go in there to brush his teeth, do his business, but he undressed and changed in the bedroom. I did the same. I didn't know if this change was because he didn't want to see me naked or he thought I didn't want him to see. What I knew was I was ending it right now, before it festered.

That was why when he came out of the bathroom, I was standing by the bed naked as the day I was born.

This was hard for me. I was bruised from my throat to my belly button and my face didn't look that great. So as you could imagine I wasn't feeling sexy or pretty. I felt like I'd been run over, backed over, then run over again.

But this was important.

Reese came to a juddering stop as soon as he opened the

door. He diverted his attention, his jaw clenched, his fists balled, and his body did this weird twitch.

"I need you to look at me," I whispered.

Immediately his gaze came to mine. Straight to my eyes. Nowhere else.

"No, I need you to look. At. Me. All of me."

His eyes dropped to my throat and after a millisecond came back to mine.

"This is when I need you to love me regardless of how hard it is for you to see. I need you to look at what Sam left around my neck, then look at what Davis gave us. The bruises Davis left behind, those are for *us*, Reese. Next to your love, those bruises are the best gift I've ever received."

Reese's eyes started roaming my body. Neck, torso, neck, the side of my face, then back to my torso.

CPR was not like the movies. It was violent and required strength to manually force oxygen into someone's lungs. Ribs broke. Sternums cracked. Considering how long Davis had worked on me, coupled with how easily I bruised, it could've looked worse.

Reese slowly closed the distance between us. When he got in front of me, he dropped to his knees, carefully rested his cheek on my stomach, and even more gently wrapped his arms around my hips.

My hands lifted to his shoulders.

The normal noises of the house faded away—the dishwasher, the fridge, the hum of the humidifier to keep all the wood in the cabin from drying out. All of my concentration was on Reese, the feel of his breath fanning over my stomach with every exhale. The sound of his lungs filling with each inhale. The tremor in his hands as they lightly rested on my hips. And finally, the tears I felt on my skin.

The show.

I was safe. I was alive. We were moving on.

The silence stretched for a long time. Reese giving me what I needed. Taking his time to take what he needed.

He slowly lifted his cheek off my stomach, shifted, and brushed his lips across my belly—from hip to hip. Then he went higher and lightly pressed kisses up my torso. I felt him shuffle to his feet, careful not to jostle me, and he continued to kiss the bruises on my ribs, between my breasts, higher still until he got to my throat.

Over and over, kiss after kiss, he worked his way over my neck and back again. Sometimes he paused and his tongue peeked out, licking my flesh. In some places, he grazed his teeth. Some kisses were barely there. It was sensual but not sexy. It wasn't about sex or lust. It was profoundly beautiful.

When he was done with my throat, he kissed my jaw, moved to my cheek, kissed me there, and trailed up to my temple.

"Your strength amazes me," he whispered. "I am in awe of you."

I wanted to remind him that I'd woken up last night with a nightmare that had me sobbing in his arms. But I refrained. If he thought that was strength, I wasn't going to argue.

But he needed to know why when I was scared and in pain, I could be strong.

"It's because I have you. It's because right before I blacked out my last thought was that I was loved. While I couldn't breathe, I was thinking about you smiling at me. How lucky I was to have a man like you love me. I found strength in that. Last night I woke up scared, but in your arms, I found strength. On my own, I'm stubborn and deter-mined. But when I stand at your side, that's when I find real strength. The kind that makes me feel like I can do anything."

There was more I wanted to say but couldn't. My throat was on fire and getting scratchier. I wanted to wrap my arms around him, but I couldn't lift my arms without the muscles in my sides pulling and putting pressure on my ribs. So all I could do was stand there with my arms dangling at my sides.

Reese dropped a kiss to my forehead and stepped away. He didn't have to go far to find the new button-up pajama shirt Brooklyn had bought me. Reese helped me into the shirt, left me to button it, and went to the dresser to get me a pair of panties. Once he helped me step into those, he pulled the covers back and got in, shoved a pillow behind his back, and leaned against the headboard.

"Crawl in, baby," he directed and opened his legs. "Your back against my chest."

I wasn't sure if this would work but did as he asked. Reese added a pillow on his chest, and I found it was the perfect angle. Once I was settled, he reached over, shut off the light, and I was totally cocooned. His thighs pressed against mine. His arms around me. One of his hands held mine, the other went under my shirt and rested on my stomach.

"Sleep, baby."

That was what I did. I slept like a baby the whole night through.

29

"YOU CHEAT," I groused.

Sadie, Letty, and Brooklyn were sitting opposite me, River, and Rhode. Davis, Jack, and Wilson filled three remaining chairs at Wilson's poker table.

The women all had blank expressions. The men were cackling like hyenas.

"I cheat?" Sadie asked with mock innocence. "I thought you said Letty cheats."

"You both are cheats," I amended.

"Listen, big man, just because you lose don't mean someone else is cheating," Letty explained.

She, too, was feigning innocence.

I didn't know how they were doing it. I'd watched the two of them all night; their hands had never gone under the table, they hadn't gotten up for a refill in the middle of a hand, but Letty and Sadie were cheating. I knew it.

My gaze went to Brooklyn and she quickly looked over at Rhode.

Guilty.

She knew how they were doing it.

She knew but she would never rat her friends out.

"What's he up to?" Letty asked Sadie.

Sadie glanced down at the paper on the table. Yes, she needed a piece of paper to keep track of what she'd won.

"Reese owes me three foot massages, a manicure including polishing, and he's on laundry duty for..." she trailed off and counted the tally marks, "twelve days after that last double or nothing."

"Don't forget," Wilson started. "You owe me a dozen cupcakes and a coffee cake."

Sadie smiled at Wilson and shook her head.

"Like you pay for your cupcakes," she returned.

Her first day back in to work at the bakery had been an exercise in control.

Controlling my fear. Controlling my need to stand guard at the back door. Controlling my mouth.

It had been the same for Wilson, Davis, Jack, and Rhode. Each of them had gone into the bakery at different times. Sadie knew it was to check on her and she didn't utter a complaint about it. But she'd refused their money. And the men had complained about that. Then she used emotional blackmail and the guys backed off and took their freebies. None of them would tell me what she'd said to them, but they did explain that if there ever came a time when Sadie and I were arguing I'd be fucked. She'd also told her employees that if any of them accepted money from any of the guys they'd be fired—tips were the only thing allowed. Of course, she was joking, or at least I thought she was. But she was serious about the guys not paying.

Wilson's phone rang. He excused himself and I took that as an opportunity to refill my wife's wine.

Though I didn't dare call Sadie my wife, or Mrs. Turmel, or mention the wedding at all in front of Letty or

Brooklyn. It wasn't that they weren't happy for us. It wasn't like they weren't there and didn't stand at her side while we exchanged vows, it was simply because we were married before them.

The circumstances were such that Sadie's parents had flown to Idaho the day after Sadie had called them to fill them in on her attack and everything that had happened prior with Nate. I learned quickly that Frank Pierce was who I thought he was, a father who worried endlessly about his children. Especially his son, who continued down a path of no return. It was rumored the Horsemen would be patching him in by the end of the month. It had taken Wilson and Letty's father to talk him down from seeking out his son. No good would come from an irate father getting in his son's face about his life choices when that son was connected to Zeus. Josh Pierce was no more. He'd fully embraced Grinder and the Horsemen way of life. Sadie was over it. Her brother didn't come up in conversation. She told me and her parents she'd mourned the loss of Josh like a death and that was what he was—dead to her.

At the end of the Pierces' weeklong visit, I took Frank to see the piece of property I'd purchased that wasn't too far from Rhode and Brooklyn. Like my friend, I enjoyed wide-open spaces. The ten acres I found would do for now, but only with the hopes we could buy the adjacent property when it became available. I asked Frank for his permission to marry his daughter. After a long, candid discussion about his concern that we hadn't been together long enough to make a lifelong commitment he came around and offered his blessing.

Frank and Mary stayed another two weeks. My parents flew in, my siblings did not. It was hard not to fall in love with Sadie, and my mom was no exception to this. She'd instantly fallen in love. My mom, Mary, Sadie, Brooklyn, and Letty pulled off the reception Sadie wanted. Rhode and Brooklyn hosted it at their homestead. Sadie decided to get married at the courthouse instead of having a justice of the peace come out to Rhode's place.

Since I didn't care about the particulars, I only offered my opinion when asked.

It was lowkey, it was just us and our closest friends and immediate family.

Bottom line was, it was perfect.

Sadie was my wife.

Brooklyn and Letty were salty because Sadie beat them to the altar.

They were still in the planning stages, but at least they'd set a date for their double wedding so that was progress.

"You need more wine, baby?"

"Yes, please."

"Brook? Letty?"

"Yeah, Reese. Thanks," Brooklyn answered.

I glanced at Letty and her still-full glass of wine. Then my gaze went to River who was hiding a smile.

The kind of smile that said he and Letty were sharing a secret.

"No thanks, I'm good."

Then she immediately engaged the women in conversation about a new author who'd sent a box of books for Letty to read.

Total diversion.

There was a reason she hadn't touched her wine and she didn't want the girls to notice.

I made my way around the table, reached between Sadie and Letty to pick up Sadie's empty glass. I kissed the top of my wife's head and gave Letty's shoulder a squeeze.

She tilted her head back and to the side. When I had her attention, I gave her a wink.

The smile she returned was one I'd never seen on Letty. Soft and tranquil.

Before the other two could pick up on our silent communication, I let go of her shoulder and made my way to the kitchen.

I hadn't even picked the bottle of wine up off the counter when the men, sans Wilson, joined me.

"They're bitching about you and Sadie getting hitched," Rhode informed me. "We took that as our cue to leave."

"I'd say I was sorry but I'm not."

"If I could get away with putting Brooklyn and Remy in my truck and eloping, I would've done it months ago. But the Welshes are involved. They want Brook to have a big wedding. Then River shows up, finally gets his woman, and now the Welshes are beside themselves with glee and want both their girls to have the be-all-end-all of celebrations. I'm not sure if a double wedding was a brilliant idea or if River and I just signed up for months of misery."

River stayed suspiciously quiet on the topic. But when he changed it altogether, I wanted to laugh.

"Has Winegarner called you yet?"

Over the last six weeks since Sadie's attack, I'd talked to Detective Winegarner a lot. But not recently.

"He finally tracked down that hutch Sadie sold. The flash drive's been recovered."

The flash drive that had gotten Sadie nearly killed. Bateman's insurance policy. Brasco and River had worked Fredrick Bateman until he admitted he wanted out. After he'd fucked over Sadie a small piece of decency had awoken and he wasn't feeling like sticking with the scams any longer. Unfortunately for him, Steve Binder and Sam

Barker didn't feel like dissolving B Cubed. Bateman was good at the con, much better than Barker. And Binder never worked the women, so they relied on Bateman for the big scores.

"Where'd he find it?"

"The couple who bought it moved to Utah. They're staying with friends while their house is under construction. That's why it took him so long."

"What was on it?"

"Everything, Freddy said. Names of all the women they worked. Bank accounts, crypto passwords, pictures. Everything. As you know, Bateman's already pled guilty. Binder and Barker proved they're morons and are fighting the charges. I'm thinking tomorrow when the prosecutor calls their attorneys with the new evidence they'll flip."

"Good news." I smiled.

"Yep."

"You got any other good news you wanna share, brother?" Davis asked.

River didn't flinch at the question. He was smart enough not to bullshit a group of men who paid attention.

"I've got great news," River returned.

Wilson walked into his kitchen with a look on his face that was hard to read.

"Care to share with the class?" Davis pushed.

"Are we talking about Letty being pregnant?" Wilson asked.

River smiled huge. The rest of us busted out laughing.

When I got my laughter under control I asked Wilson, "There a problem?"

"I need to go to California."

Damn. Last check-in, Asher reported that in his opinion everything was on the up and up. Joi was what it claimed to be, a sex club with a heavy emphasis on voyeurism. But at no time had he witnessed anyone partici-pating acting uncomfortable or coerced. His reports indi-cated the opposite—the members were polite, happy to be there, and the club had a strict, no second chance policy about consent. Ask before touching, period. All members adhered to this. And it wasn't the men who gave consent for their partners to be touched, it was a two-way policy. Both partners had to say yes. Asher hadn't seen anyone at any of the parties who looked under thirty. The SOIP was happy with Asher's finding and were ready to pull the plug and get Asher out.

"What happened?" Jack set his beer on the counter and gave Wilson his full attention.

"Tonight, Asher met Lorenzo Kelly, Marco's son. He doesn't like the vibe this guy gives off. But more, he picked up on how some of the female members shied away from him. The atmosphere of the party changed when Lorenzo showed up. Before he called, Cole did some digging, and the week before the police went to the Kelly mansion Lorenzo was in California. He left the morning of the police visit."

"What kind of vibe?" I asked.

"The kind that made Asher call me and ask me to come to California to check the guy out. Rhode, I need you to call Shep and ask him to get me a cover. Lorenzo's in real estate, I don't much care what my cover is as long as it will get me a meeting with Kelly. While I'm gone, Reese, stay on top of the deputy. Zeus is gonna make his move soon. Butch is antsy as fuck. If possible, I'd like the deputy approached and flipped before he turns dirty. River? You and Brasco still good watching your guys?"

"Yeah, we're keeping an eye and IA has been notified. Surprisingly they agree; watch and wait and when Zeus approaches, we flip them. The sex tapes will have to be addressed but it's up in the air how that's gonna happen."

"Anything else that needs to be wrapped up before I go?" Wilson glanced around the kitchen.

Everyone shook their heads in the negative.

"Good. Let's finish watching Reese's wife fleece him."

Refills were poured and the men all went back to the table.

Sadie got another week of laundry out of me.

————

I WAS DRIFTING off to sleep with my wife's warm naked body draped over mine when she whispered, "I have a confession."

"Yeah?"

"I cheated."

I smiled into the dark.

"I know."

"Do you want to know how I did it?"

"Nope."

"You don't care?"

"Nope."

"But I swindled you. You're on laundry detail for almost a month and you have to paint my nails and give me foot rubs."

"So?"

Sadie made a disgruntled noise and snuggled in closer.

"Would you *like* to tell me how you did it?"

"No. But I was hoping my confession would lead to you pretending I was in trouble, and you'd pretend to punish me."

My body started to shake with silent laughter. Sadie

huffed out another annoyed noise and shifted her leg resting over my thighs.

"Do you want more, baby?"

"How'd you guess?" she deadpanned, and I barked out a laugh.

"I'm just smart like that."

I adjusted the pillow under my head then tapped her leg.

"Climb up and turn around. I want your mouth on me while I eat you."

Sadie squirmed, then scrabbled to do as I asked.

When I had her beautiful ass facing me, I gave her a sharp smack.

"Hmm," she hummed.

My hands went to her hips, I pulled her back, then down, and gave my wife what she wanted. Her lips wrapped around my cock, and just like always she gave me everything.

30

Sloane Ellis

There I was, standing in a beautiful mansion, surrounded by beautiful people all in varying degrees of undress, watching them mingle and converse. And I was wondering not for the first time or the third or the tenth, how on earth was this my life.

I'd been to enough of these *soirées* that the nudity didn't bother me. At first, it did, until I came to the realization that the members of Club Joi paid a hefty price to be there. They paid for the opportunity and the privacy to safely, willingly participate in a lifestyle they enjoyed.

However, as the nights progressed into the public sex, I found any reason I could to leave the area. It wasn't that it was a free-for-all wild orgy. Everything revolved around consent and that included touching as well as watching. No one was forced to watch. There were designated spaces throughout the mansion where sex acts could be viewed, but no place else.

So, when the penises and vaginas came out, I skedaddled.

I actually knew how this had become my life. Every time I walked into my apartment and didn't see my roommate's smiling, pretty face I was reminded. What I was really wondering was why on earth I thought I could find out what happened to Elise. I'd been a part-time waitress, part-time event planner for God's sake. I had no idea what I was doing or what I was looking for. It wasn't like during cocktail hour one of the members was going to announce they'd kidnapped my friend. Or during an orgasm, someone was going to scream, "Oh, yes, so good! I killed Elise Keller and buried her in the backyard."

I'd been working at Club Joi as the executive event coordinator for over six months and I hadn't heard Elise's name uttered once. At first, this made me ultra-suspicious, now I understood it was part of the respect and privacy the members extended to each other. There was zero gossip at the club. Which was frustrating. No one asked questions, more frustration.

Six months of nothing.

Elise was gone without a trace. The police were scratching their heads with no leads. Her parents were beside themselves with worry and heartbreak. And I was destroyed.

"Excuse me." A smooth, rich voice pulled me from my thoughts.

I pulled my gaze from the scantily dressed women drinking champagne in front of the fireplace in the great room to a man who interrupted my thoughts.

Adam Newcomb.

The man was a real-life, walking, talking, billboard ad for something manly.

It was a shame he was a member of a sex club. If I'd met him out in the real world I would've done something outrageous to catch his attention, and if that didn't work, I would've approached him and asked him out for a drink.

Sandy-brown hair, nice eyes, carried himself with an air of confidence. Not the kind that was cocky and screamed douche bag. His came from someplace deep, he was comfortable in any environment. He was the master of his universe, and he was that because he was good at what he did and knew it.

He was sexy as hell.

But he belonged to a sex club and that was a hard pass.

"Hello, Mr. Newcomb. Is everything alright?"

"I was going to ask you the same thing."

He was?

"Everything is wonderful, is it not?"

I glanced around the room. Everyone was smiling and happy. Having a good time talking to their fellow members, enjoying light hors d'oeuvres and the two-glass maximum for those who would be playing later. There were also strict rules about intoxication, and a drink limit for anyone who was participating in any kind of sex.

"It is," he confirmed. "That's why I'm wondering why you're standing off to the side, frowning. Do you find something particularly distasteful or is it the party as a whole?"

Damn.

Shit.

"Of course I don't find consenting adults participating in activities that are mutually satisfying distasteful. If I was frowning, I apologize, I was thinking about the champagne. More to the point, if the staff had ordered enough."

Semi-lie.

I don't find it distasteful per se, it just wasn't my scene. And it was not something I wanted to witness or be a part of.

Adam leaned closer, his mouth dangerously close to touching my ear when he whispered, "That sounds rehearsed." I felt his breath against my neck, I caught the scent of his woodsy cologne, and against my will, I shivered. "Or more to *my* point, it sounds like bullshit."

He straightened and I felt that, too. The loss of his closeness. It was only for a second, but I didn't miss the way his heat had surrounded me.

I tipped my head back to catch his gaze and vehemently deny his accusation. That denial was swept away by his smile. I couldn't muster any of the professionalism I'd mastered over the months I'd worked here. My resolve was slipping faster than I could remind myself that Adam Newcomb liked watching and having public sex. Not that I'd ever witnessed this firsthand. I'd never seen him bring a date, which as a top-level member he was welcome to. I'd never seen him wander back into the viewing rooms or even sit in the lower lounge, which was referred to as the Hunting Ground, because that was where either unattached female members went to find a partner for the evening, or couples went to find a third or switch. Negations happened down there. And other than his tour of the property and the rooms, I hadn't seen Adam use any of the amenities.

Strange.

"Perhaps I should ask you if you find Club Joi distasteful," I returned.

In the last couple of months, I'd become an expert on body language, so I didn't miss the stiffness in Adam's shoulders or the way he tensed.

"Why would you ask that?"

"You've been here over two months," I noted. "Have you not found our club acceptable? Is there something I could provide for you that would make your time enjoyable?"

Holy shit.

There were some things that, when thought in your mind, sounded better than when actually spoken out loud.

I felt my face heat.

I felt sweat trickle between my boobs that were pushed together to the max by a fabulous, but expensive bra that made them look at least a cup size bigger. I had more cleavage on display than I ever would in my real life. Though, in real life, I also didn't wear low-cut cocktail dresses and high heels.

"If I thought for a second you were offering what it sounded like you were, I would take you up on it in a hot minute. However, to answer your question, the club is perfectly acceptable."

I didn't know what to say to that. I wanted to offer what it sounded like I was. And I would be offering it if he wasn't a member. As a part of my employment contract, I had the same membership Adam had purchased. I could participate any time I wanted.

"Have a good night, Sloane."

I was still recovering from the sexy way my name had fallen from his lips, wondering how it would sound while we were in bed, naked, and he was deep inside of me, when I felt the faintest brush of his hand against mine.

Barely a brush.

But forbidden.

That slightest touch without my permission could get him banned.

His eyes danced with a dare. A naughty, filthy dare.

"You as well, Adam."

His lips quirked up into the hottest smirk that made my thighs squeeze together.

That smirk turned primal.

And I had a feeling I'd unwittingly issued a challenge.

Check out Sloane and Asher in Dangerous Encounter

ALSO BY RILEY EDWARDS

Riley Edwards

www.RileyEdwardsRomance.com

Takeback

Dangerous Love

Dangerous Rescue

Dangerous Games

Dangerous Encounter

Gemini Group

Nixon's Promise

Jameson's Salvation

Weston's Treasure

Alec's Dream

Chasin's Surrender

Holden's Resurrection

Jonny's Redemption

Red Team - Susan Stoker Universe

Nightstalker

Protecting Olivia

Redeeming Violet

Recovering Ivy

Rescuing Erin

The Gold Team - Susan Stoker Universe

Damaged

Flawed

Imperfect

Tarnished

Tainted

Conquered

The Collective

Unbroken

Trust

Standalones

Romancing Rayne

Falling for the Delta Co-written with Susan Stoker

AUDIO

Are you an Audio Fan?

Check out Riley's titles in Audio on Audible and iTunes

Gemini Group

Narrated by: Joe Arden and Erin Mallon

Red Team

Narrated by: Jason Clarke and Carly Robins

Gold Team

Narrated by: Lee Samuels and Maxine Mitchell

The 707 Series

Narrated by: Troy Duran and C. J. Bloom

More audio coming soon!

BE A REBEL

Riley Edwards is a USA Today and WSJ bestselling author, wife, and military mom. Riley was born and raised in Los Angeles but now resides on the east coast with her fantastic husband and children.

Riley writes heart-stopping romance with sexy alpha heroes and even stronger heroines. Riley's favorite genres to write are romantic suspense and military romance.

Don't forget to sign up for Riley's newsletter and never miss another release, sale, or exclusive bonus material.

Rebels Newsletter

Facebook Fan Group

www.rileyedwardsromance.com

facebook.com/Novelist.Riley.Edwards

instagram.com/rileyedwardsromance

bookbub.com/authors/riley-edwards

amazon.com/author/rileyedwards

ACKNOWLEDGMENTS

To all of you – the readers: Thank you for picking up this book and giving me a few hours of your time. Whether this is the first book of mine you've read or you've been with me from the beginning, thank you for your support. It is because of you I have the coolest job in the world.

Made in United States
North Haven, CT
11 January 2024

47309305R00200